Presenting…
The Fabulous O'Learys

Presenting…
The Fabulous
O'Learys

by
Caron Freeborn

www.hhousebooks.com

Paperback ISBN: 978-1-910688-35-9

Cover design by Jo Dalton: Studio 59
Typeset by Polgarus Studio

Published in the USA and UK

Holland House Books
Holland House
47 Greenham Road
Newbury, Berkshire RG14 7HY
United Kingdom

www.hhousebooks.com

Printed and bound in Great Britain by TJ International Ltd.

For Gabe, Jude and Holly

When we are born, we cry that we are come
To this great stage of fools

Delia

Clouds
Tree bark
Purcell
Dandelion and Burdock
Rabbits
The Tomorrow People
The collected works of Alexandre Dumas
The letters of Sylvia Plath
The Penny Whistle
Staying at 6 stone 13
Girelli's Circus
Salad Cream
The novels of Iris Murdoch
2001: A Space Odyssey
Marigold the dachshund
1981
   (sub-category:
   Lady Diana's wedding)
Gem stones
   (sub-category:
   rhodochrosite and moonstone)
Pebbles
Eddie

The list is itself lovely, of course. I looked at it for one hour after making it. All the things I've loved in my life. Daddy and Raquel and Auntie Lesley aren't on it because they've always been there, like my hands or my feet. My lists are about things I chose or that chose me. As I like new things, the old ones drip away until all that's left is a word on a list. And a warm feeling around the word or around me when I see the thing. Orangey, sunsetty.

When I was three or four, I'd lie for hours on my back, watching the clouds shift. I even liked rain clouds but someone would bring me in when the drops made me screw up my eyes, so the clouds went long and thin like the liquorice in a Sherbet Fountain. Suppose it must have been my mother who moved me. Or maybe Raquel.

Candy floss was when I was about six. Maybe being able to eat the clouds was one better than watching them. I was a teenager when I got really good at the penny whistle. Used to play for hours. Then one day I put it in a beer glass on a shelf and never moved it. It's still there, in the room that used to be mine and Raquel's and now has a desk and a sofa-bed in it. Nothing else of ours is there, just that glass with the whistle, some pens, some paperclips, a dried-out lipstick. That definitely wasn't mine because of course I never wear make-up except for mascara – I like the little wands – and some rouge because Raquel once told me I look dead without it. I know I don't really, but.

Some things stay a while. I've been 6 stone 13 pounds 0 ounces for ten years now and I really really like that. When I slept all the time and got fat, my face bloated-closed like that purple jellyfish at Southend. After I threw the pills away, after the ants stopped crawling, I thought I'd decide what number weight to be. I still like salad cream, though for one year I didn't eat it and had mayonnaise instead. It didn't last.

But most good things don't stay. *The Tomorrow People* didn't, and I didn't want a telly after that. Girelli's didn't stay or not for us and I still miss, miss, miss the circus. 1981 didn't stay, and the years in between didn't make it. But perhaps 1984 might turn out to be on the next list. It must have made George Orwell's. It's going well so far. Mostly. So far.

Eddie minds about losing the money. He pretends not to, but he looks angry when he talks about it. Anger only looks like one thing, it's easy to read. Actors get that wrong, they make it too complicated, but it's simple. A moving ugliness. Glittery eyes. Too-tight skin. Happiness is much harder to read because it's not how I used to think – people don't smile all the time when they're happy. I know because I've looked in the mirror when I've been happy and I don't catch myself smiling.

If Eddie minds, perhaps I have to mind. I'm not sure how much difference it will make, really. I don't spend much. Even Eddie doesn't spend much. He likes tobacco and sometimes he likes rum or beer, but he doesn't buy things. His list would be quite short, I think. Mostly, he wants to be famous and you can only buy that if you're properly rich. I know four thousand's a lot, and I know people haven't got jobs, but it's not silly money. Eddie will be okay. He's talented. And that's true.

When Daddy asked what I thought about not having my allowance any more, I said *I can't say it*. They all believed I was being difficult, but I wasn't. Sometimes, I can see my thoughts on the other side of my head but I can't get to them, I can't make them come clear and come out. What I wanted to say was, I do sort of mind if Eddie does but I don't know for myself, so I think it's fine. But that wasn't precise enough. And I didn't think Eddie would want me to talk about him. By the time I'd sorted out what I thought, the conversation had moved on. That's always happening. *I can't say it.* Wasn't hiding a truth *or* hiding a lie, I just couldn't get to the other side of my head.

Daddy wants us to do something special tonight. A Daddy and daughter thing. My choice. I hate choices. Made my list again, hoping that would help but it didn't, even though it was all choices. Though I might take him my newest, smallest grey pebble, in case he needs it.

'Thatcher, fucking WHORE, Thatcher.' Pause. 'That's not a tic, I just hate her.'

The audience screamed with laughter. Daddy laughed too, turning round as though he expected people to be looking at him. A few were. On the stage, Tom opened his mouth wide, gave a big shudder that looked as though it was on purpose but it wasn't. I've always liked the way Tom looks: tall, thin, humpbacked, with a lovely long red nose and long red fingers to match. His hair's all zhooshy like Auntie Lesley's. He's gorgeous to draw: all long lines, nothing too tricky. Raquel tells me I drew people as just heads with arms and legs coming off until I was seven, but now I like the feel of a 4B pencil as it sweeps lines of bodies. Drawing didn't make my current list, though, because I only like it and sometimes not even that.

'I see we have a celebrity in the house.' Twitch, gape, shudder. 'Mr Ken O'Leary BUGGER star of stage and screen. Late of stage and screen, because he's retired. Retired from resting. LAZY CUNTS.'

Now most people were looking at Daddy, who raised his glass at the stage. I couldn't tell if he was happy or annoyed, but I did know he had to seem happy.

There was so much smoke filling the air that it was hard

to see faces properly, even the ones near you. Not that I minded that. Faces are tiring. But I think people were pleased to see Daddy, probably because he's a little bit famous.

'Still, at least I've got charm. Charm! CHARM! CHARM! Yip yip heeheehee! Sorry sorry sorry sorry fuckers sorryfuckersorryfucker... yaaaah that was a good one right? You never know. It just sort of builds up, like a like a FAT BASTARD LOOK AT YOU! Oh dearie me, as me old mum says and wishes I could. We're in for an evening of it, know what I mean? I knew it shaving this morning, you do it in your own head, in your thoughts, I'm shaving away, left side, right side, chin and then the itch starts in your head and I'm doing my top lip and it's like my brain suddenly shouts QUASIFUCKINGMODO! You can't imagine it, pal. You're shaving away and your fucking MIND starts making Hunchback Hunchdick Huncharse WHOA Hunchback of Notre Dame *jokes FUCK OFF SHUT THE FUCKING FUCK THE FUCK UP.* That's what I shouted. You didn't know whether it was me then or one of me turns, did you? *FUCK OFF SHUT THE FUCKING FUCK THE FUCK UP...*I know I'm repeating myself but that's what I said. *QUASIMODO! FUCK OFF SHUT THE FUCKING FUCK THE FUCK UP!* There was blood everywhere. FUCKING POSH BITCH THE COW. You're not even thinking, are you? You don't have to ask. You know it's not one of me turns and you know who MILKSUCKING TITS it is. I should go into Parliament, me. Liven the place up. Looks, charm, I'd end up shagging Thatcher SHAG SHAG SHAG SHAG TORY WHIG ARSEHOLE ey, yip yip hmmmm...that was a turn. Honest...I could be a secret weapon. I could be a spy. A plant. Concealed yip up a tree, in a tree. Like the SAS, Iran Embassy. BANG BANG BANG yip yip smash windows, stun grenades whizzbang flashbang bangbang UP A WOG'S ARSE, that's me. In a tree. Concealed fnn fnn yip… shhh… *I'M IN THE TREE YOU CUNTS COME AND GET ME FUCK ME IN MY SNOWY WHITE HUNCH-HOLE ARSE ARSE.* Yeah. That would go down well…'

It was getting too loud. I slipped my fingers into my ears for a bit, under my hair, where no one would see, and tried to get a proper view of Tom's mouth, the way it got damp when he talked a lot, the way he licked at the corners as though they tasted good. When I was young, I used to walk around with my hands clamped over my ears all day long, but Daddy trained me out of that with Galaxy Counters.

By the time Tom had come round to our table, men patting him on the back as he passed them, Daddy had got a bottle of champagne in. Tom always drinks pints of lager, but I suppose Daddy didn't know.

'Very funny. Very funny indeed,' Daddy said. 'Reminds me of Larry Olivier in *The Entertainer*. End of the end of the pier stuff.'

'You got that?' Tom smiled, slapped his knee. 'People normally don't realize, what with—'

'How much of that is non-volitional?' Daddy asked.

'Used to be all. Now, maybe I give it full rein, something like that.' Twitch, gape, shudder. 'Most like me don't shout out stuff, I don't think. Not bad stuff. I'm just—'

'Lucky,' said Daddy, and Tom laughed. Hate it when people do that, jump in each other's sentences like hopscotch squares. I want to hold my stone, not throw it. It's hard to pick out voices in a crowd, anyway. Don't know how people manage it. Maybe they're just pretending, so they jump on the squares by accident because they can't hear properly. Buzz, buzz, buzz, I wonder why they does.

There was another comedian on now. I tried to blot out his voice. Buzz, buzz, buzz. Daddy had poured me half a glass of champagne. I dropped a mint into it, to watch the tiny bubbles ping off as if they were trapped sunshine.

'Can't drink too much of this,' Tom said. 'Got to get over to Soho in a bit. PROZZIES. Got a late show.'

'Get much work, do you?'

'Yeah, not bad. Never going to get telly, though. NIGGERS.'

'No, well, quite.' Daddy put down his glass. 'But there's always editing.'

'You'd have to be brilliant for them to want that much FUCKING BOLLOCKS trouble.'

'Yes, I can see that.'

'And it's my schtick. There's no me without...Sorry. MOOSE.' She had a very fat bum and her man was trying to make her go faster than she could through the small space. 'Always pumped after a gig, but even noisier than normal tonight, I am. Meeting someone new.'

'Don't give it a thought.' Daddy waved his hand in front of his face.

'Wasn't an apology.' Tom spoke quietly.

'Good for you.'

Neither of them was looking at me. Daddy had forgotten I was there, I think. That happens a lot – to me. Not sure it happens to real people. They hopscotch right through, as if they're terrified of being forgotten, but I don't mind. It's hard to see how three people can have a conversation, anyway.

'Dee? Dee?' Tom leaned across the table, tapped the back of my hand.

I looked up. The smoke from all those cigarettes made heavy patterns in the air, almost still but not quite, like they were not quite finished.

'She's all right, leave her,' said Daddy. 'Could always entertain herself, that one. Used to park her for hours in her pram under a tree, looking up at the leaves. She didn't sleep, didn't cry, just looked.'

Maybe I should have put *Leaves* before *Clouds*. Because they are.

'Not ignoring you, Dee,' Tom said. Twitch, gape, shudder.

'Doesn't matter,' I said, because he seemed to expect me to say something. 'I don't care,' I added, for good measure. Fantastic expression, that: *for good measure*. It means a generous measure, making it up to the top, adding more than you need. Reminds me of Auntie Lesley, and Raquel too in a way, so it's another orangey-sunsetty-warm thing, although you wouldn't put it on a list.

'Don't be rude,' Daddy said. But I wasn't being rude, so I went back to watching my mint.

Tom lit a cigarette. That made me look at him, because it's always interesting to see if he gets the flame to the end before his hand jerks up. Once, he caught his hair on fire, and had to beat his head with his hand. He said it didn't hurt. A little bit of me hoped it would happen again, but only because it was beautiful and it didn't hurt.

'So d'you have a day job, Tom?'

'No. Never have had. IDIOT. Who'd employ me?'

'Fair point.' Daddy finished his glass of champagne and topped it up, wiggling the bottle afterwards above the table. Tom put his hand over his own glass and shook his head. Twitch, gape, shudder. 'Day jobs aren't a good idea unless you really have to,' Daddy said. 'They make you feel less committed, so you are. I've seen it time and time again in the profession – promising young men and women losing all their ambition in the waiting of tables.'

'Lucky old me again, then,' said Tom. His look picked

me up. 'You look pretty, Dee,' he said. 'Did you make that necklace?'

'Yeah.' I ran my fingers over the polished amanzonite, held it out so he could get a closer look. 'Do you like it, Daddy?'

'Very pretty,' he said. But I don't think he even saw, really. So I fished my half-melted mint out of my drink and ate it.

'Have you eaten anything else today?' asked Tom. 'Dee?'

'Me? Uh-huh. One ounce of Bran Flakes. One slice of toast with tomatoes and salad cream. A Ski yoghurt – raspberry. Two Ryvitas with jam, no butter. A Rich Tea biscuit, an apple, a Dairylea triangle. Five other tic tacs.'

'He doesn't want your shopping list, child,' said Daddy.

'That's not much, Dee.'

'It's fine,' I said.

'Want some crisps? SKINNY BITCH.'

'No thanks.' But I leaned across and stroked the inside of his wrist because he was being kind. He rubbed the end of his nose, very hard. It went redder. I took his hand away, held it. 'Don't do that,' I said. But that was silly, he can't help it. 'Sorry,' I said. He smiled, put out his cigarette, went to stroke my cheek I think, but slapped me round the head instead.

Whoa! said someone on the next table. And, *Steady*, said another voice. *Watch it, pal.* It didn't hurt, not one bit, it's not as though he had the cigarette still alight, but Daddy half-jumped-up and looked like he was going to say something too.

'God, sorry, sorry Dee.'

'You didn't mean it.'

'No. HA HA HA.'

'You're a dangerous man to have around,' Daddy said. Not very nicely.

'Got to make you right on that one,' said Tom. 'Got to run, anyway. Pity, brass monkeys out there.' He stood up, bent to kiss me. Warm, soft, nice. Then he shook Daddy's hand. 'Good to meet you at last,' he said. And he was gone.

'Strange fella,' Daddy said. 'Tragic, really. Nice enough chap, and he's got stage presence, have to give him that. But ugly as all get-out.'

'I like the way he looks.' My eyes filled with tears. I felt as though Daddy was telling me I was wrong about my lovely friend.

'Of course you do, he's your pal. Very commendable and all that. But nature played a cruel trick, giving him that thing and those looks.'

'Does it make a difference to Uncle Glen-Glen that he's so handsome?' I asked. Not because I wanted to know but because it didn't, it couldn't. That's called a rhetorical question.

'No.' Daddy picked up my hand, kissed it. 'Always say there's more going on with you than people realise.'

But that's just a nice way of saying I'm a bit stupid, I think.

'What're you going to do, Daddy?'

'Hm? What d'you mean, Princess Pea?'

'With your time. Everyone's always asking me what I do, but I have my things. My walks. My stones. You don't have a list other than acting.'

'A list? What the buggery…? D'you mean hobbies, for God's sake?' He drank off his drink, looking angry. 'What d'you think I am, defective? Shall I go and weave a basket with Glen-Glen?'

'He doesn't weave baskets, does he?'

'Of course he doesn't weave baskets! Doesn't know where his hands are.'

'Thought not. What d'you mean, then?'
'Hobbies aren't for people like me, Delia. They're for—'
'People like me.' Hopscotch.

Raquel

'Raquel darling, you look lovely. Don't she, Ken? Lovely.'
Auntie Lesley gave me one of her hugs, heavy with perfume,
and reached up to kiss me on the cheek. 'You've lost weight,'
she added, opening my coat. 'Wasting away.'

'You only saw me a fortnight ago, Lesley - was ten stone
four then, same as I am now. And I really should be nine and
a half.'

'Load of old nonsense, slimming diets.'

It was hard to remember that she was only ten years older
than me. Even when we'd worked together, she'd seemed
like a very different generation, almost a mother. Too much
a mother. 'Tell that to my stage frocks,' I said.

'You just fill them out better.' Lesley smoothed her skirt
over her hipbones, tucked in her shirt. She was barely any
heavier than in her aerial silk days. *Don't mind, don't mind,
be happy for her.* I handed her the bottle of Liebfraumilch
and managed to manoeuvre myself into the flat.

'Hello, sweetheart.' Daddy blew a kiss, raised his G & T.
Delia was fiddling with the table lighter, Eddie helping
himself to a cigarette from the heavy onyx box. He winked
at me.

'All right, Raquel?' he said. 'Straight?'

That always hacked me off, him calling cigarettes *straights* to show the whole world he smoked dope too. Well, whoopee-do. They were Lesley's ciggies, anyway.

'Thanks, darling,' I said. Doing a quick round of cheek kisses. Dee didn't look up from her fiddling, but she did press her cheek into my lips for a brief moment. 'Dee-Dee, can I borrow that a sec to light my ciggie? Dee? Delia?'

She looked at me, vaguely. Palely.

'The lighter, Little. Can I have it?'

'Yes.' She opened her hand but I had to take it myself. Thing weighed a ton. I put it back in her palm. She seemed to have lost interest, leaving it to pin her hand to her jeans. Eddie leaned over and took it from her, scratching her palm with his nail in a gesture of reassurance or possession. She stared into the vacated hand as though it contained more than any of us knew.

We weren't quite used as a family to Eddie, yet. Well, she'd only been seeing him a few months. He was one of those men who expects to be the centre of attention – lots of actors are like that of course – but it was more than that. He was chippy. Restless. Daddy didn't really... No, I don't mean didn't approve, quite. The surprise of Eddie, of his rather spiked hair, his sharp jaw, his lean body in the inevitable 501s and weather-inappropriate tucked-in tee-shirt with some crass slogan or, as today, CND symbol on the front, of the fact that *this* was the man who had chosen Delia, was what Daddy couldn't seem to get.

'Everyone all right, then?' Lesley appeared from the kitchen, an apron now covering her skirt. She patted her hair, which barely yielded under her touch. 'Won't be long, it's only salady bits,' she said. 'Who needs a drinky? You haven't got one, Raquel. Bacardi and Coke?'

Lesley always made drinks a little too strong. Worst thing you could be in our family was tight. But even by her standards, this was choke-making. I put out my cigarette in the green marble ashtray that I rather coveted and took a more cautious second sip.

'I'll have a freshner, if one's going,' Eddie said, holding out his glass without standing. 'Rum, neat.'

'Not senile yet,' Lesley said. 'Can remember stuff from quarter of an hour ago.' But she patted his cheek, taking the sting out of it. He winked at her.

Never been struck on winkers. They always have an inflated sense of their own charm - assuming they can get you onside no matter what. Reminds me of the end of the pier or the comics at the club. If Eddie wanted to play Stratford rather than Stratford East, he should watch those habits. Daddy looked over at me, winked with just a touch of over-emphasis. It was like being hugged. He was still a good-looking man, Daddy: a bit on the plumptious side, and he'd never been as tall as he'd have liked which made the tummy rather more noticeable, but he'd kept most of his hair and he really wasn't lined. Could pass for early fifties easily. Of course, it was Uncle Glen-Glen who'd got the devastating looks. Rather a waste, when you thought about it. Uncle Glen-Glen could have taken Hollywood, no problem at all. 'Raquel, lovely, want to give us hand?' Lesley had a piled-high plate on one palm and a saucer of beetroot on the other, as though she was about to toss them in the air and catch them. 'Pass these to your dad, I'll bring out the knives and forks in a minute.' She always plated up, probably because there was no dining table.

Lesley and I made sure everyone had food, water, wine, cutlery, salt; Delia stared at her fingers, wiggling them. When I passed her plate, she placed it carefully on her lap and immediately began picking out lettuce, folding it, dipping it in the salad cream, popping it into her mouth, without waiting. Never failed, bless her. *Use a bloody fork* I wanted to shout, but even when she had one it lay limp in her left hand. Must have driven her mother crazy, trying to teach her to use cutlery. I do know I still had the job of it after she'd gone.

Once, Delia asked me if she was the reason her mother left. She was only a little girl when she said that, maybe eight or so. I was about sixteen and I told her no, but I was never sure that was true. Wasn't even sure for myself: my mum left when I was even younger. On balance, I'd have to say it was probably Daddy, I told Dee, even though neither of us could see why. Not really. Suppose he had other women, I said loftily, but Dee didn't think that would be enough reason to leave, and I think I agree. Of course, I was left twice: by my own mother and by Dee's, but I've never pointed that out to anyone in case the finger starts pointing my way.

'*That man that hath a tongue, I say, is no man, If with his tongue he cannot win a woman,*' said Daddy, spearing a slab of cold tongue.

'*Merry Wives?*' asked Eddie.

'*Two Gents.*' Daddy picked up the small fork for his beetroot. 'Not his greatest work, but I had a bit of fun with it in the Northern provinces in my youth.' He looked at Eddie, clearly appraising. 'Must have been a good ten years younger than you are now. What are you again, thirty?'

'Twenty-nine.'

'Twenty-nine, thirty, feh. But things are different now. When I was young, we worked all the time, learning our trade. Now it's all *drama* courses and waiting jobs and the odd part until the big break.' Smiling, waving his forked beetroot. 'Bound to come though.'

'I've just finished two plays back-to-back, well, near enough back-to-back, and a telly,' Eddie said. Not, I imagine, for the first time. Daddy could be so naughty, playing a doddery fool twenty years older than his real age.

'Course you have, yes. Fine parts, I'm sure.'

'You saw the telly, Daddy,' said Delia, as though coming round from a trance. 'Remember? *Purple Sky*. Sci-fi. Eddie played the hero.'

'Third lead,' said Daddy. 'Course I remember, what d'you take me for?'

'He was ever so good,' said Lesley. 'Took a lovely part.' She leaned over, stroked Dee's soft blonde hair.

'Filming an ad next week,' Eddie said. 'Not what you might call acting, but it keeps the wolf from the door.'

'Cadbury's,' said Delia. 'Eddie says he'll bring me some.' She put her plate on the coffee table. All she'd eaten was the salad-cream-drenched lettuce and a slice of chicken. Her wrists were so thin they looked as though they had difficulty supporting her hands, which dangled, heavy and inexpressive, between her knees. I quickly finished the rest of my food and reached for a cigarette. Didn't smoke much anywhere else – well, ciggie or two at the club perhaps. But at Lesley's flat, where they were in the abundance of a decade ago, I couldn't resist. Sometimes, we all need it to be 1974 again.

Eddie pulled out a tobacco pouch.

'Oh, don't roll one, help yourself,' said Lesley, as he must have known she would. 'Hate roll-your-owns,' she added. 'All them bits of baccy everywhere, and men pulling them off their tongue. Bloody horrible.'

'As it happens,' Eddie said, 'got a chance of a biggie coming up. British, but it's the male lead. Nostalgia thing, sort of *Local Hero*ish.'

'Miles to go before you sleep, boy,' said Daddy. 'You keep that in mind.'

'Well yeah, course.' Eddie shrugged, casually toked on his cig. My strong guess is that he didn't have a flipping clue what Daddy meant. Not a bad performance, though, not at all. He leaned back against the sofa, draped his arm along the low cushions, behind Delia but not touching her shoulders. She turned to look at him then, and smiled, a sight so rare that I found myself rather staring. He smiled back, leaned down, kissed her full on the mouth. Her arms went round his neck, feebly pulling her to him. *In front of Daddy*, for heaven's sake.

'I'll get the afters,' said Lesley. 'Come on Dee, there's tinned peaches if you're that hungry.'

Didn't dare look at Daddy, but the bellow of fruity laughter told me how he'd decided to play it. Dee pulled away and got to her feet as though to help Lesley, but then simply stood where she was, swaying ever-so-slightly in that way of hers, that when we were kids made me want to knock her over. Eddie put out his cigarette, going for insouciance but not quite pulling it off.

'Vardi the chat,' Lesley added to me. I nodded. Look at that indeed.

Daddy ate his peaches and most of Delia's with his usual gusto but he wasn't saying much. Stupidly, I thought that was down to Eddie being there, to Daddy still trying to suss him out. When I was a teenager – this was before Girelli's, so I must have been about sixteen – I was going out with the rhythm guitarist from The Shysters, and didn't Daddy go silent on us then. Didn't speak to either me or even Dee for a good three weeks, except for Pass the salt, You're not going out in that, Move your backside Dolly Daydream. The minute my fella left to go on tour, Daddy was his old self again, but I always wondered if he'd said something to Billy before he started speaking to us. Billy never rang or sent a postcard, I do know that much. Rotten b.

'Now, have we all got a drink?' Daddy said, putting Dee's empty bowl on top of his own. 'Come on, look lively. Drinks.'

Lesley bustled round collecting bowls and checking glasses, sending me to refill this and that, but I could see she wasn't pleased: at her suppers, *she* set the agenda thank you very much, not her show-off much-older brother who couldn't host a chimp's tea-party.

'Some people are getting too big for their batts,' she said to me, in a whisper that wouldn't be out of place in panto. 'Mentioning no names.'

Daddy took a big sip of his drink, and stood up. Ran his hand through his still-plentiful hair. Made eye-contact with each of us in turn.

'I'm fifty-nine,' he said. 'Fifty-nine and been in the business for over forty years. Fifty-nine and,' he swept his free hand round, including us all, 'I'm as successful as I'm going to be.'

'But—'

'No, Raquel, let me finish,' he said. Too kindly. 'As successful as ever I'm going to be. It's not been a bad career.' A modest shrug. 'Though the list of people who pipped me to the bloody post is a damn sight longer than it ought to be. They thought of me for *Bouquet of Barbed Wire*, you know. O'Toole's *Hamlet*? Mine. But to be fair, so was a part in his you-know-what.' He crossed himself. 'Even bloody Jack Hawkins slipped in there with that nice bit in *Ben Hur*.'

For a moment, it seemed we were going to be treated to the entire list.

'But I can't complain. I've always worked, and not much that I need to hang my head for. It's been all right.' A wry laugh. 'It's been a riot, if you want the truth. But,' and here he looked at each of us again, 'enough is enough. Tonight,' he raised his glass, 'will mark the end of my career. Tonight, I retire from this business some fools call show. Feh.' With that, he swallowed his drink down.

It was as though he'd told us we were adopted or he was off to save the whale or join the burn-their-bra brigade. Retire. Impossible to get my head around it. *Daddy* retiring? As likely as the Pope stepping down.

'What'll you live on?' Lesley tapped her fingers against her mouth. 'Glen don't come cheap, you can't take that back.'

'What the hell d'you take me for?' Daddy looked properly angry. 'I signed it over *knowing* I'd never go back on it.'

'You're not going to tell me you got secret savings?' she said.

'No, I'm not going to tell you that.' Daddy shot a glance at Eddie, as though wondering how much to say in front of an outsider.

'It's our money that'll have to go, isn't it?' said Delia.

I went all funny. Sweet heaven, she was right, little Dee was right. If Daddy didn't have an income, our allowances had taken their final bow.

'Well, up to a point,' Daddy said. 'I need to know how you girls feel about that.' Daddy sat down, looked first at Delia, his baby, his pet, and then at me.

'For goodness' sake, Daddy, it's your money,' I said. We've been lucky to have it this long. The most important thing's that you're happy.'

'Raquel.' He smiled, leaned over, touched my face with the back of his hand. 'Should have known you'd be like that. All grown up now.'

Selfish old *cunt*.

'Dee?' he said, turning to her. 'What about you?'

19

She lifted her head as though pulling against its immense weight. Looked into Daddy's face. I knew her gaze would be on his mouth.

'I can't say it.'

'What d'you mean, Princess Pea?'

Dee shook her head. 'Nothing,' she said.

'Must be something. You must have an opinion.'

'Just tell Daddy you're fine with it,' I said.

'Be surprised if either of you was fine,' said Lesley, laughing. 'More like riled. But it'll all come out in the wash. Dee'll be married soon, won't you, love?'

Dee rested her face on her hands; impossible to tell if she were mourning the probable loss of her income or simply wearied by the effort of conversation.

'In fairness, sir,' Eddie put in, 'she can't earn, can she? She's—'

'Delicate,' I said. Leaning over to take a another ciggie from the box, conscious as I did so of the growing roll of fat round my waist. 'Well, there you are, Eddie – she's your responsibility now.'

'*Raquel.*' Daddy glared at me, rested his hand on Dee's head for a moment, then sat down. 'When my father returned from wherever his desertion of us had taken him, I was only interested in getting Glen what he was due. You girls never saw the place... But,' he shrugged, 'forget and forgive. My father wasn't much older than I am now when he died. I have to make my peace with all, and time's the one thing the profession never gave me.'

Cobblers. He was scared the work was drying up.

'We understand, Daddy,' I said.

'Good girl. Dee?'

But she said nothing.

Shrewd. Didn't have to hide your feelings if you didn't

express them – she'd always been like that.

'You've been an actor since the war,' said Lesley. 'What was you, eighteen? Even me, when I left the circus—'

'I'll always be an actor,' Daddy said. Rather coldly. 'Does a doctor get struck off because he reaches retirement? I'll just be…' He swept his arm out as though about to give a bow. 'I'll be done with the workaday bollocks.'

'That's lovely language,' Lesley said.

'Oh, fuck off.'

'I can't say it,' whispered Dee. With the focus elsewhere, she ought to have taken the opportunity to keep her mouth shut. Hard to believe this was the same person who'd screamed and thrashed and bitten as a child, unable to contain her anger, unable to connect with attempts to soothe. On my forearm there's still a faint scar from her six-year-old teeth. We'd had to remove one from my flesh to put under her pillow for the tooth fairy. Mouths do bleed dramatically so no one noticed at first that some of the blood was in fact mine.

'Let's all have another drink,' I said. 'Come on, this is a celebration. Will you make a *Stage* announcement?'

'It'll be expected of me,' he said, with a modest dip of the head. 'But the rag's not the same since Hepple took over.'

'That was over ten years ago.'

'Was it? I suppose it was.' He looked over at Lesley. '1943, Algeria. Doing my poor man's Alice Faye.' Laughing now. 'Remember how skinny I was?'

'I was four, Ken.'

'So you were.' Not looking best pleased. 'Don't think I was cut out to be a drag act. Mummy was horrified.' He drained his glass.

'So how will this work?' I asked. 'Will our money stop as of now? Not that I mind,' I added, 'but it would be useful to know.' A third of my income. Yes, it would be useful to know. Felt like one of Thatcher's millions.

'Good God, am I some sort of brute to you? Sort yourselves out first, couple of months, whatever you need. It's not final, I'm not in Debtors' Row yet. Though I did once play Micawber – Christmas '72. Bit of fun, that.'

'That's all I wanted to know. Thanks, Daddy.' I got up, went over to kiss his cheek. 'Want another drink?'

Eddie suddenly stood, muttering something about nature calling, then made his way painfully round the table, dragging one cowboy boot, his limp more pronounced than usual. Impossibly romantic. He stopped at the hall door. Turned.

'What's she meant to do?' he said. 'What's she meant to do, sir?'

Daddy stared at him. The silence went on too long. Even Dee lifted her head to look at it. Silence lurched round the room, the doubtful guest. Then Daddy spoke,

'*Now...*' he intoned, heavily, '*is the winter of our discontent.*'

I caught my breath. Oh my goodness, he might as well have called Eddie a cripple. Eddie didn't flinch, didn't appear to react in any way: one hand on the door handle, one hooked into his jeans pocket, his bare arms ropey, sinewy, flexed.

'That's not the sense,' said Dee.

Everyone's eyes on her now.

'It's *Now is the winter of our discontent / Made glorious summer, by this son of York.*' She wetted her lips. 'It's not about being discontented. The sense was wrong. It's about happiness.'

Dee bent her head again, letting her long hair fall forward. For a second, I thought I was going to laugh. I bit my lip, aware that my teeth were gripping which meant my lipstick had worn away.

Abruptly, Eddie left the room and a few seconds later we heard the toilet flush. Daddy lit a cigarette, gave a flourish with his hand, laughed his deepest, most charming laugh.

'Ladies and gentlemen – presenting the Fabulous O'Learys.'

Eddie

That family, man, they took some swallowing when they got together. But they weren't the whole story, that was for sure. So this morning, I went there. Bus came along, like it was fate. Took me nearly all the way to Highgate.

'Sorry, I don't understand.' The receptionist looked at her white nails, then at me. Most birds seem so shiny compared with Dee, like they wash more. Even the sorts who're a bit Nice Legs, Shame about the Face, like this one, seem better put together. Give her my killer smile but she was having none of it.

'I'm Mr O'Leary's niece's fiancé,' I said, pulling off my Spurs hat, mussing my hair to spike it back up.

'Well, I've only got your word for that.' She went back to the very important job of doodling flowers round the edges of an appointment book.

'Why would I lie?'

'You could be a journalist.' Sounding bored.

'Do I look like a journalist?'

'Wouldn't know.' She pushed the book aside and unwrapped a two-fingered KitKat. Pointedly, she bit across the fingers instead of snapping them into two.

I believe in euthanasia. Means good death, someone told me. What's the point of keeping around a mirror you never want to look in? Cracked. According to Dee he spits, shits himself, rocks, hits his head. He talked until he was two but by three, not a dickie-bird. Never played with other kids, even Ken, never did much at all except for stripping the wallpaper through the bars of the cot he still needed at four. Was in a home by seven or eight. Even with just them few details – she's a crap story teller – you can see that's not a life. You'd put a dog down for less. Most would, anyway. Dee told me about a miniature dachshund she'd had, called Marigold. Just as many details of the dog as we'd had of the uncle. Not right in the head, it weren't, used to sit in a corner facing the wall, twitching its face like it was trying to get the same view over and over with its one good eye, or walking round and round the table leg for hours, with a chop bone in its mouth. Lived till it was fifteen, she reckoned, and she cried when the vet finished it.

Suppose Glen's money would go to Ken, but he wouldn't need it all, would he? Must cost a fair few bob, that joint he's in. Not exactly St Clements, more like a bloody hotel. You could even say it's immoral, taking money out your daughters' mouths to pay for a bloke who'd be better off dead.

Hard to say what she believes. There's stuff going on there, she's bright enough, but you have to take a lot on trust. Even how pretty she is. She's not a serious looker, not sexy either, but she's symmetrical – everything matches, the way it doesn't on most people, then there's that transparent skin, those big grey eyes that never quite look at you, and you just have to keep staring. Once you've clocked it, hard to pull away. First thing I saw was that she's all edges, sharp elbows, jutting hipbones, great big jaw, and I didn't like it much but then she scratched her head, hard, pushed that long blonde hair away from her face and that was it. I noticed.

Don't love her. Not sure I even like her, much. Not like
we got anything in common. She's not got a Scooby what
it's like to have to go to the library in secret and tell your old
man you're going to football when you're standing in line
for matinee returns. She's not got the first bloody idea about
politics. And I don't give a stuff about stones and the little
gems she spends all them hours polishing. But no one's ever
wanted to sleep with me as much as she does. Tom says she's
the type men want to protect, but I don't. I just want to fuck
her.

Of course, I was sure who she was right from the start.
Tom's known her for years, since they lived in the same
block of flats. Not that I know Tom all that well, but he's
funny, I like him, so I'm always up for meeting the weirdoes
he hangs round with. And be truthful, he's a prize, might be
able to use him one day in my work. Never look a gift tic in
the mouth.

She didn't laugh once. Not one solitary crack of her face
through the whole gig. She wasn't sitting there all offended,
just serious. As though she'd stamped a Reserved on her
forehead to mark the one gag she was waiting for. It never
came. Once or twice, she glanced round the club, watching
the laughs (Tom was on form that night or the crowd was
generous), not with any kind of bafflement, just observing I
think. Curious. Interested, but only up to a point. Later, I
found out she'd seen him work quite a few times, but you'd
never have known, it wasn't a *Yeah, seen it, next* thing. She
tapped her cheek a lot, with three of her fingers, her mouth
open, like she was making sounds only she could hear. Looked
about twenty at the most, but turned out she was twenty-
seven. And then she pushed her hair back and that was it.

Ken O'Leary's hardly really big time, but he'd still have
contacts. Everyone still knows him, in and out of the

business. A fuckable daughter and a useful father. Not like anyone was begging for my Hamlet. It weren't the set-up I'd planned for myself, but it definitely had potential. Definitely. Now this retirement and nicking back his dough. Mouldy old bastard.

In the end, the receptionist let me in. Wouldn't've took quite so long, I reckon, if I'd said I was a nephew or something. Could've asked her for a drink. But saying I was engaged to Dee put the kibosh on that one. Always a mistake to go on as yourself. Made the decision a bit too quick to hide the bastard limp too – reckon she'd've been one of them who'd've gone for it.

'Don't try to touch him,' said the little coloured nurse. Least needed advice in history. She showed me up a dark wood staircase – very *Upstairs, Downstairs* – and along a corridor that smelt of lemon polish to a room at the end.

'Glen-Glen, visitor for you, my darling,' she said. And to me, 'Don't stay long. I'll just be next door.'

The bloke was wearing a thick jumper as if he was outside in the bitter winter wind instead of sitting on a chair next to his bed, very straight, a book on his lap. For some reason, I'd thought he'd be watching telly, but there weren't one. Upside-down, I could make out a boat on one page of the book, a lighthouse on the other. He never looked at me, and he was staring at the window rather than at the pictures. Wished I'd thought to bring him something.

'I know your brother,' I said.

Nothing.

'And your nieces,' I said. Bit louder.

Nothing.

And I had nothing left to give. What a pillock, coming all this way without spending five minutes to think it through.

He moved his head, but still he never brought his stare anywhere near me. Bloody handsome. Real shocker, that – had him down as a dribbling idiot. But he looked like Ken would kill to look - slim, fit even, with a right strong jaw, loads of hair – with these amazing eyes. Most amazing thing was that they never seemed to look outwards but inside him, like he had them on the wrong way round. You'd put him at ten years younger than Ken, too, at least. *One Flew Over the Cuckoo's Nest* meets *Picture of Dorian Gray*.

Suppose he was drugged up. My heart was going a bit quick, but I could see he weren't going to attack me, nothing like that. He was just going to sit.

'Thought I'd drop by, say hello,' I said.

Nothing.

No, this was no bloody life.

Not that I want to marry Dee. Not that I ever asked. She assumed, and it was too hard to put her off. Different if I'd wanted to dump her, but as it was, couldn't come up with a good enough reason to put her right.

'If I ever have a son, I'll call him Laurence,' I'd said a couple of months ago. 'Larry for short. Teach a kid to aim high. My parents called me after my mum's uncle, and he was a bin man. Nothing wrong with that but as a role model they could've gone up a bit.' Just running off at the mouth, can't ever imagine having a kid, never mind calling him one name more than another. Don't even know how I got my name, but it certainly weren't an uncle. All of Mum's family worked for Dagenham Ford's, anyway.

Two days later, in the club where her sister sings – though we managed to miss the act through Dee's vague grasp of timing - she turns to Raquel and tells her that when we have a son, we're going to call him Larry.

'Didn't know you were that serious,' said Raquel. She raised one perfect eyebrow. You and me both, girl.

'It's best for children to have two parents.' Which was the most assertive thing I'd ever heard Dee say.

'Meaning what?' Raquel asked, lighting a fag. 'Not marriage, surely.'

Dee nodded. 'Of course we're getting married if we're going to be parents.'

I didn't exactly panic – after all, could always do one, she couldn't force me to stay with her – but it was like being hit in the chest with a brick. Was she actually round the bend? Yeah, all right, she was a bit odd, but could she really not see the difference between a bit of pretend day-dreaming and a fucking proposal?

'Parents. Right.' Raquel looked at me, and I swear man, she was looking at the bastard leg. Swear.

'It's not hereditary,' I said. Arsey.

'Glad to hear it.' Bitch actually smiled. Had to give it to her – she had front. 'Many congratulations, then,' she added.

To be fair, Dee didn't start buying *Bride* magazine or any of that shit. She hardly mentioned it, unless someone asked. It was Delia's thing and we all humoured her, but no one – except maybe the aunt – bought it. And it's not like Dee seemed to give a shit about marrying me. Weird. It's like someone was writing her lines and she was made to say them, but she was the girl forced to be in the school play when she'd rather be at home watching *Grange Hill*.

'Dee?'

She hadn't looked up as I'd come in, sat there on the floor in the living room, running her little stones through her fingers. Not that my voice startled her - she just raised her head, smiled.

'Are you staying now?' she said. Holding out her hand

full of stones. Wasn't sure if I was meant to take them, so I crouched down, swirled them round a bit on her palm with one finger.

'Sure,' I said.

She stared at my finger in the polished pebbles. I could hear her breath, feel it on my cheek. I changed the swirl to anti-clockwise.

'Are we going to have sex?' she said, and let the little stones drop back into their box, took my hand, pressed it to the side of her face.

'Sure.' It didn't shock me any more, but I still wasn't sure I liked her approach. Bit – well, cold.

Without even bothering to close the curtains, she started taking off her clothes - jumpers, jeans, knickers. She didn't really need a bra. I watched her for a minute or two, watched her sitting there waiting. Then she pressed my hand into her, rubbing herself against my wrist.

'Come on,' she said.

When I was inside her, that's the only time she seemed more than other people instead of less. Most of the time, she kept her hands pressed into the sides of my head, forcing me to look her straight in the eye, to see who she could be. I tried to turn her over, but she'd never let me, wanting to keep us locked together in that stare. Man, that's a powerful thing, to know your fucking brought someone to life.

But minutes afterwards, with my spunk still running out of her, she was back with her stones, sitting like a naked fairy, pebbles running through her fingers as though the box was a stream. Make a great little film scene if it was. Her spine was fishy - with her hair falling forward, I could see the bones from her bum to where her neck disappeared into her scalp. For a second I felt bad, as if I'd scraped the flesh off with a fork. Soon as I thought that, I was starving.

'What you going to do for dosh now?' I asked, rolling a fag. My stomach rumbled but it weren't worth apologizing, she wouldn't have heard it.

'Do for dosh? Money?' Letting the stones trickle slower and slower.

'Yeah. Dole's not enough, is it?'

'Isn't it? Suppose not. I don't seem to spend a lot. There were lots of savings before I met you.' Few months ago, when we'd not long met, that would've seemed like a pop, but I knew better now. She looked at me. 'There's still *some* left where Raquel moved it so the dole didn't see.' Interesting. She hadn't thought to tell me that. But *some* probably didn't amount to more than a couple of grand. 'Anyway, you'll get work,' she said.

'Yeah, well, it'd be a fuck of a lot easier if your dad would help.' Hadn't said nothing that straight out before, but I could see the brother in my head still, draining the money away into that inwards stare.

'Ask him.'

'Don't work like that.' Felt like slapping her sometimes. Don't get me wrong, not like punching her, but clipping her round the ear, the way you would a kid. 'You don't go cap in hand to someone like your old man, specially if they've just packed it all in.'

'How do you know?' She was watching my mouth, the way she often did.

'Trust me, Dee. Just do.' Pulling a bit of tobacco off my lip, I managed to rip a bit of skin. '*Fuck's* sake, that hurt.' It crossed my mind – not for the first time – to ask her if she'd have a word, but I just knew it would all go tits up. Now Raquel, that girl could ask and get an answer, maybe even the one you wanted. Hard to credit, even with different mothers, that those two were sisters.

'Maybe I'll get a job,' Dee said. But even she didn't sound convinced.

'As what? Keeper of the Stones?'

'Is that a real thing?' She lit up.

'No.' Put my fag out in the saucer she kept around for me as an ashtray. She'd stuck tiny purple quartz bits round the rim since I'd seen it last, but she hadn't bothered washing it up first, so the middle was still stained with brown. 'Got anything to eat?' Zipping up my jeans.

'Eat? Don't know,' she said, as though I'd asked for a couple of rolls of velvet or a gramophone or some other weird object she'd heard of but not seen. 'I've got some fruit,' she added, like she was inspired.

Two shrivelled oranges and a brown banana.

Slung her the kimono she had draped over the back of the chair. Suddenly didn't want to look at her bones.

'I'm going to get some chips,' I said. 'Want anything?' To be truthful, didn't bother to wait for her reply.

Delia

'FUCK OFF Delia.' Almost before he'd opened the door to me.

'Hello.' I touched his arm.

'OFFFUCKFUCKOFFHOFFMIESTERBEARLARE. Didn't expect to see you this morning.'

'I'm learning to be spontaneous.'

'You planned it?'

'Of course.' I knew Tom was teasing me, I kind of got the joke, and it felt warm, nice, not like when Eddie does it, and I get confused and I'm not sure what he means. That's the wrong way round, I know it is. That's not how it's meant to be.

'You want to come COME UP YOUR BUM in, or go for a walk, what?'

'Will you come up the museum with me?'

'Sure.' He looked pleased, I'm sure, but something else too. Something harder to read, even with his nice-and-easy face.

'You've never been, have you?'

'Nope.'

'The dolls' houses are so fabulous. All that detail.'

'Dee…No, never mind.' Twitch, gape, shudder. 'Just let me put some shoes on and grab my cigarettes.' He banged

33

the door three times, then another three, and another. That was a new one, I think. Lucky I stepped back in time. Then he managed to leave the door open while he sorted himself out.

I looked down at his feet, with their long, hairy toes. They were clean, well-cared-for, as though he had ten tiny pets.

It was a pity when he covered them with his new plimsoll things.

'Too aspiring Joey Ramone?' he said.

'No idea but it's chilly out.'

'You're *such* a relief.' Twitch, gape, shudder. 'I love it that you never PISS POOR pretend.'

'Oh, I do,' I said. 'But not with you. Only with people who mind.' That's another thing that shouldn't be true with Eddie, but it is. When he's glittery-angry, I soft-cloth-polish, laughing when he does, nodding, anything I can think of to stop him being cross at all the things Der-der-Delia can't understand.

'Then I'm honoured, mate,' Tom said, with a little bow. 'Come on, let's hitch a ride to rockaway beach.'

'Thought we were going to the museum?' I said, but only to make him laugh. I knew he was talking about something else, some poem or song or something. Raquel always tells me I'm so literal, *You are darling, really. As literal as an encyclopaedia*, but I'm not. And I think she's wrong, anyway – I'm not sure encyclopaedias are all about the literal truth. Some explanations are stories, really.

It was only a hop and a skip and a jump to the museum. And it was cold. Still frosty under foot and the sky baggy-sagged with snow. That would fall by this afternoon.

'Why are we skipping TRIPPING?'

'I'm testing out a saying.'

'Cool.'

When Tom skipped, his long long legs kind of twisted round each other, and I kept thinking he was going to fall flat on his face. He was faster than me, but he kept having to windmill his arms to steady himself, skidding on the frost and the iced-over puddles, sliding off the kerb. I didn't stumble or slip once.

What you two on?

Andy Pandy's coming to play...

'Ow! No, don't worry.'

'Was that your toe? Sorry, Dee—'

'I've got more.'

Eddie would never, ever skip or hop or jump with me, and Raquel would tell me off, massively, with one of her Looks. Tom and I skipped and we hopped and we jumped, and it really didn't take many of any of them. Guess Tom was so used to people looking at him that he didn't care.

No. That's wrong. He never drew attention to himself if he could help it, not off the stage. Never. I took his hand when we got to the gate.

'You're a great hopper,' I said. 'Thank you.'

'You're EMBARRASSING TWAT welcome.' He kissed the inside of my wrist and just for a second, maybe not even one elephant, it made my stomach flinch. But in a good way.

'You'd better not do that,' I said, and did it to him, to show him what I meant. After I kissed it, I gave his wrist a little lick. He tasted salty, of sweat, of something sweet but slightly off.

Tom looked down into my face, and made me hold his gaze. 'See what you mean,' he said. I let go of his hand and went along the gravel to the big heavy doors. He'd be behind me, I knew that, I wasn't worried he'd walk off or anything.

Hope my Eddie stays. He says we'll get married but I

don't know. People do get married. They fall in love, get married, have children. That's what people do. I love Eddie. I love the way he sounds – actory, half-posh, half-London-common, a bit like Daddy but younger – and I love the way he smells, like limes. His skin smells as though he washes in limes but he doesn't, it's just him. Limes and tobacco, mossy-damp. Sex. I've had sex with lots of men. Twenty-five. That's a lot, I think. Raquel says she's slept with nine men and I mustn't think she's a slut. She's eight whole years older than me as well. I didn't tell her. She probably thought I was a virgin when I met Eddie. But I've always liked sex. I went on the pill when I was 16 because of something I read in the newspaper about protection. Then three weeks later, I did it with the director on Daddy's play, and then with the boy who worked in Rosa's café. One was 57 and one was 17. I did it with them both for six months.

I didn't have a bag to hold open for the guards, but I showed them my coat pockets, with my cloth purse and three pebbles and a box of tic tacs and a tissue.

'FUCKFUCKFUCK. FUH- Look mate, it's not BOLLOCKS YOU NIGGER CUNT sorry, look, here's my pocket. KUNTA KINTE.'

'If you don't leave, I'll have to call the police,' said the biggest guard, barring our way with his arm.

'No. He doesn't do it on purpose,' I said.

'He doesn't?' Curling his lip, like Elvis Presley. Only not.

'Tell them, Tom.'

'Perhaps you can tell us, madam.'

'DO HE TAKE SUGAR UP THE ARSE?' A fleck of his spit landed on the guard's shoulder, but everyone behaved as though it hadn't happened, though the smaller guard took a hanky from his pocket as if he was going to hand it to the spat-on guard. But he didn't.

'He can speak for himself. Honestly. *Tom—*'

'We have children here. This is the Museum of Childhood. Girlie, we can't allow him to—'

'ARSE ARSE ARSE ARSE.' His arms thrashing so hard that his sleeves were runched to his elbows. 'Sorry.'

'Children hear those words all the time,' I said.

'I don't know what sort of children you know, but—'

'KIDS' COCKS.' Slapping himself on the cheek.

'Sir, I'm afraid I'm going to have to insist.'

'Shall I call the Old Bill?' the other guard said.

'FUH-FUH-Dee, let's go.' Twitch, gape, shudder.

'But the dolls' houses. I want to see the dolls' houses.'

'You go in TRAITOR. I don't mind, really, BOLLOCKS.'

'No way.' I tried to look the main guard in the eye. 'We're just here to see the dolls' houses. Like anyone else. They're my favourite. I like the twenties' one best. Don't you like it? With the bendy people, especially the diving man.'

'Just take your friend away.' Waving his hand as though he was a traffic cop and we were cars.

'I can't take him anywhere. He's not a shoulder bag.'

'SHOULDER ARSE.' Tom was pulling at his hair now, sweat or snot dripping from his nose. 'Dee. Come *on.*'

Oh. He really wanted to leave, I think. He wanted that now.

'You're both very horrible men,' I said to the guards. 'You don't deserve to look after interesting things.'

Tom grabbed my arm but not hard, and we walked away quicker than we'd skipped. I turned back, and saw the quieter guard making circles at his temple with his finger. He thought we were mad. Der-der-Delia and her shouty sweary friend.

'We're going to report you,' I shouted. But that just made them laugh.

'FUH-FUH-FUH…Oh Dee.'

'I'm sorry, Tom.' I was trying to stop the tears coming, but I couldn't. 'I did it all wrong, didn't I?'

'*No.*' He didn't stop, but sort of dragged me even faster. 'It was nothing to do with how you were. If everyone FUCK YOUR ARSE was like you, the world would be a very different place.'

'That's true,' I said. And then we both giggled, just a bit, because it was funny, just a bit. 'I really did want to show you the dolls' houses. It's all spoilt now.'

'You can tell me about them,' he said. 'I'll make you a FUH-cup of tea, and you can tell me.'

'I've got some postcards,' I said. 'Lots.'

'We can get them on the way.'

I've never wanted to make a list of all the things I don't like. Too many of those stay and stay, like lolly sticks and the fat on meat and public toilets and squashy crowds. Like the dizziness that comes and sometimes stays so long I worry that it will never leave. But I especially hate lolly sticks, the feel of them, the look of them, their woody blindness. And now I especially especially hate stupid guards.

So I showed Tom the twenties' house with its still pool and all the lovely Victorian ones, with their teeny-tiny china and proper painted pictures on the walls. And I showed him the people with their fob-watches (I used to call them wob-fatches) and bustles and shiny shoes and maids' caps. And I showed him the gas lamps and the grandfather clocks and even a tiny dish of anchorite and amethyst on a dressing table. But it wasn't the same.

Ken

What you have to remember is most people don't give a tuppenny toss for anyone but themselves. Not a tinker's damn. Our grandmother used to say that,

Oh, that one, he don't give a tinker's damn for no one.

No idea why a tinker's damn should be worth any less than anybody else's damn, but there you are. Do you remember that, Glen-Glen? No, probably not. Sensible chap. Probably too busy staring at your shoes or some such.

Did I tell you the definition of a gregarious introvert? He stares at *your* shoes. Stupid joke, when you think about it - assumes you make a difference between your shoes and mine, when you probably don't, in fact. Well, quite right, why should you?

You okay there, Glen-Glen? Comfy? I like the way they've painted in here – institution green always was your colour. Bet really you'd love to tell them to stuff their regulation paint up their backsides. Maybe I should tell them for you. Still, at least they did give it a freshen up. Bet it'll be years before they get around to the corridors. Much better, having your own room. Privacy's important – I loathe being overheard by pathetic creatures offering cups of tea and misplaced sympathy. Feh. Don't know why they took so long to realize privacy matters to you, too. Not sure they ever would have done if I hadn't been your brother. Brown-nosers, the lot of them. You'd laugh, I know you would – not as though I'm all *that* famous, am I? Not really. Not really.

Never mind them. What do you make of these lace-ups? Just Bally, but they're a decent enough shoe, though they want to be brogues when they grow up. Went home from a party once wearing Cubby Moore's brogues. Haven't the foggiest how. He'd inked his surname in them, like a child. Got his number from my agent the next day and telephoned him, but he'd apparently gone home barefoot, so God knows what happened to my Beatle Boots. Never liked them, mind – present from a dollybird – and those Cuban heels were the devil to walk in. Careful with that banging, darling boy, don't want to bring old Nurse Pillow Tits running. She might knock herself out.

Funniest thing, that - never owned a pair of brogues in my life. Not till then, anyway - Cubby told me to hang on to them. Suppose if that was twenty years later and it was *Roger* Moore's shoes that, that let's say Bob Lindsay had gone off with, they'd have ended up in some auction. Feh. Wore them till the soles went through then put them in the bin, same as I would with any. No one can say I was ever a starfucker, though I've attracted a few in my time - the ones who aimed rather low.

Was that a laugh then, you old devil? Did you like that? Always say there's far more going on in there than you let on. Bet *you* always tell me to mind my own bollocking business, too – and you're utterly, utterly furious you can't say it out loud.

Cold out there today. Freezing. Can you see the frost on the window here? Look, darling, turning face. Look. Pretty, isn't it? This damn place framed like a Christmas card. Never did send my cards out on time, or not since the wives went.

Do you think I'm right to do this? I'm only 59 – *we're* only 59 come to that, you and I – there's time enough yet. Plenty of meaty parts left to me. Thought I'd work right through the eighties at least, take me up to sixty-five and the bus pass. But I don't want to end up like old Patrick G, getting two lines here and there out of pity. His last telly was a witness in *Crown Court*, for... *I'm* not made to be an attendant lord, no bloody way. Was fifteen when I first heard that line. Wasted on me then – not that I thought so, little know-it-all shit that I was. Funny, when you think about it, how many teenage boys fall in love with Eliot through 'Prufrock'. Did myself, used to recite it with tears rolling down my face, d'you remember? And yet it's a poem about aging. Don't think I've ever really understood it until now.

Bollocks to it, ought to have been a GP after all. Used to want that when we were boys, didn't I? Not that we'd have had the money for the fancy-dan training. And I'd probably have taken that just as personally, been furious if one of my patients died. Personal rejection. The ultimate bad review. Or I'd be saying, 'Ooh, you suffer with that, do you? Know how you feel, I get it terrible.' Remember the review I had for *Titus*? Well, of course you do, no way you could forget that.

Mr O'Leary appeared less excited or repelled by the maiming of Lavinia than concerned that it might be catching.

That was one of the Bastard Boys, having a pop – made the mistake of telling him when we were on the toot once that I booked regular doctor's appointments in advance, in case I turned out to be ill that day. Am-dram error that, Glen-Glen. Critics are always Other People.

You look tired, old boy. Want Kenny to stroke your

elbow? No? Hey, I forgot – brought you something. Bar of the old Old Jamaica – paper shop got some in. About bloody time, that's what we say. Blamed the snow, silly buggers. Bit of snow's not going to stop lorries getting through. Mind you, enough to freeze your vitals, that's for sure. There you go. Not all at once. Steady on. Wonder you don't choke yourself. Look, I'll wrap the rest up for later, give it to… No, quite right. There you go. Bollocks to it. *Eat yourself pleasant*, as Mummy used to say.

I've told the girls. Was no point putting it off - too easy, then, to keep postponing retirement as well. Speaking makes it so. I need to announce it now, don't I? Of course I do, quite right. Thanks for this little chat, it's been helpful. Cleared my mind, far as anything could be said to do that. Got a hug for me, have you? Hug for your Kenny boy? No? Next time, then. Next time. Love you.

Raquel

It's still the same old story
A fight for love and glory
A case of do or die
The world will always welcome lovers
As time goes by

No more than polite applause, but though I was shattered, it was early - third on the bill tonight. Maurice likes to mix us up. Not that I deserved more than a hand, as to be fair I wasn't very good, concentration right off. No real expression there, couple of pitchy notes. Mickey asked if singing sharp was my new gimmick, cheeky b.

'Barcardi and Coke.' I heaved myself onto the ridiculously high bar stool and lit a cigarette. The skirt was too tight for me to cross my legs easily but I couldn't sit like a navvy so I hoiked it up a bit, squeezed one leg over the other. For a sec, I couldn't get my breath. As discreetly as I could, I touched my tongue to my wrist, three times.

I'm all right.
I'm all right.
I'm all right.

It was much worse since Daddy's little announcement last week, but that was hardly surprising.

'Can I buy you a drink, darling?' A beery leer, too close to my cheek.

'Just got one, thanks,' I said, as Sid put it in front of me.

'I'll get that.' Mr Beery-Leery waved a fiver across the bar. 'And a large whiskey mac, mate.'

He was about fifty or so, slimy with fat, a greased pig in a bad suit. Didn't look as though he was bothered by the unemployment statistics, but that was about the most you could say of him. Dearie dear – was he really the best I could do? Was the only offer on the horizon, I knew that much for nothing. Slim pickings, these days. Oh blow it. I gulped my drink.

'Want another in there?'

'Sure.' No harm in taking a drink off a man, I wasn't about to sleep with him.

'Voice of an angel, you got.'

'Thank you very much.'

'No, I mean it.'

'I'm sure you do.' Pound to a penny his wife didn't understand him.

Lisa had started her set with a too-upbeat version of 'Downtown'. For my money it ought to have a bitter undertone, a kind of irony, but there we are, she always was a crowd pleaser. Being twenty-two helped a lot – that pleased enough on its own. I crushed my cigarette into the over-full ashtray.

Mr Beery-Leery put his hand on my knee, his hand lifting slightly for a fraction of a second after he made contact, as though startled. I looked at it, pink and podgy against my dancers' tights. Bet he'd thought it was naked flesh. He squeezed, far too tightly. Obviously thought he was on a promise. Incorrectomundo.

It was a long time since I'd let a man go home with me.

Almost six months. Even longer since my last proper relationship – more than a year. Two. Drinks didn't grow on trees. I emptied mine again and let him buy me another.

'You're a very beautiful woman,' he said. 'Doesn't your husband mind you doing this job? You must get approached all the time.'

'He's not the jealous type,' I said. Never even been close really to marriage. Not really. Thought once or twice – maybe - but that's just the way the cookie crumbles. *My wife won't let me.* Least I can please myself.

'Got kids, have you?' He fumbled in his trouser pocket. Oh God God Goddington, here come the family snaps. 'There are, that's mine - boy and a girl.'

'Lovely,' I said, lighting another cig (my little packet of ten wasn't going to go far at this rate). He wasn't going to ask again. Pity - I'd decided to call mine Peter and Lee.

'Good little club you got here.'

'It's not mine.' But he was right, it wasn't a dive. Daddy didn't understand why I stayed here – *You clock in and out like some factory girl* – though it's fortunate for him now, selfish bugger. Not been too badly hit, what with the passing sales trade and the naughty boys and the regulars. We were surviving. All the same, five or six nights a week of the same standards got a bit much. The other girls had different jobs, so they were here just the two or three nights. All right, they'd still be singing 'You Made Me Love You' wherever they were, but at least the crowd would make a change.

'Can I get you some peanuts? Or pork scratchings?'

'I'm a Jewish vegetarian,' I said. Which was technically half-true, as my mother had been Jewish. Not that she'd hung around long enough to bring me up with any feeling for it one way or the other. Mind, I was peckish, could have gone for the eggs and bacon – the club speciality - so I kicked myself for saying it.

'Sorry. Peanuts it is, then.' Motioning to Sid over the bar. 'Don't think I've ever met a vegetarian,' he added.

'My family hasn't eaten meat since the nineteenth century,' I told him.

'Really? Bloody hell. Sorry.'

'That's okay, sweetie.' Bored with that now, I balanced my cig in the ashtray, tore open the nuts, poured a few into my hand. The salt gleamed like dandruff on a bald head. Unthink. Unthink. Unthink. Would make myself sick at this rate.

'You got some salt on your lip there.'

Thank you, Claude Rains.

'Let me just...' He leaned in for the kill.

'Raquel! Darling, have we missed you? Can't believe it.' My auntie had slipped in between the two stools, pulled me into a hug that dislodged me from mine. Nearly sent it flying as my feet hit the ground.

'This is...' Oh buggery bugger.

'I'm sure it is. Nice to meet you.' Lesley nodded in Mr Beery-Leery's direction, took my packet of peanuts and dumped them on the bar, and linking her arm through mine steered me away to a table where people were leaving. From behind me, I heard a faint 'Hey!' of protest, but it was clearly token - he knew when he was beaten. I felt like a teenager caught snogging in her bedroom. Lesley slid into a group who were collecting their bags, putting out cigs. 'Jump in your graves as quick, we would,' she said to them, as she pushed me towards a seat. A woman who'd just stood had to tug at the wrap I'd sat on.

'Excuse *me*,' she said.

Lesley had always been able to get me where she wanted

me. When the family was worried that I'd get married too early (there was no boy, mind you, they simply said *Raquel's the type*) and have a fate-worse-than-death, moving out to Basildon where I might sing in a Working Men's Club on a Sunday, or – horror of horrors – become the star of the local Am Dram, she took me to the circus.

Lesley had been a josser for a few years before I ever saw her perform. Daddy – utterly uncharacteristically – didn't approve of animal acts, so we were never taken to the circus as children, not even our auntie's. Apparently, the tigers once made Uncle Glen-Glen cry when the trainer cracked the whip, *Quite right too, barbaric stuff*, but I don't think either of us girls would have cried.

I was eighteen, or nearly, and Lesley about twenty-eight, when I went to Girelli's. Not so much Big Top as Small Top; as soon as we walked in, I knew trapeze wasn't on the agenda. The troupe was basically eight adults and one little girl, about three, obviously the offspring of Gerry and Ellie, who were in nearly every act. When the rather tubby tightrope walker – four feet from the ground – did his stuff, the children ooed and aahed as though they'd seen something special, and that was it. Hooked, I swear. Oh, so much more glam than anything I'd seen Daddy do. Then we had acrobats - one also juggled with his feet afterwards – and the African running ducks (their act was to run), the pigeons and their sweetie-pie old boy handler, who mouthed *Sorry* to the audience each time the birds refused to climb ladders or twirl on rings. And the clowns, a traditional white face who was also the ring mistress – Ellie – and the auguste, Gerry. Very like the vaudeville acts I'd grown up watching, straight man-funny man, so familiar ground there. A rather tatty ancient tiger, a baby elephant, a Big and Small horse act in training, and then Lesley came on.

There's nothing quite like a good aerial silk act. The woman – always a woman – twists herself into a great swathe of material hanging from the ceiling, suspending herself with willpower and core strength. Lesley had been a British gymnast (made County but not Nationals), at a time when all the other little gym girls were from big houses in the country. She'd danced as well, of course, though never more than front row of the chorus. But here, among the burnt sweetness of spun sugar, she twisted soft red fabric round her ankle and made tissu magic happen.

The highlight, new for '68 we were assured, was the Wild West show: the auguste, the ring mistress, the tubby tightrope walker, the acrobats, Lesley, even the horses, all in cowboys hats, which the ring mistress was using to accessorize her Indian dress, twirling lassoes, performing the worst knife act in circus history (Indian Squaw flinched every time the cowboy with dark paint still round his eyes missed her by an arm's length). That's mean, it is, it's mean. Anyway, it didn't matter. The applause was what mattered, and that was real and long and loud and I loved it.

A week later, I was singing a couple of numbers, selling candy floss and windmills, and a couple of months after that, I juggled with my feet too. I've still got the strong lallies from those days, although it's been ten years. Daddy says I've been left with footballer's calves, rotten b. Bloody earned that muscle, I did – could crack a walnut in these thighs even now. For a little while, we tried a singing and foot juggling routine but it never worked, just couldn't get the breathing right, and you got laughs when you weren't expecting them. One day, I filled in for the squaw, who had tummy trouble, and that was it: after that, I was the one to look death in the face. Tried not to flinch, but dearie dear, sometimes had to. By the time the new auguste arrived (to replace Gerry, who'd drunk himself out of a job and a marriage by being a bit too obviously fond of the kiddies), he took me for a seasoned vet at first, which was a compliment in and of itself for a real josser like me. I never went near the silk though, or anything higher than a step-ladder, in case I threw myself off. Baffles me that anyone could do it without that impulse, or maybe fighting it is part of the attraction. You never know about other people, of course, not really.

Even Lesley was never really accepted; I certainly wasn't. But it saved me from marriage, and kids, and a chance of real happiness. Suppose we have to say it's fate. For eight months of the year it saved Delia from my care, too.

'Don't you want a drink, Lesley?'

'Dee's bringing them over.'

'*Dee's* here? And you've left her to go to the bar on her own?'

'She nipped to the loo while I fetched you, then she'll get the drinks. Said she wanted to.' Lesley touched her hair, nervy. Bloody well ought to be. 'Going to pay and everything,' she added.

'What on earth were you...?' Looking round the club for Dee. Quiet tonight, though average for a Wednesday, but there still must have been a couple of hundred people, well over half of them blokes, to get between me and my sister.

'She'll be okay.' Lesley lit a cig, slid the packet across the table to me. I tapped the packet on the sticky table, then gave in and took one. 'She's often here.'

'Yeah, clearly I know that, but it's not the same as getting a round in.' Did she even know how much a round might cost?

Lesley's gaze was fixed over my shoulder, and mine over hers. Neither of us said anything. It was obvious Lesley was as freaked out as I was, but she wasn't about to admit it. She

shook her head, reached for her bag, took out her pale pink
lippy. It still amazed me that she could touch it up without
a mirror, even though I must have seen her do it on a
thousand occasions. From time to time, tried it myself, but
never managed to cover the lips if I didn't cover the
surrounding skin too.

'*Here* she is.' Lesley waved, just a tad too big. Too jolly.
I swung round, saw Dee carefully making her way over to
us, gripping a tray, head bent towards the drinks, watching
them rather than where she was going. The bar was more
behind Lesley than behind my back, so how Dee had
managed to come that way was beyond me. She must have
walked right round the edge of the club or something. Lesley
jumped up, took the tray, nodded to a spare seat. 'Park your
bum there,' she said.

'Bacardi and Coke, Cinzano and lemonade, lemonade
with a dash of lime,' Dee said. She looked at us and beamed.
I swear, a proper beam.

'Thanks, lovely.' Aiming for casual but ever-so-slightly
missing.

'Had to wait a very long time.' Dee picked up her drink.
'The man didn't see me for ages and ages. Then someone
else told him I was waiting, so that was okay.' She took a sip.
'That's delicious,' she said. 'Wonder how they make it?'

'They add a splash of Rose's to a glass of lemonade.' Dear
God.

'Well, it's delicious.'

'And mine's delicious too,' Lesley said, gamely. 'This is
proper R White's in me Cinzano, unless I'm very much
mistaken.'

'Yeah, and the Coke's real. Well, real Pepsi,' I said. Well,
whoopee-doo. 'But I can't see that lasting much longer, not
the way things are.'

'Is it nice?' Dee asked.

'What?'

'Your drink – is it nice?'

I took a sip. 'Oh look, mine's delicious as well,' I said, not bothering to keep the edge out of my voice. Dee would never hear it. Lesley threw me a disapproving look but quite honestly, I'm 35 years old and can be sarky if I want to. 'Anyway, what're you two doing here?'

'Visiting you. Sorry we missed your set,' Lesley said.

'So you said. No, come on, really, what's the score?'

Dee was tracing patterns with her finger in the little line of spilt drink on the tray. Softly, she hummed under her breath. Couldn't make out the tune.

'Delia O'Leary – give.'

But Dee affected not to hear. Oh well, no, that's probably a bit mean, she doesn't always hear, but sometimes you'd think she was slow or difficult or both.

'Where's your young man tonight?' Lesley asked her. Still overplaying jolly.

'Hm?' Still tracing. 'Told you, he's gone to see a man about a job. He said dog, but I think he must've meant job, don't you?'

Lesley was trying not to meet my eye. 'Yeah, that'll be it,' she said.

'Have you really not—'

'*Sigh no more, ladies, sigh no more / Men were deceivers ever.*'

He was three tables away, his arms outstretched, projecting to the gallery.

'*Much Ado about Nothing,*' Dee said to me, lifting her head.

'I *know.*' So this was it: his little surprise. But why hadn't he bothered to find out what time I went on? Typical, just typicular. 'Hello, Daddy,' I said, standing. He strode over to me, crushed me in one of his more public hugs. 'I've been on.'

'No, don't tell me that.' Pulling away from me, covering his face with his hand. 'I'm devastated, just devastated. Reminds me of the time Pinky Greene was supposed to see me in *Revenger's Tragedy* – his train was delayed and he arrived just in time for the curtain. Never did employ me. Timing, my dear girls, is all.' He bowed his head in mock-sorrow. Then he sat, picked up my Bacardi, drained it. 'Don't know how you can drink this muck.'

'Load of old toffee,' said Lesley.

'I beg your pudding?'

'Never mind.'

'No, come on, out with it, woman.'

'I *said*, never mind.' Lesley waved her hand dismissively, but you could see she was *not* best pleased. Had something happened earlier on?

'How's business?' Daddy asked.

'Like you care.' Lesley took an angry-looking sip of her drink. Dee started that damn humming again. Lesley'd been in the rag trade with the man Dee called Uncle Lou for eight or nine years now, but Daddy never really accepted it. I've no idea if Lesley and Uncle Lou were ever lovers. He certainly had an unattractive wife. He was nice, though: used to save the paper parasols out of his fancy drinks for Dee. She must have been twenty at the time. He liked a bacon sandwich too, used to tell us not to mention it to the Rabbi, even though I doubt he'd been near a synagogue between his own wedding and his daughter's. She was a miserable mare, that one - his wife, not his daughter. His daughter was a pretty miserable mare too, mind you. No wonder he spent all his time at the factory. But it's possible he was just a beard. 'Business is bloody bad everywhere,' Lesley added, after an awkward gap.

'Yes, I suppose it must be,' Daddy said, raising an eyebrow at me. She must have seen. 'Feh, you'll be all right. You're a survivor.' He turned to Dee. 'You okay, Princess Pea?'

'Yes.'

'That's the trouble with you,' Daddy ruffled her hair, 'chat, chat, chat, can't hear ourselves think.'

Maurice appeared at my elbow.

'Mr O'Leary, sir – honoured to have you here again.' He shook Daddy's hand as though Daddy was Robert de Niro. Daddy did that two hands over Maurice's one that we associated with him doing humble.

'Man of leisure now, Maurice old boy.' He pulled over a chair from another table. 'Can you sit for a moment? Have a drink with us?'

'I'm sorry, I can't.' He laughed in that way people sometimes did when they were trying to pretend Daddy wasn't well-known or that they were used to mixing with the semi-famous. 'Clubs don't run themselves.'

'How'd this one do tonight?' Daddy patted me on the knee.

'Fine, fine. She's reliable as—'

'A Reliant Robin?' whispered Dee. She wasn't joking of course, but I wished she were, that we could laugh about the ridiculous men.

'Well, yeah,' said Maurice.

'Her school reports used to say *Competent, as always*,' Daddy told him.

'No, that was just the only report you read,' I said.

'Good hit,' he said, nodding.

That report was the worst review I ever had.

Maurice put a daring hand on Daddy's shoulder.

'I know I say this every time, but if I can ever persuade you to give us a number, I'd be eternally grateful.'

'Hell man, I'm no singer – like I always tell *you*. Did a Sondheim once, and a musical *Hamlet* – don't ask, though you wouldn't think a confessional prayer would suit ragtime would you? But I'm more Telly Savalas than Mario Lanza. Sorry.'

'Pity.' Maurice shrugged. 'Well, I'd best—'

'Tell you what,' said Daddy, as though a marvellous idea was that very second occurring to him, 'why don't I say to hell with it? You've been good to Raquel, and not like I've got anything to lose any more. Retired now, of course.'

Oh no, please God no. Not here. Wrong, wrongage, wrongest.

Don't show it, don't show it, you're the daughter of the talented Mr O'Leary. Proud smiles, big clap, nudge your sister to make her clap. Get it right or something bad will happen. Some nameless Bad Thing that will make you die.

Maurice looked as though he didn't know quite what to do. He made his way to the stage as Lisa was finishing her set – impeccable timing, Daddy – and shuffled over to the mic.

'Uh…ladies and gentlemen. Tonight, we have a very special treat for you. The famous actor Mr Ken O'Leary has agreed to give us a number.'

Daddy stood up, the spot found him, and he did a self-deprecating little mock-bow before joining Maurice on stage. The applause sounded startled, as though the hands were caught on their way to doing something else. To be perfectly truthful, I think half the crowd didn't know who Daddy was. He took the mic, turned to whisper to the band. They insisted on being called that even though it was just a guitar, piano, couple of drums. I saw Mickey, the guitarist, shake his head but Daddy patted the air as though to say it would be okay. Then he held out his free arm to the audience.

You must remember this
A kiss is still a kiss
A sigh is just a sigh –
The fundamental things apply
As time goes by

He's singing my song. My bloody signature song. The one I sing here five or six nights a week, forty-eight weeks of the bloody year. The one I finished three-quarters of an hour ago. Lesley can't look at me. Dee, bless her, stares right at me which quite frankly I couldn't do without. She doesn't know what to think, she's waiting for a cue, but I'm going keep this smile on if it kills me.

The selfish fucking bastard. He knows. He must remember. He's swaying there, loving the way no one's talking, everyone's listening to his cracked old wheezy pipes giving the most hackneyed performance of their career. He's belting it out like it matters, like he can sing, like I'm nothing, nothing at all, and I have to keep smiling fucking smiling while the bastard gets away with it.

That's... Beery-Leery's gone right up the front. He's holding his lighter in the air, like he's at a rock concert. His shirt's come untucked in his excitement. Daddy reaches down, pats his cheek for God's sake. Who's he think he is, the Pope? Bet Beery-Leery won't wash for a week.

He's not right in the head. Look at him, that's not right. Some people are laughing, they are, they're laughing, I can see them. A few are on to him. But some are looking at me, it's me they're laughing at, surely. He knows he can't sing, usually he knows that, can barely even hold a tune. But he can't resist, has to do it, has to give it the… Oh my God, the big finish. Please, no. He is, he's going for it. You watch, it'll break… And it has.

As time goes by.

'Going to ask me in, then?'

'Sure, I guess. Come in.' I led him down my too-narrow hall to the living room. What on earth did he think he was doing here? And it was far too cold to be wearing that denim jacket. 'Do you want tea?'

'Please. Two sugars. And I brought these with.' He held out a packet of dubious-looking lemon puffs. Bet your sweet life he got them at an Indian shop, one of those where no one seems to buy anything. Don't know how they keep going.

He hadn't mentioned Dee, so I didn't think he'd come with a message. Interesting. You could bet your sweet life double or quits that the reason he was here was to benefit himself, even if he dressed it up some other way, as he no doubt would. I left him kneeling on the floor, flicking through my records, while I went to the kitchen part of the room to make the tea. Stuck a few of the biscuits on a plate, but I didn't have a tin for the rest.

'There you are.'

'You not having one? Got them for you.'

'Slimming.' I patted my stomach. 'A Chinese fan brought me Fortune Cookies the other night. He kept saying, *Go on, go on, don't worry, aren't fattening, you can eat. Not fattening at all, very light, very nice. Not fattening.* I took the hint.'

Eddie laughed. 'What was your fortune?'

'*Don't let friends impose, work calmly and silently,*' I said.
'So that's me told then.'

'Are we friends?' I sat on the armchair, even though I usually chose the sofa.

'Hope so.' He stood, with an album in his hand. 'Wouldn't've had you down as a Cohen fan.'

'Misery and heartache? What's not to like?'

'Fair point.' He slipped *New Skin for the Old Ceremony* out of the sleeve, limped over to put it on the record player. Cheeky b, might have asked if I'd minded. 'Nice place,' he said, as 'Is This What You Wanted?' drifted into the room. He turned it up a fraction. It *was* a nice place: small but full of rather lovely things, my cushions and my hangings and My Important Bookshelf, with *The Tao of Pooh*, the *Alice* books, *The Prophet*, my Bradley Shakespeare that Daddy gave me when I turned 18, Christina Rossetti, the biog of Bette Davis, Beatles song book, my Walter de la Mares. Telly hidden inside the dark cabinet, that I liked to pretend was full of drinks instead of loneliness. *My* flat. Almost too perfect for me.

'So are you living with Dee now or what?' I said.

'What's she say?' Through a mouthful of lemon puff.

'She isn't sure.'

'There you go, then. Sort of.' He flashed me a cheeky-chappie grin, and pulled his tobacco pouch out of his back pocket. 'Don't suppose you want one of these.' Khaki Che Guevara tee-shirt today. From a distance, he'd pass for early twenties: he was so slim, so physically confident despite (because of?) his leg, but up close, the lines at his eyes and mouth, the hair just beginning to recede, could put him at older than the nearly thirty he admitted to. 'Her place could do with a woman's touch, though,' he added.

'She doesn't like drapery. It bothers her.' Sounding more

defensive than I felt. He was right – her flat was far too Spartan, except for those bloody rocks everywhere, and the dust gathering on her past.

'Yeah, well, that's fine if it's just her.' He sat cross-legged on the floor, lit a roll-up, noisily slurped his tea. 'But is it just her? Hard to know where you stand.'

'You could ask her.'

'She's got a bad cold, I'm steering clear.' Confidently, as though that was relevant. And what cold? She'd been okay the other night at the club. Hope she hadn't given it to me – that'd be all I needed, time off work. Then he shook his head. 'Ever get a straight answer from your sister?'

'Course,' I said. No. 'You just have to know how to ask.'

He pulled hard on the roll-up, narrowing his eyes against the smoke.

'You're not a bit like each other,' he said.

'Hear there's a new cop show starting in the autumn. Called *The Bill*. You'd be a shoe-in.'

Eddie laughed, and did that finger point that I loathe, just a whisker away from pulling a pretend trigger. He was a bit of a tosser, really.

'Eddie, I'm not being funny, sweetie – but really, why are you here?'

'To—'

'And if you say to see me, you're likely to get a lemon puff up your nose.'

'Just as well you never said up your arse.' He winked.

The smoke from his roll-up hit me; I breathed in. Would have loved a ciggie, but I seldom keep them, and no way would I smoke his - nasty soggy things.

'Don't suppose you fancy the pub, do you?' he said.

'No, don't suppose I do at five-and-twenty to five.' I took a sip of my tea. 'Some of us have work to go to, you know.'

'Thought club singers all went on half-cut.'

'Sobbing into our gin? Yeah, that's what we do.' Cheeky so-and-so. He wasn't doing himself any favours here, but he thought he was, you could tell. Sat there cross-legged like an overgrown leprechaun, smirking away as if he was a younger, handsomer version of Jonathan Miller. More like Windy Miller.

Leonard Cohen was imploring his lover to come back to him. With the tobacco smoke, and the tea, and the album, all when I'd normally be doing my ironing or my stretching exercises to Radio 2, the years rolled off, and not necessarily in a good way. It was on the tip of my tongue to say Sod it, let's go to the pub after all, but I bit the inside of my cheek instead. Eddie looked up at me, appraising.

'Roll me one of those, would you?' I said.

He raised one eyebrow: bet he'd spent hours and hours practising. I could do it better, though. And he reached for his pouch when the eyebrow slumped down again. 'What did you want to be when you grew up?' he said.

'What did... An actress. Singer. Dancer.' Oh God, those awful afternoons at Madame Fifi's (I was always confused when her sister arrived to walk her home and called her Doris), *Tap spring, tap spring, tap step-ball-change. Everyone stop. Raquel O'Leary, do it again, this time we'll trouble you to do it on the balls of your feet if you wouldn't mind.* 'There were only a limited number of things I knew you *could* be.'

'But was you ever proper ambitious?'

'That's hard to say.' None of this was unreasonable, of course it wasn't, but it felt as though Eddie was asking questions that were too personal, too naked somehow. Resented it, yes, but it was nice at the same time: a relief, somehow, to be asked something real. I traced my eights with my middle nail on my thumb pad, until I'd reached twenty-four. 'Not ambitious as such, no. Couldn't say that I've been disappointed in life, just, well, unsurprised really.' *Shuffle-hop-step, shuffle-hop-step.*

'I'm ambitious.' He moved to his knees, edged forward, handed me a skinny, perfect roll-up, sparked his lighter and I bent to the flame. The toke was bitter, like bonfires. *Remember, remember, the fifth of November.* 'Would've put something in if I'd thought to bring any,' he added. 'Don't like to walk around with it.'

'Haven't smoked dope in years,' I said. Sounding bored.

'Definitely should've, then.' He hadn't moved back. Disconcerting, to have a man kneeling before you. 'You've gone out.'

Gathering my hair into a ponytail to protect it from the flame, I lent over again. He held the lighter for a beat before running his thumb down the wheel.

'Thanks.' I sat up, pressed my shoulders into the back of the armchair.

Still, Eddie watched me. He tapped a counterpoint to the music on his thigh. Gave me a half-smile.

I'm not a stupid woman. Nor am I naïve or what Daddy would call a natural ingénue. Eddie wasn't coming on to me, not that, but he was definitely buttering me up, wanting to make me think he might kiss me or at least that he wanted to. When I thought of poor little Dee it made me mad. That he was just *playing* for whatever motive made it worse, somehow. Couldn't even say he was carried away, though I suppose it's something that he had no intention of being unfaithful. He wasn't one to trust, that was for sure: skinny malinky with a fat heart of stonio, that one.

'You might as well come out with it,' I said.

'As the actress probably never said to the bishop.'

'Don't be so sure about that,' I said, then was cross with

myself for flirting. 'Come on, Eddie.' I put my cigarette in the saucer we were using for an ashtray; it had gone out again. 'What are you here for?'

He held up his hands, in a gesture of surrender from a 50's Western.

'Help,' he said. 'I mean, that's what I come for. Help. I'm nearly thirty years of age, and I'm dying on me feet here, girl.' His accent suddenly was much stronger. I almost expected Julie Andrews to burst in with a cheering ditty. 'Your old man must have a black book the size of the Yellow Pages—'

'And you want him to let his fingers to do the walking.'

'Well, yeah. Basically, yeah.' He threw his cig on top of mine, started to roll another. 'He's retired. Don't matter now if this one owes him or he owes that one, not like it would've a few month ago.'

'Wouldn't it? I see.' I took a mouthful of lukewarm tea.

'So will you?'

'Will I what?'

'Make me work for it, why don't you?' Rubbing his hand over his face. 'Will you suggest to him he might be able to help me? For Dee's sake? And don't ask me why I didn't ask her. Just don't.' He stood up, walked over to the window.

'Wouldn't dream of it.' I got up too, went and stood next to him. We were almost of a height; he probably had an inch on me, no more. I put my hand on his shoulder, felt him tense underneath my fingers. 'I could mention it,' I said. 'Yes, I could do that. But what you have to understand is that Daddy's – well, a law unto himself. It could go the other way.' I could smell his aftershave, something citrusy. 'When I was young, a boy asked Daddy if he could court me. Really, he did. Sure, we'd been out a few times, but he wanted to let Daddy know his intentions were honourable.' Sean

Callaghan. Twenty-two, gorgeous, a stage hand, probably gay I now realize. 'Daddy saw him off, even though if we'd just carried on going out, he wouldn't have said a thing.'

Eddie turned his head. I moved my hand away. Our faces were so close that I could smell the tobacco on his breath, the tannin.

'Got to risk it,' he said into my air, holding my gaze.

'*He flies through the air with the greatest of ease / That daring young man on the flying trapeze-*'

'Yeah, all right.' He moved his head, fractionally, closer to mine. 'Will you?'

'If I can.'

'You can.'

'Okay, you can stop working it now.' Taking a step back, I looked at my watch. Pointedly. 'Got to get ready in a tick, so if you'll excuse me...'

'Right, yeah, cool. I'll be off, then.'

'You do that. And give my love to Dee.'

He laughed then. 'Oh, you're good,' he said.

But *he* wasn't good. You could see that in the arrogance of his grin, the wicked creases at his eyes, in the way he stood with his legs too far apart, clearly refusing to favour the good one. Not being famous by now must have surprised him in and of itself; he'd have chosen his Desert Island Discs and his quotes for the theatre pages long ago. No, the film pages. He'd have practised his autograph – generous, spiky, illegible – and decided which drugs to admit to. He was every man I'd ever gone out with until I was thirty, when the landscape changed for me rather and I was left with what was left. But before then, I'd had my pick. Bad boys playing badder ones. He didn't have a trick I hadn't seen.

'I know I'm a bastard,' he said. 'But I'm serious about acting. That's where *I'm* good, Raquel – proper good. And I do love Dee, it'd be good for her, straight up.' He shrugged. 'Can you sing?' he asked. 'Really?'

'I'm not bad. I can fake it okay.'

'Wouldn't be enough for me.' Eddie shook his head. 'Rather go get a job in Dagenham Fords.'

He meant it. I'd seen him in that awful telly thing, I knew he was okay, but just maybe he did have real talent after all. Thousands believe they have and they're quite mistaken, but maybe, just maybe, he wasn't one of them.

When he left, I ate four stale lemon puffs and decided not to call my sister.

Delia

When the dizziness comes, I sit on the ground. Sometimes, I have to sit on the ground a lot. The world rocks and wobbles as though it's a ship and I'm the only sailor. Everyone else walks around on solid ground, but they only jiggle my world more. It lasts for hours, days sometimes, once or twice it lasted a week. When I was little, I pretended to be a pirate. I didn't play pirates exactly, not exactly, I didn't walk the plank or have fights or make x mark the spot but I wore my special hat and said *'eave, 'o, me 'earties* instead of yes or no. It was handy because yes and no were difficult for me, then. I can manage okay with them now. Yes. No. Daddy told me once that my minnie was a pirate. I had my hand down my knickers, and Daddy said, *Don't do that, Dee-Dee, your minnie's a pirate*. So that's when I started playing pirates and stopped touching my minnie. Or I stopped when people could see, anyway. Mostly, unless I forgot. I told Raquel that a few years ago, and she said Daddy must have said *Your minnie's private* which I suppose does make more sense.

The first time it happened I assumed I was going mad. People have called me mad all my life, so I thought it was my mind catching up. Then I thought maybe I was going to start having fits, like Uncle Glen-Glen. But now I think it's just me. It happens once in a while and I hate it and then it stops and I'm okay except sometimes I get really anxious, thinking that if I move my head wrong it'll come back. Things I hate aren't black or red like you might think, they're that horrible olivey-brown that you get when you mix all the paints or all the plasticine together. If you don't keep things separate, the colours merge until they don't mean anything any more. Nothing shines. Meanings are hard to pin down as it is, without the mixing.

Mostly, I don't mind being alone. I like it. You can scrunch up your eyes really small and hard, and make the colours come, without anyone saying, *What the bloody hell d'you think you're doing, Dee-Dee?* So good they named me twice. You can sit around in your pants and there's no one to fuss over meals. You can eat a whole lettuce with salad cream without anyone bringing you a fork or pressing beef. You can polish your gem stones and your pebbles until they shine like angry eyes. You can get up in the night, before six. You can be.

But when the dizziness comes, I'm afraid to be alone. I don't know how to hold my head, where to rest my look. I don't know how to be me.

'For fuck's sake, get to a doctor, girl.'

'I'm not ill.'

'Well, you're not right.'

'That doesn't make me wrong.'

Now I hide it from Eddie. It's better to be afraid and alone than to be got at, peck, peck, peck in my face-feelings, like a carrion crow. I don't want any more happy pills, that take away your over-and-overs, that put single thoughts in your mind instead. Single thoughts aren't enough. I'm a rubbish liar, Raquel always says that, but if I just tell Eddie I've got a bad cold, he doesn't come round.

'Can't afford it in my game.'

He doesn't ask questions, just puts a flower on the doorstep sometimes and tells me to ring him when I'm better. So I do. I think of the dizziness as Delia's special cold. But I'm never left entirely by myself, not for all the time. And that's a good thing. Something I ought to feel grateful for.

'You look FUCK IT better today.'

'I'm better, yes. Nearly normal.'

'As normal as you get.' Twitch, gape, shudder. Tom smiled at me, tucked my hair behind my ears. He wasn't swimmy today, barely flickering. Yesterday had been awful, but it was almost over. Wished I could trust it, though. Do other people trust their bodies and their minds? Tom doesn't. But Tom isn't like other people. Raquel thinks I don't notice difference but I do, or I think I do. 'I'll make COFFEE BEER BUGGERY LEMON tea,' Tom said.

He's such a kind man, so gentle, soft. I like his voice, too – it never gets loud or hard, not when he's just saying his normal words. It's like someone singing to you when you're little. It's like a secret. Usually, I don't like other people fiddling about in my kitchenette. Not even Eddie – he leaves puddles of tea and grains of coffee and bread crumbs on the side. Raquel is okay, because she likes to bleach for me. The smell reminds me of when I was young, before she ran away to join the circus. But only Tom seems to have a right to be there. It took him two years. He stood and chatted to me at the doorway. Then he came in and sat on the side. Then he got the milk out of the fridge for me. Then he put it in. Now, he makes tea and even toast sometimes. I almost never mind.

'How you FUH-feeling?'

'Okay now. Nearly okay.'

'Your eyes look better. More in focus.'

He sat next to me on the floor – he didn't kick the teas over this time - put his arm round me. We leaned back into the sofa. His hand rested on his knee, the knuckles red, bitten, sore, the fingers all long and jointy.

'How do you know when a man would rather be somewhere else?' I asked.

'How the EDDIE hell should I know?' Tom stroked my arm. 'You worried?'

'No. I don't think so. But he likes not being here, I know he does.'

'He must like being here too.'

'Suppose so. Just...I'm not sure how you tell.' I leaned over to pick up my mug. 'You know him. You know him quite well.'

'Oh, baby, don't put me in the FUCKING FUCKING FUH middle.'

'Am I? I didn't know.' Carefully, keeping my eyes steady, I turned my head to look at him. His hair was more zhooshy than ever today. If he dyed it, perhaps he'd look like someone in a New Romantic band. But probably not. He was a punk once but that's not the same, though I'm not sure why. 'You can't sing, can you?'

'No.' He looked down at me, breathed onto my face. A mixture of toothpaste and tobacco and tea. Suddenly, he stood up. He knocked his elbow on my head. 'Left my cigarettes CANCER BAG in my jacket.'

'Whose friend were you first?'

'Yours. His. Don't know.' He fumbled with his lighter, but got the flame to the cigarette okay. 'It's not easy, Dee.' Twitch, gape, shudder. 'Was weird for me, two friends of mine getting together. You. I've known you longest. Best.'

'What if we split up? Whose friend would you be then?'

He laughed. 'You never BITCH WHORE give up.' He sat on the hard-backed chair, put the ashtray on the little table. 'You, Dee. It'll always be you.'

'Good.' It made me happy, him saying that. Made me feel safe. You don't know whether someone will leave you, just go after tea when you're in bed, but he said he wouldn't and I believed him. It wasn't something I'd have asked Eddie.

'Why?' Tom asked. 'D'you think you might split up?'

'People don't know things like that.'

'Half the time they don't, no.'

I pulled myself up backwards onto the sofa. The room tipped, just a bit. Too quick, that's all it was. I kept very still, and slowly, the world righted itself.

'You okay, Dee?'

'Mm.'

'Oh BUG…BUGGERUGLYBUGGERBASTARDLIMP DICK.' Tom slapped himself in the face. Hard. I heard it slap across his skin, tight. 'TOMTOM.' His eyes were all watery. He minded, I knew he did.

'It doesn't matter,' I said.

'Yes it FUCKING does. FUCK IT. STUPID WHORE.'

'I love you,' I said. Because I did.

Tom sucked so hard on his cigarette that the tip glowed fierce, like rage.

'If I try to suppress it,' he said, after a bit, 'the bad thoughts come.'

I waited for him to explain. He looked at me, his nose red like his cigarette. Perhaps I was meant to say something.

'Do you know what bad thoughts are?' he said.

'I know what my bad thoughts are.'

'You don't have them.'

'I do.' No one knew about this, but he was going to. I

wasn't just pathetic little Dee with her harmless funny ways. I was bigger than that. Worse. Bad. 'Sometimes, when Raquel or Auntie Lesley give me a fork, I have to stop myself sticking it in their hands. Or I think I might throw myself onto the tube line. Or push my fingers in my eyes till they pop.'

'Really?' Tom put his cigarette out, came over to me, knelt on the floor. 'Is that true?'

'Of course it's true.'

'BOLLOCKS. Like, I see a baby. And I want to kiss it but I get the FUCKING FOETUS urge to pick it up and throw it under a bus.' He put his hands on my knees. 'And I hate myself. FREAK. I can't handle it. Thinking like that's a lot worse than the tics, tell you. So mostly, I don't try and stop them.'

'Maybe everyone gets them?' This was amazing. 'If *we* do, maybe everyone does. Maybe Raquel and Daddy and Eddie...Maybe the lollipop man and Mr Kumar at the shop.'

'And Uncle Tom Cobbley and all. Doubt it, Dee.'

'You don't know they don't.'

'Think I FUH-do.'

But we couldn't be the only two, no way. I could have been the only one, Tom could have been the only one, but as there were two of us, there must be others. Lots of others. And that would give the bad thoughts a lot less power if they were just ordinary. Nothing special. One of the crowd. The discovery of ordinariness was the biggest thing that had happened to me in a long time. Surely it must be for Tom, too. Surely ordinary was what he wanted more than anything. And I might have to subtract Purcell from my list to make room to add *Ordinariness*. I moved my head too quickly, had to grab the world as it passed.

Tom was still kneeling in front of me, looking at my face. He really thought it was just the two of us, I think, just the two of us with the bad thoughts. That would make us a special unit, and there was something I liked about that, but it couldn't be true. Maybe he was too frightened to see. Maybe he was scared ordinary might not be what he thought. Sometimes, it's not me who doesn't see what's obvious. Sometimes, other people get it wrong.

'It's logical, Tom,' I said. 'Thought I was telling you something really big. A confession, like to a priest. But where there's two, there'll be more.'

'Safety in numbers,' he said. One of those strange things people say that are more about a conversation they're having with themselves, than about getting others to understand. And I didn't, but I didn't say so. He might have meant that the bad thoughts weren't powerful if they weren't special but I don't think so. That was *my* conversation with myself. We don't all see things in the same way. Raquel says I think people can see inside my head, but I really don't. I just can't believe sometimes that they can't see the obvious.

Daddy says when he prepares for a part that he doesn't hold with *All that interior bollocks. Just say the lines convincingly and get the clothes right. Clothes right, voice right, the audience will believe you've got a whole other person going on behind the eyes*. Eddie believes in living a character, getting inside them, asking *If I* questions. *You got to be someone else. People outside the business think actors are one massive ego, but we're not, man. Acting's about banishing the ego.*

That's not right, I think. Daddy's been believed by loads more people than Eddie has, so you must be able to act without becoming someone else, and I can't see how Eddie's ever banished the ego. But they're both saying no two people are actually the same. No matter how hard it is to really feel that, most people do understand it logically, I think. I'm no different there.

'Dee?' Tom's breath was warm on my face again. 'Dee? You okay?'

'Fine,' I said. Even lovely Tom feels the need to ask that too much. I almost never feel the need to ask it, unless I can see someone needs actual help. Sometimes, I think that what they really mean is, *Talk to me*. It's like a theme tune that tells a programme it has to start. People often say one thing when they mean another. Raquel says she wants to find somebody kind, but what she means is somebody who's kind to her. Don't suppose she'd care one bit if he was nasty to his neighbours. If everybody would just say what they meant, no sub-text, then we'd all be okay.

'Not dizzy? DOZY COW Dee? Not dizzy?'

'No. Aren't your knees hurting? You've been kneeling for ages.'

'No. FUCKIT. Now you mention it...' He walked on his knees to the side of me, sat down, rubbing his legs. That couldn't have been comfy. 'I've been BUGGERYBOLLOCKS offered some film work,' he said.

'That's great.'

'Not so much. Just a tiny film about stand-ups. Docu-drama. Playing QUASIMODO ME ME ME ME myself. Only a couple of hundred nicker in it.'

'Still, it might mean more work.'

'Maybe.'

'Will you do it?'

'Maybe.'

'You should talk to Eddie about it.'

'Don't think...COLONEL MUSTARD. Maybe.'

The scraping at the lock made me jump, setting off the world again. But I pulled it back.

'Think that must be him now,' I said. Odd. He didn't

usually come until he was certain Delia's special cold was gone.

'I should go.'

Scrape, scrape. Then we heard voices, laughter. Suddenly, the front door burst open and we heard what sounded like a couple of bodies falling into the hall.

'Eddie? Is that you?' I didn't get up. Best to conserve movement when I'm just getting over a dizzy-attack.

Eddie opened the living room door and stumbled through it, followed by Daddy. *Daddy*. I don't think I've ever been more surprised in my life. Had they met on the doorstep? Daddy knocked straight into the little table, sent my dish of special gems everywhere, but Tom leaned over and scooped them back in before I really felt it. Eddie fell to his knees in front of me, gave me a big wet kiss. I tried to kiss him back, but his was too sloppy.

'Tommo!' he said, clapping Tom on the shoulder. 'You all right, mate?'

Daddy walked over heavily, sat on the sofa behind me, put his hand on my head. '*Drink, sir,*' he said, '*is a great provoker of three things … nose-painting, sleep, and urrrrrine.*' Ruffling my hair. He pointed at Eddie. '*Lechery, sir, it provokes and unprovokes: it provokes the desire but it takes away the performance. Therefore much drink may be said to be an equivocator with lechery: it makes him and it mars him.*' Weighing it out with his hands, like scales. '*It sets him on and it takes him off.*'

'WHATTHEFUCK? Excuse me?' said Tom.

'Come on, boy, come on,' said Daddy. 'That's a fool's question. Starter for ten. *Macbeth*. The porter.'

Eddie was giggling like a star pupil. It was like being in my dizziness without the actual dizziness. Or like a dream where your old history teacher is having tea with the Queen and invites you.

'Have you both been drinking?' I said.

'She makes it sound as though we've been to an opium den!' Daddy said.

'*Dost thou think*,' said Eddie, with his consonants all blurred, the vowels limping, '*because thou art virtuous, there shall be no more cakes and ale?*'

'No, of course not. I just can't make it out.' Turning to Tom, I added, '*Twelfth Night*.' Because after all, he hadn't even known the porter.

'FUCKFUCKFUCKUPTHEBUM. BUMCHUMS.'

'What have you been doing?' I asked.

'Little bit of this, little bit of that,' Eddie said. 'Watched some *Grandstand* in the pub. The Owl's got a telly in the corner now.'

'Daddy hates sport.' I shifted my body so that I could see him properly.

'People watching, Princess Pea,' Daddy said, resting his hands on his tummy. He had his goatee at the moment. In that green pullover, he looked like Father Christmas in one of those Victorian pictures. 'You never lose the impulse, even in retirement.' As though he'd been retired for ages instead of a few weeks.

'We was talking shop.' Eddie was rolling a cigarette, dropping tobacco all over my carpet. I didn't like it but I knew that if I cleared it up straight away, he'd call me *Uptight* and Daddy would get cross because I'd *broken the laws of hospitality*.

'You mean talking about work?' I asked.

'And brotherhood,' said Daddy. Eddie spread his arms wide, like people do when they're saying sorry but they don't mean it.

'I should BUMCHUMMIES go.' Tom was rubbing the

end of his poor fierce nose, hard. He didn't look happy, I was pretty sure of that. When people are drunk, it's easy to feel left out.

'*Strive mightily, but eat and drink as friends*,' Daddy said.

'Shit,' Eddie said. 'I do know it.'

'*Shrew*.' Daddy threw himself back into the sofa. 'Got a coffee for your poor old father, have you? Your poor old pensioner father?'

'You're not a pensioner.'

'In spirit, my darling girl, in spirit. You're as old as you feel, and right now, I feel like Methuselah's grandfather.' He slapped his knees. 'Do you know, it's absolute bollocks that you're only as old as the woman you feel. In my – modestly vast – experience, the younger the girl, the older you become. That barmaid was nearly a case in point. What was she – twelve?'

'What's FUH-nose painting?' Tom asked.

'What?' Daddy leaned forward. 'Nose what? Oh, it just means your nose gets red in drink. In your cups. Cu-psss.' He and Eddie burst out laughing, sounding as though they might choke. Daddy's did end in a great cough.

'I'll get you that coffee,' I said, standing carefully.

'*Everybody'th been tho kind*,' Daddy said. 'Crip parts get the awards, you know.' He nodded at Eddie, who went dark red and definitely looked angry. Glittery and angry.

'Film,' said Tom. 'John Hurt in *Elephant Man*. Even I MEMEMEME know that one.'

'She gave me whithkey, whithkey,' Daddy said, reaching his hand out to me. I ignored his Charles Laughton and went to make the coffee.

'Me an' all, gorgeous,' Eddie called through.

Tom appeared at the door.

'Not my scene,' he said. 'I'm going to split.'

74

I measured a spoon of Nescaff into Daddy's mug, one and a half into Eddie's.

'Dee? I'm going to go.'

'Yes, I heard.'

'You be okay?' Twitch, gape, shudder.

'With Tweedledrunk and Tweedledrunker?' That was a Raquel line. 'Course.' But I did feel abandoned. It was stupid-wrong, I did know that, I think I did, but it's how I felt.

Tom came to kiss my cheek, though in fact he licked it. Slimy, warm, but really no worse than Eddie's sloppy kiss before. I rubbed my cheek on my shoulder and that was that.

'Sorry, Dee.'

'Don't be silly.' I slipped my arms round his waist, gave him a quick hug. He made one of his strangled noises, and pulled away. I think he minded about licking me, but really people lick each other all the time. Smell each other's bottoms. Not actually lick and smell – though some must do – but we're all little animals in the end. 'Why do you think they're together?' I asked.

'They said work. Maybe your old man's helping him out.'

'That's nice.'

'Only you,' he said, touching my other cheek with the back of his hand. I nearly flinched, but luckily he didn't hit me. It's funny, he's never hurt me. Daddy has, with the way he thinks I'm not capable of the things others are capable of. Eddie has, for the same reasons, really. But Tom, even when he's slapped me or smacked his arm into my chest, hasn't ever hurt me. He never, I think, will.

Ken

Didn't expect it to be so tiring. Don't know how you do it, old boy. All this sitting, can't be good for the bum. Remember Mummy would never let us sit on concrete, in case we got piles? Still can't, to this day, even though it's a load of old bollocking bollocks. Mind you, she told Lesley she'd get preggers if she showed a man her backside. Well, fair enough point, when you think about it: one thing leading to another. But she was wrong about the piles – they're an ailment of the armchair.

Thought I might get a call about the Big Red Book, thought Eamonn Andrews might be there to pretend to have gathered my loved ones personally. Feh. Remember when they did lovely Hattie, God rest her soul? Early sixties, that would have been. Everyone knew she was schtupping that driver, and poor Le Mez was playing the loving hubby – she looked horrified, poor dear. Mind you, when you think about our loved ones, probably it's just as well no one's called yet.

They haven't, have they?

Sorry, don't mind me. Just pulling your leg.

What d'you think, Glen-Glen? You want to be on the telly-box? Course you don't. Though my God, you'd look the part – *Mirror, mirror on the wall, who's the fairest of us all?* Handsome devil. Maybe you could stand in for me. Could work, could work, not as if it's live, not after that boxer chappie couldn't stop swearing last year. Fucking buggering fool, that's what we say. They could edit to make us seem like the Waltons. Could even get Dee's friend with the funny turns on – he'd bring the house down and still be safe for the kiddywinks by the time it was broadcast.

My pal Peter Walshaw turned it down in '74, '75. Remember that? They had to show an old one. Was due to speak on it. I'd just done that Dickens for the BBC, so I'd got a bit of currency, not to mention I'd known Peter for thirty years. But he didn't have a happy war – think he was scared someone'd mention that. I wasn't going to, of course, was going to talk about the frocks and the melting greasepaint.

You all right there, Glen-Glen? Nurse said you had a bit of a do yesterday. Little fit? Never mind, brighter this morning she said. Knocked your poor old eye there, though. Brought you a nice iced bun ring today - the bun that cheers. You want it? Well, course you do. Here you go, have just... No, you take it, yes, why not.

Got offered a VO the other day, for cigars. That's what retirement means for a lot of us – the graveyard of the lucrative voice over. Well, always done a certain amount of course. Remember when everything was mono, and I once did a whole take into the dead? Missed the mic entirely. Was just a cub then, of course, and bloody mortified when the director said we'd to go again. Public health warning about VD, of all things – not something you want twice. Told Beryl to turn the cigars down. Retired means not working, I told her. It doesn't mean just doing the bread and butter gigs, avoiding the real stuff. But I didn't like saying it, I won't lie to you. Went against the grain. Never turned much down, handful of times in a whole career.

Not used to this. Spring used to mean a new season, now it's nearly here it's just a few dreary old bits of blossom. Almost always been in work, haven't I? Not like Delia's young gentleman, doing bits and bobs here and there, thank you very much, single hand and off down the Job Centre. He's a funny one, Glen-Glen, can't make the fella out at all. Don't suppose you'll meet him; can't imagine it'll last. Can't imagine he will. Got this limp, he has – that's not going to help. Only so many Richard IIIs for your money. Suppose he could play the hunchback, maybe Byron, get a sideline in crips going.

What have you done?

Polio, road accident, birth defect, stubbed toe, gangrene, done them all, me.

But he's never going to be Michael J. Fox, poor devil.

I don't trust him. He's after something… Me, probably, what I can do for him. If he hurts our baby, I'll swing for him, promise you that.

Want a nip of this? No? Quite right, keep that baby's bum complexion. Had this flask some years, haven't I? Ollie Reed gave it to me back in the day, and it went everywhere with us for a while, even to that party Sweetie Brown had at the Ritz, when he was casting *Five Roses*. That waiter nearly asked me to leave, but I gave him the old glad-eye and he relented. Funny, you'd have thought that would've been my big break, but no one really noticed me in it, did they? We could have moved to Hollywood permanently on the strength of that, if it'd really come off. Mind you, don't remember much of that shoot. Sip, sip, sip like a bloody maiden aunt wondering where her next sherry's coming from. Difference was, I had the girls to think about. Hard to be a hell-raiser when you've got a Parents' Meeting. And I must've gone to *some* Parents' Meetings, I'd have thought.

Good God - that's a big laugh, Glen-Glen. Do it again. Two of us, having a laugh over a drink. Do it again for Kenny.

Look at me. Turning face, come on. Look at me, Glen-Glen. Look at me. Don't know if I did the right... Look at me. Please.

Look at me.

Eddie

'The beggar was treading on my laugh every night. He's the type. *Can I crash on your line?* overly polite, obsequious even, Uriah bloody McGovern, but he'd get there any way he could. You must have come across them.'

'Yeah, a few.'

'Of course, you haven't worked much yet.' Ken let out that big roaring laugh, the one I remembered from his cameo in that Burt Reynolds film. Comedy thing. Something II. Punters in the pub turned round, stared.

Shit, not like I was on strike, was it? Not like I was stood on a picket line refusing to work and waving a bucket at passing people to get them to pay my wages. I was at Watford for two years playing all sorts - it's not like I *never* got offered things. Even in the last five, done more than my fair share of ads, and I was in *Crossroads* for six straight episodes, then there was *Purple Sky...* Bit my tongue, though. Couldn't afford to put him straight just because he got on my wick.

'Not got the right voice for radio,' I said.

'No? No?' Ken raised his eyebrows. Could've bred rabbits in them. 'Suppose you haven't, now you come to mention it. Can you do other voices?'

'Not really. Bit posher, bit more common. Few accents.'

'You're a tenor, aren't you? Light, rather thin.' Mimicking me as he spoke. 'No, I can see that radio wouldn't be your milieu. Pity, it was always a nice bit of bread and butter for me. With jam on, sometimes.'

It was knackering, talking to Ken. He made you work for it, man, no joke. When I rung him that morning, I screwed my courage to the sticking place and asked,

'You free?'

'Free?' A ripe pause. 'No one is ever free.' You could almost see the sad shake of the head, swear it.

'Fair enough.' I traced a CND sign in the filthy glass. 'But apart from being in chains, you free?'

'I don't know what you mean by *free*.'

At that moment, was right tempted to put the phone down. But then, like he knew my part better than I did, he added,

'Lofty Baines used to ring up and bark, *Yes? What do you want?* Did it with so much conviction that once or twice I found myself answering.' He laughed. 'D'you mean am I free today? Nothing in the work diary.' I heard him take a sip of something. 'Are you going to ask for my daughter's hand? Officially?'

'Well, no, I'm not as it goes.'

'Right, well in that case it must be a professional call. Raquel told me I'd to be nice to you. Bollocks to that, but I *will* be fair.'

'Good enough for me, sir.' So Raquel had come through. Sweet. Weren't at all sure she would, but they were close, them girls. In a funny sort of way. She'd be doing it for the team.

'Cut the Sir, I'm not Larry Olivier.'

The pips went, making me jump. Knocked my pile of coins onto the floor and I had to fumble for some more shrapnel, quick. Hadn't thought it was going to be a full-on conversation. Seemed a good idea at the time, getting an incoming calls-only phone, but having to come out to the box for important shit was a pain in the arse. Had to wait for some Skin to leave before I got in here, and he weren't making a phone call, tell you that much for nothing. Place reeked of Copydex.

'You fancy a pint?' I said.

'Do I fancy a pint?' Taking the mick. '*Do* I fancy a pint? Do you know, I haven't been asked that in twenty years. Do I want a *drink*, yes. More times than I care to recall. But…Well, there we are. Miscast, certainly, but beggars can't be choosers. Yes, I'll take that pint. Do you know The Cow and—'

'Was thinking The Owl, near Dee.' But I sounded pathetic, even to myself.

'A pub crawl! Excellent. The Cow and Calf, on the corner of my street, followed by The Owl and the Pussycat. And any other creatures we may meet along the way.'

He was playing me, I knew that, but quite obviously that was something I'd have to put up with. Bloke was a legend, in a small way. Legendette. Legeling. As Raquel might say. And in fairness, he was bloody good. When I was at school, about fifteen, we had a trip to the Old Vic. Twenty years ago now. Saw this totally amazing production of *Measure for Measure*, and his Angelo was the best thing in it. The Duke was good, and Lucio was hilarious, proper funny in the way Shakespeare's comic parts aren't very often as I later found out, but it was Angelo and Isabella who took it. You could believe they both wanted to fuck, in a fucked-up way, it wasn't just him being turned on by her chastity – he made her feel it, too. And he made me understand that, even though I was just this spotty teenager. Acting was a way to get the birds, that was for definite. Could never tell him – he'd never believe they took ten-year-olds from round my way to see Shakespeare, and man, wouldn't get away with making my birth certificate a liar. Don't know why he never quite made it big. Luck's a major player in this game.

Was chilly, on the way to the tube. Late-winter early-spring's a bugger to call. Wished I'd put the bomber on, but the denim's more youngish actor. Ankle-deep in rubbish at some points along the Waste, had to kick it out the way, and a bastard Kentucky box hit me in the shin where the wind took it. Could hear my mother, *It's a disgrace. So dirty these days, never go up there no more except to see you. Not being funny, but it's them Pakis what've done a lot of it. Keeping their shops open so late. Kids throw the rubbish, course they do. Well, it's the parents.* She's a stupid cow, properly thick. Sometimes think I must have been switched at birth. The old man worries that I've not got a proper job, says my mum's cousins could get me in Fords even now, but her, she's just disappointed. And my God, she has to let you know it. I was clever, meant to be a teacher; that was the point of getting me the complete Shakespeare one Christmas. God forbid you should ever want to make the thing live. Heard her once, talking to my aunt, *He just don't realize, you'll never get a crippled Paul Newman. But I could just see him being called Mr Muir.* Thick as shit.

The pub was one of the done-up ones that do food. Knew it would be. Not pies, but scampi in a basket, chicken in a basket, that type of thing, as though to make food better you only had to stick it in a bit of fake raffia and shit. Spotted him in the corner next to a battered piano that for now had survived the renovation, and was well annoyed with myself for hiding the limp as I went over. Not like he didn't know about it. Bad move. That's something a lot of actors get wrong - they walk too slow, too deliberate, if they're playing someone trying not to limp. Noticed it three, maybe four times. But the trick is to move quick, so people don't know what they've seen.

He looked up, and for a split second I could see Raquel in him. And then Dee.

Raquel has such a strong face, big featured, like her dad. Dee's frail, almost mousey from some angles. But there they both were, just for that moment, looking out at me.

Two pints of bitter on the table. I'm a lager man these days. Younger drink.

'Thought I'd better get into character,' he said. 'Not that I approve of the Method. Expect you do, though.'

Knew better than to try to answer.

'Drank pints of cold tea in a telly once,' I said instead.

'That's in case you have to go for multiple shots.' Ken picked up his pint, drank from it, pulled a face. 'Feh. Not that it mattered in film back in the day. There'd have really been a mutiny on the Bounty if the booze had been fake.'

'That right?' Trying not to sound too eager. But come on, the legeling knew them all. The whole madding crowd.

'Could name you three Oscars earned by Johnnie Walker, off the top of my head.' Another swallow on his pint, this time without reaction. 'And that's just the men. The women, trust me dear boy, were worse. Or perhaps I mean better.'

As I leant forward to hear more, I knocked the table leg, a bit of my pint splashing onto the top. There was a wodge of tissues in my pocket. Mopping up the spill, I was embarrassed to see they were purple, yellow, green. Must have been a handful I'd grabbed out of a box at Dee's. Or maybe Raquel's. When I rolled a cig afterwards, it smelt of beer and lavender. Ken put his hand on the damp table and then looked at his palm, with no expression, before wiping it on his old tweed jacket.

'Shit, sorry,' I said.

'So you want my help then.' Not a question, a statement. Be truthful, I'd expected him to string me along for half the afternoon before we got down to it.

'Yeah, I do.' Of course I'd rehearsed that. Calm, confident, no bullshit. Not quite entitled, but nearer that than supplicant. Though at College, they'd told us that supplicants – who held on to the legs of the person they was asking – had to be given what they asked for, so maybe it was a wrong call. Tragedy class. When I'd still reckoned myself as the next Olivier. Year full of bastard Oliviers and Suzmans.

'What's in it for me?'

'Sorry, what?'

'What – if I help you – might be in it for me? The satisfaction of altruism?'

'Your daughters'd be happy,' I said.

'Both of them. I see.' He sipped his pint. In a script, the wryly would be (thoughtfully). 'You'd want what? Introductions? My agent - my *ex*-agent - to call yours, that sort of thing? Not that agents are known for helping the clients of others.'

'Introductions, yeah. To directors or whatever. Listen,' I re-lit my fag, 'it's not like I'd show you up. I'm good. Just need a chance to prove it.'

'Of course you do. What happened to the big British Film?'

'What?'

'The one you said you were up for.'

'Didn't happen. You know how it is.' Shit, forgot I'd bullshitted about that.

Suddenly, he stood. Moved over to the piano. Started banging out a few chords, then slipped into 'It Had To Be You'. Everyone was staring. Place weren't packed, it was lunchtime on a weekday after all, but there was enough people to make me want to tell him to stop. And then, oh shit, I knew what was coming.

'Think of it as your audition!' he projected over the music.

Maybe I could laugh it off. Maybe I could refuse. Maybe I could leave. Look, the guy was after humiliating me, that was obvious, and it could be that I let him and he said *Next*. But on the other hand, what did I really have to lose?

Before I can think any more, I get to my feet.

It had to be you
It had to be you
I wandered around
And finally found
Somebody who…

Not got a bloody Scooby whether I'm getting the words right, but man, I keep going. Right on until the end of the lines. Giving it some, too - moving around, blowing a kiss to some blowsy sort up at the bar who's wearing make-up she'd put on in the fifties and never took off, close my eyes near the end. Raquel goes through this night after night after night - got to admire that, in a way. I finish with a mock-finger point and a wink. Hold still for two beats. Then I make it to the chair, to a little scattered applause. Thank Christ I don't live round here.

Ken closed the piano lid.

'Two large whiskies, if you'd be so good,' he called to the barman, as though this was a hotel instead of a slightly ponced-up pub. Sitting down heavily, resting one hand on his big belly, he looked right in my eyes. 'Balls,' he said. 'I must give you that. Balls.'

'No frigging choice,' I said. He nodded.

'I'd have sung. Su-uu-ung!' he sang. Could hear a few piss-taking laughs. Back of my neck prickled with embarrassment. Something felt well off. Surely the bloke couldn't always be this OTT. Was he hammered? Maybe he was on something off the doctor. Eyes looked dark enough. 'Had to play,' he said. 'Don't ask me the reason. Sometimes you still need to do these things, even though you've retired. Probably wouldn't be such a wrench for you, being more of an occasional chap.'

I rolled a fag. Had I got the gig or what? Or did he do that to make a mug of me. Most likely, truthfully, but I'd had to chance it. Didn't want to stay a fucking occasional chap. But he weren't wrong.

The barman brought over the drinks, rolling his eyes at me. Ken gestured him away with the back of his hand.

'Put it on the tab.'

'Cheers.' I raised the whiskey to my lips, but as it burned them, right before I properly had a mouthful, he leaned over, closed his fingers round my wrist.

'Why did you visit my brother?' he said.

Fuck knows what I was doing there again. It'd been risky enough the first time, but man, this was beyond a joke. Woke up at Dee's with a hangover Dennis Hopper would've been proud of, and sloped off back to mine before she woke up. As it goes, I think she might've been awake, wanting me to go - she's a right early bird as a rule. But, be truthful, can't blame her if she *was* faking. Can be a bit of cunt when I'm pissed. Not proper nasty, just a pillock. Dee likes consistency. *Don't know why people can't always be the same.* Heard her say that more than once, and she means it, she really *doesn't* know.

Got a breakfast at Luigi's on the way home, then had a shit, shower and shave, and put my head down for another hour. Took some more Disprin when I got up, but still felt rough. Not headachey, just paranoid, banging chest and that, light-headed, dry mouthed. Couldn't sit around wallowing in my own head, so thought I'd take a stroll, maybe get a hair of the dog – if I could face it.

Never meant to get on that bus. Never meant to get off here. But here I was, with no reason at all to back me up, ringing the bell. Must be out of my frigging mind.

'You again.' She never even sounded surprised.

'Yeah, like—'

'If you say like the proverbial bad penny, I'm going to shut this door now.'

'Wouldn't dream of it.'

Raquel turned her back on me and went back indoors, leaving me to follow and shut the door behind me. She had on a pink dressing gown over some of them lounging pyjama things. I could see the movement of her bum.

'You only just got up?' I said. The place smelt a bit of bleach, and more strongly of lavender. That'd be one of the dishes of that pot pourri stuff she had about. Even Mum had got into that recently.

'No.' She sat in the armchair, tucked her feet under her. Definitely weren't wearing a bra - could see her tits - full, pretty firm - easy through the thin material. Now I looked at her properly, I realized she had a bit of make-up on, so quite obviously she hadn't just got out of bed.

I sat on the floor, got my tobacco out my jacket. It was a really nice place, this. You could tell a woman lived here and that she liked being a woman. Loads of floaty stuff and ethnic shit and colour. Dee's place was bare almost, not like a bloke's where we can't see the point of all the drapery and want a table made out of a keg like Tom's got – and fuck off is it for a joke - but as if she couldn't imagine herself in a room with ordinary life clutter in it.

'Did I tell you I like your pad?'

'What do you want, Eddie?' Raquel said.

'Not got a Scooby, quite truthfully.'

That made her laugh. She had a nice laugh, low and a bit dirty, bit like Barbara Windsor. She was much more my usual type, though of course girls like Raquel were ten-a-penny - busty, just a bit plump, dark, pretty, older than they wanted to be by five years at any given point after twenty-five.

'Got pissed with your old man last night,' I said.

'With Daddy? Really?' Pushing her heavy hair back from her face, in a way that reminded me of her sister, even though Dee's was so light. 'How'd that go?'

'Plays his cards close to his chest.' I lit my fag. 'He all right? Seemed a bit...odd or something.'

'Hard to say.' She passed me the ashtray from the little table the side of her. 'He's never not odd, exactly.'

'That's what I figured.'

'He's probably bored. You're talking about a man who was hardly out of work for forty years. Don't think he knew what he was letting go, not really.' She rubbed her arm, thoughtfully, then started running her index finger quickly over her thumb pad, again and again, as though it helped her think. 'That sounds mean, I'm sure he thought it through beautifully. But it must be tricky. Reality's always different to the fantasy.'

'Yeah, he said as much.'

'He did?' Now she did sound surprised.

'Not in so many words, maybe.'

'Ah.' She picked up a mug from the table, drunk from it. Knew I'd be pushing it to ask her to make me one. There was a book open on the table as well, a tatty paperback, but it was upside down to me and I couldn't make the title out from here. Raquel was watching me, sizing me up I reckon. Made me feel a total dickhead. My mum used to say all the time that I acted before I thought – *You don't never use your head, boy* – and I was starting to see she might have a point.

'Can I buy you dinner some time?' I asked. 'To say thank you.'

'For what?'

'Putting a word in with your old man.'

'That was for Dee.' Dismissive. 'And who knows if it'll even do any good? He's a moody b, my father, a law unto himself. Don't think he likes you much.'

'Fuck. Really? Fuck. What makes you say that?'

'His warm and charming manner when you're around?' She smiled then, made a rolling gesture with her fingers, indicating I should do her a fag.

'Thought that was my paranoia.'

'Nope. He seems to pretty much think you're a waste of space.'

'Don't hold back, will you,' I said. 'Tell it like it is, don't mind me.'

Her lips were full, pink, shiny with gloss. No doubt about it, she was a looker, in an overripe way. Tasty. Second lead. The naughty best friend. I looked away, opened my tobacco pouch.

'You're a chancer, Eddie. You don't even care, so long as he'll do it for Dee.'

'Yeah, well, I need to support her now there's no money—'

'That'll be it.' She nodded. 'Selfless for your woman.' She took the fag I held out to her, bent her head for me to light it. I touched her hand to steady the fag against the flame. 'Dee's my baby sister,' she said.

'Yeah, I know.'

'Just make sure you do.'

She weren't silly, she knew I wanted to kiss her. Wanted to fuck her, I think – not that I'd've been capable of fucking anyone this afternoon, the night I'd had. Guts was churning now, but hard to say if it was thrills or the need to throw up.

But she weren't shocked, tell you that much for nothing. And she weren't turned off. I'm not trying to say I thought she'd let me jump her, nothing like, but there was something there, some thin thread of connection that she might've followed up in other circs. Might. And I'm not silly, either - I knew I'd come here, really, just to be around her. But it'd never be a goer. And I could always find another Raquel. Another Dee was out of the question.

'Come and have an hair of the dog that bit me,' I said, throwing my fag in the ashtray and standing, brushing my hands on my jeans. We'd be safe in a public place, and she'd take my mind off what Ken might or might not do for me.

'Working tonight.'

'Just the one won't hurt.'

She eyed me, nodded slowly.

'You really reckon it'd be just the one?'

'Yeah.' Putting my hand on my heart. 'Scout's honour.'

'Okay. Give me two minutes to change.'

Part of me was wondering what the hell I thought I was doing - could mess everything up here. But I felt like shit, I wanted a pint and maybe some chips or a pie, and I didn't want to be alone. Nearly thirty-six years of age, man, despite what I told casting agents and everybody else – more than capable of looking after myself.

She really was only two or three minutes. Black leggings, oversized pink tee-shirt with Marilyn Monroe's face on the front, maybe a bit more lip gloss and blusher. Soft pink slip-on plimsoll things. No effort.

'I'll come with you,' she said. 'But I've got your number, darling. Don't try and tell me you didn't do Youth Theatre instead of joining the Scouts.'

But as it happens, she was wrong. I was a Cub Scout. And I'd never been near a Youth Theatre until I was almost too old for it to be of any use at all.

Delia

'Get off me!'

'Nowhere near you, you mad bitch.'

'Leave me alone. Please.'

'Fuck's sake, don't go into one. Look, I'm going.' He holds up his hands, traffic-steady. 'See? Going.' Walking backwards, as though scared that if he turns round, I'll shoot him in the back. Perhaps I would, if I had a gun. Bang, bang, you're dead. But I always wanted to be the Indian.

Yes, it's true he only asked me the time, I know that. But he leaned in, close as close, envelope-letter, and breathed in my face. Right in it, dirty air all over my mouth. I needed baby lotion and cotton wool, but I didn't have them out here in the street. I didn't have anything. *You got a tongue in your head.* Yes, and I used it and then he backed away so as not to get shot.

It's dark. Even round here, where most of the street lights work, it's proper dark, as if it's the middle of the night though it's only early evening really. Some people won't even have had their tea. But I'm not scared of the dark – nothing ever happens to me in it, so what's there to be afraid of? I'm just scared of people breathing right into my face, too too close. No, not scared, not that, but I've got a right not to breathe the filthy air. I've got the right just to walk and not be bothered. He didn't just want to know the time. I used to think that people only wanted what they said they did, but that's not true. Words can mean anything people want them to, and I think his meant he wanted to kiss me, to do it with me, and that was the most horrible thought. I don't like ugly people, I mean people who are ugly through and through, and that man – he had ugly eyes. Mean and peering like he needed glasses, and he stank of alcohol and mints and ash, as if he'd come straight from a funeral. Corpse-thin and hard he was, too. No softness anywhere.

I want Tom. He's just the best at making the unwanted ones go away. Not away in real life – I can do that by myself, I *did* do that by myself – but away from the inside of my head. The pictures can run and run and take the skin off the inside of my thoughts if someone doesn't help stop it. Raquel's good if she's in the mood, Eddie can distract me with sex or confusing conversation, but Tom is the one who can shoot them in the back.

He'll be working tonight, but not yet. I think not yet. And if he has to, he'll take me with him. Tom should make my list, even if *The Tomorrow People* has to be subtracted to make room. I really think he should make it and maybe for always. He won't leave me while the man is still inside my head.

'Lovely FUCK ME Dee, this is HARD-ON, FUH-FUH-FUH great, but I have to get a move on.' He was shivering in the cold. We should have gone inside really, but I liked being the doorway, a not-in-not-out place.

'One more minute.' I wrapped my arms tighter round his back, ran my hand up to feel his hump. Must be lovely, to have interesting parts of yourself to stroke, to know that they were always there. As long as they didn't hurt, of course. And he said his didn't. I asked, and he said no, so I had to hope that was true. His body went tense against mine as I moved my hand so I stopped in case he didn't like it. Maybe it did hurt.

'Oh God, I'm going to FUH-FUH hate myself for this, but I've TART got to go, sweets. Come with?' His breath was sweet, like rainbow drops.

'Do you do it in your sleep?' I said.

'Yeah, apparently. But not in my dreams. My dreams FUH- FUH- are silent.'

I'd asked that before. I liked hearing the answer, liked the way he said it as though it was something to be proud of, somewhere he could rest. It should have been sad maybe, but it wasn't, it never was. Or not for me.

Tom pulled me in close close close even though half a second before he'd been pulling away. I could feel his heart through his thin shirt.

'Dee-'

'What was that?' I jumped back. Out of the corner of my eye, I'd seen something, someone small and scurrying. 'Was that a grown-up man?' I asked.

'FUCK! Didn't see a thing. BLIND CUNT.'

'Along the corridor, there. Into the stairwell.'

Delia.

'F-F-F—'

'He said my name.'

'Who did?'

But then I couldn't hear anything or see anything. Well, no, of course I could – Tom's tee-shirt and the doorway, a drunk down below shouting *Come here and say that* at no one, I think at no one – but nothing I didn't expect to see or hear. It was probably my imagination. Too much imagination. Sometimes, it runs out of me - hot, shiny wax

– because I can't hold it inside, being more of it than there is of me.

'Can we go to your gig?' I said.

'We can go to my FUH- gig.' He touched my hair, just for a sec.

One of the best things about Tom is that he never, ever asks me to see his act. *Come with*, but no, *You not coming to hear me?* No, *You don't want to check me out?* It's about them, so what do they want me for. There'll always be another gig, another show, another question. And I never know the right answer. Sometimes I've said yes when I can tell that was wrong, so now I just tell the truth. I don't want to go.

'It must be nice though,' I said, watching Tom get his sneakers on.

'What?'

'When I say something, zillions of people have said it before.' I looked at my palm. The lines were so busy. Inroads you could imagine small figures making, scurrying down, whispering your name. 'But when you talk, every single time it's new. Bosh. Like magic.'

Tom laughed. 'That's me, baby – a complete CUNT original.' He shrugged on his jacket – which was awkward, as his shoulder kept on shrugging after he needed it to - and banged the door shut behind him. 'But language is communal. So I'm not part FART HEART FART START FART FART FART…' Twitch, gape, shudder.

'Don't think I'm very communal,' I said.

'There is that.' He grinned right at me, hitting my feelings, making the little figure move out of sight. It wasn't a man, it was imagination. My waxy imagination. I was safe here. 'Storm's blowing up, I reckon,' he said. 'You warm enough?'

'Do you ever get the feeling you're being followed?'

Nearly tripped over my feet, following him down the corridor.

'No. Sorry Dee.' He took my hand, but then looked around quickly and let it go. I think he was probably worried Eddie would see him. Eddie wouldn't care, I think, but Tom would assume he would. Even Tom makes assumptions, sometimes.

'S'okay. Most probably not true anyway.' I hooked my thumb through the belt loop of his jeans, to help me keep pace with him. 'Be funny tonight, okay?'

'Okay.'

And he was. Especially funny. For me.

Ken

Hark at that weather. Spot's paradise, they used to love making days like these, got to rattle the old metal sheets and drop dried peas into pans. Different now, of course - though it's not all as hi-tech as people think. Funny thing - real storms never sound quite as real as radio ones to me. But then, real people never sound as real as actors, do they?

You all right, Glen-Glen? Not making you jump? No, you don't care. Used to as a little boy, you'd hide under the blankets. Look at you now – come a long way, old son. But that certainly is teeming down now. *Careful Kenny, there's going to be a lot of weather – better take a brolly.* Remember? Mummy always said there was more weather, nights like these. Remember? Not looking forward to going back out into that. Just made it here in time, only got a few drops. Shake it off like a dog. That's it.

You've got a new neighbour, I see. Noticed her as I was coming in. Frail little voice, she had – then I turned and saw this great whopping creature, greasy chins and tiny piggy eyes swallowed by all that flesh. She smiled at me, Glen-Glen. That's it, like that. You always know, don't you? But it didn't light up her face, not like yours. Remember how much Hattie hated being fat? And La Mia Piccina. You might not recall her – most don't. Soprano, beautiful. Face by Medici, body by Mrs Beaton. Feh. I always thought her suicide had a lot to do with her weight. Bollocks to all that fading career rubbish - she just wanted to be thin.

That girl can only be in her early twenties. Younger than our Delia. D'you know, I've never really looked at the others before. All these years, and I never really looked, not unless there was a ruckus or some such. Averted the eyes. Not proud of myself for that, old man. Not proud at all. Now you're not looking at me. Don't blame you, frankly.

Do you ever want to be different? Sorry, I know it's all bollocks this, but I've been thinking about it lately. You know...different. The same... Do you ever want to be me? No, why should you. Quite right, who'd want to be me? It's just that when we were babies, Mummy couldn't tell us apart – did she ever tell you that? She couldn't, even though we're not identical. Used to tie a bit of cotton round one of our ankles. Took her weeks to know who was who without it. Sometimes I wonder if she got it wrong, and I'm really Glen-Glen and you're really Kenny Boy. Used to keep me awake when we were kids. Before you went – well, you know, before you went, I'd lie awake and look and you and wonder if you were me and I were you, and the rest was Mummy's mistake. When they took you away I wanted to tell them that they might be taking me. Been remembering that just recently. How it felt to have your voice carried away in silence.

Trouble is, old man, I've got too much thinking time on my hands. Not used to it. Actors don't think much, you know we don't - wasted muscle, like that chap of Delia's leg. Giving me brain ache, it is. Audience believes because we learn reams of lines, we must be sharp. *Oooh, Mr O'Leary, how do you learn all them lines? Sharp.* I can see you, giggling away there. Well, inside, anyway. Thing is, some actors think they're intellectuals, despite all the evidence to the contrary. Gielgud, for a kick off. All that set. Mind you, didn't help him when he was found in that public lavvy, did it? Poor old bugger. The fifties wasn't a kind time to queers. My old pal Roberta Roberts, remember him? Pianist in that trio. Disappeared in the end. People said he must have left his clothes on a beach, but I always thought he might have flown off somewhere hot and forgiving. Might be playing the bars in Morocco as we speak. What d'you reckon? You're the optimist.

Ah bollocks to it, listen me, maudlin old devil. What's this in my pocket? Look, tube of Polos for you. And this is…Yeah, that's it, you have a good sniff. You're quite right, it's new. Well, last year, but we've not tried them yet, have we? Do you want…Nice, is it? *Was* it. Here, have your Polos then. Good old crunch. No, sorry my darling boy, no more Wispas - Kenny'll bring you a few next time. Didn't know you'd like them. Thought I might get a bite. No, silly of me. Why the bollocking hell should you share? I'll have one with you next time. Always a next time. Don't know what I'd do without you to talk to. Oh, look at me, daft old beggar, filling up like a housewife at a matinee. Better blow the old trumpet, that's it. You like that, don't you? Best nose blower in Bow, I was. Do it again for you, shall I?

Elbow rub is it? All right then, old chap. Glad to.

Nelly the Elephant
Packed her trunk
And said goodbye to the circus
Off she went with a trumpety-trump
Trump, trump, trump.

1956, remember it exactly. I bought you the record – well, you'll know that, you had it until a couple of years ago, didn't you? Kenny'll see if he can find it again for you. Thirty-one we were then. Oh Glen-Glen, our salad days when we were green in judgement.

Here we are again
Happy as can be,
All good pals and
Jolly good company.

Worries me that the girls don't seem to have many friends. Raquel hasn't got anyone close, far as I know. Girls at the club, on the circuit, but otherwise it's just Lesley and Dee. As for our Dee-Dee, well, she's got her waifs and her fella, but a proper girl chum would do her good. Shopping, frothy coffee, ordinary things. Maybe it's my fault. She hardly had an ordinary childhood - but damn it, I did my bloody best. I was always a one for my pals, that must have been a good model. And of course I've always had you. Don't understand them, being so bloody solitary. Do *you* get it? Bet you don't. People think you're a loner but they forget about us, don't they? They don't realize.

What d'you make of him, then? Come on, you must have known I'd ask you sooner or later. Stop the elbow rub? Okay old man, okay. That's it, that's it, Kenny's stopped now. Look, hands up, all stopped. I'll stand over here. Lovely. Wind's really getting up now. Bin's gone over out there. Made the bugger sing for his supper the other day. Bloody good job. Not sure if I should despise him for doing it or admire him, in a way. Bit of both, perhaps, bit of both. Pitchy performance, but he did it with balls, give the crip that. Clever with that limp, too. Larry O used to say if you speak fast, walk slowly and vice versa, otherwise all you're doing is demonstrating a cliché. Never forgot that, stuck to it too. Otherwise you're tearing around like a ranting avenger, or doing a professional mourner. Delia's crip makes a bloody feature of how he has to move, varies it, catches you on the hop, as it were. On the hop. Make myself laugh, swear it.

I've been getting these headaches, Glen-Glen. Maybe it's the wind. Sometimes feels as though I'm in Act V but then I see the epilogue stretching out in front of me, pages and pages of the damn thing, like one of those dreams where you don't know your lines.

You think I made a mistake? Bit early to stage a comeback. No, still don't want to end up like they all do, all those finished *old men*. This had to be the way. But it's hard, you know that better than anyone, it's hard, not being all you can be, watching yourself on your internal screen. Bugger it, I'm off again. Could have done with this on the box a few times. Save the poor make-up dolly rushing in with the drops. That vet thing was the worst, what was it called? Everyone else boo-hoo-hooing all over the show… Big girl's blouse now. Where's that hanky? Can I have one of your tissues… No, course not, course I can't, sorry. Stupid Kenny. That's it, Kenny loves you. I love you. One of these days, you'll look straight at me and say *Piss off, Kenny*. You will, you know. And I'll laugh.

Raquel

It hit me today that I'm pretty bloody broke, or soon will be. The black velvet's getting rather worn, frankly, practically bald around the backside, and I was on the point of heading for Selfridge, virtually out of the door, when I suddenly thought, Hang on a minute, missy, the new stage frock will have to wait. That's the moment I realized what not having Daddy's money will mean. Not a UB40, not that, not quite yet unless the club were to go under. Worse in a way. Secondhand Rose.

When I was at the grammar school, there was a girl we called that. Her real name wasn't even Rose, though I'm blowed if I can think what it was. Ruth? Rebecca? Her mum used to go round all the jumbles, picking out everything that was out of fashion or home-made by someone else's nan, and that's what Rose had to wear after school. Even her uniform was always bobbly before the start of the school year, and her skirts were too long or too short or not quite the right shade of blue. We pretended she smelt, though I'm sure she was perfectly clean really, poor little b. Her shoes were always new, I do remember that – ugly, cheap-looking, but new. *Sarah*, that was it. Someone started a rumour that she wanted to be a model, though I'm quite certain she didn't. I went along with it, of course. Took pretend photos just like the rest. Well, no one wants to stand out at that age.

There ought to be a happy third-act climax, where Secondhand Rose marries a millionaire or becomes a famous actress, and I bump into her one day when she's dripping in diamonds. Cobblers, frankly. Though I did see her once, about ten years ago, three kids in tow and all of them dressed in what looked like other people's cast-offs. Bloody hell, didn't the woman remember what hell it had been for her? What was she doing, having more children than she could afford to clothe decently? Made me cross all afternoon.

Don't suppose I'll have a baby now. I'll be Auntie Raquel. Bet I'll have to do more than my share of bringing it up, though. Even now, when we meet someone we used to know, I can see them looking at Auntie Lesley with pity: *You never had kids, did you, Les? Well, circus is no place for a baby.* But there were babies in Girelli's, children learning the acts. There's always lots of babies in a circus. Homey place, in its way. Suppose it was when her marriage broke up that we knew; from then on, everyone called her *Your auntie* when they mentioned her to us. I should be grateful, I know I should, but sometimes I can't help feeling we were a tad – well, *convenient* I suppose. We gave her an excuse not to have much of a life of her own, although we were all grown up really. I was twenty-five, twenty-six, for heaven's sake. Even her thing with Uncle Lou - if it *is* a thing - is on the side, nothing she has to put in the middle of her life. It's safer. *Unthink, unthink, unthink.* That wasn't fair, it was mean, it was. *Unthink. Unthink. Unthink.* She had bad luck, shouldn't say she brought it on herself. Not that I was really doing that... I can be a rotten b at times.

Stupid to be nervous. Really silly. Uncharacteristic, too. It's just a bloke, just the club, it doesn't mean anything. Well, no, it does, but nothing sinister. If he could do with some singing practice, then it makes sense, of course it does, I can see that. Daddy's quite right. If that big musical does open next year, there'll be tours, Daddy knows people, it makes perfect sense. Daddy says he's got something. It's just I don't want to be put in an awkward position at work. Nobody likes that. If he's rotten, it'll come back on me. I notice Daddy and Dee aren't coming, oh no. This one is muggins here's responsibility. Burden, more like.

If I were Dee, I'd want to go. Funny that she doesn't. But that's Dee all over. When she was a little girl, she was picked to be Mary in the Nativity. How old would she have been? Four? No, older, about six or seven. On the day, she wouldn't leave the house: she said she didn't want to see herself on stage, that she could imagine in her head how it went. Don't know how you *begin* to untangle that one, quite frankly. Like the time we were playing hide and seek, and I was It, and she offered to help look for herself. Dearie dear.

But I'd go, think most people would. I was always the reader in the Nativity plays. Never got a costume, just my uniform. I had beautiful vowel sounds, apparently.

Don't like this dress much, but I really have to retire the black velvet. It's a bloody stinking nuisance, being borassic. Daddy's far too young to have nothing to do, and I'm sure he hates it, and he'll start to hate it even more. But he'd lose a lot of face, going back on his word. Don't think he'd risk that, even for a retirement's worth of boredom or worse.

Thought I had oodles of time, but it's getting on, should be out of here in five minutes. Come on, Raquel, up you get. One, two, three. *You're all right. You're all right.* It'll be all right. Five eights are forty; I'll do forty eights on my thumb, then I'll leave. Forty eights and I won't die, and neither will he.

You must remember this
A kiss is still a kiss,
A sigh is just a sigh,
The fundamental things apply
As time goes by...

It was a bloody bad joke, it had to be. *Eddie* singing my song now? For heaven's sake, I hadn't even been on yet. Now my set would be ruined: it was built around 'As Time Goes By', echoes in the intro to two others. Buggery buggington. What would it be next week – Dee turning up to have a bash? Maybe her friend with the swearing could try it. Or Uncle Glen-Glen could drool his way through a silent chorus or two. Admittedly, Eddie had never seen me perform, so he couldn't know, but couldn't he have checked? It was a bloody standard, for crying out loud. Selfish cunty cunt. No wonder he wouldn't tell me what numbers he was going to do. Jinxing them my eye.

Pure cocktail lounge. Sub-Bogart, though Bogart doesn't even sing it in the film. Look at him, almost taking a mouthful of his scotch, but not quite, moving on to the next thought. In character - rum's his own drink. Cig burning away in the ashtray. No one ever uses that high table except for Louise. She won't be best pleased, she's funny about things like that. Wouldn't even wear a green ribbon for St Patrick's Day.

Suppose he thinks it's cool, to have his jacket sleeves pushed up like that. Suit jacket with tee-shirt and jeans, looks as though Secondhand Rose dressed him. Oh my God, he's winking. He is, I can see it from here. Bloody winker.

At that point, I put my mental fingers in my ears, turned away to light a cig, took a mouthful of my iced Pepsi. I was so going to have a large Bacardi in it after my set, on Eddie. In fairness, the first two numbers had been okay, and he was only doing the three, but it was going to be a hard act to follow, for obvious reasons, and I didn't know if I could forgive that, quite. At least Sally was on in between us and she hadn't been in voice lately.

He got a decent hand. I joined in as though I'd enjoyed it, up to a point.

'What d'you think?' He was across to me in a few uneven steps, took a swig of my drink, a cig from my packet. 'Don't mind if I nick a straight. Was it evil then, my singing?' Eddie flung himself into the chair next to me, his legs splayed. 'Nearly dried in 'Paper Moon', but reckon I covered it. Raquel? Think anyone noticed?'

'You were fine.'

'Stop it, you're killing me.' He put his hand over his heart. 'Too much praise can turn a girl's head, you know. Fuck, was it bad as all that?'

'Nope. Not bad at all. You can hold a tune, you acted it. You were fine.' I swept my arm around. 'You've given the ladies something to look at. Always thought we should have a male singer, but we hardly ever do, except as a guest.'

'Why not?' Eyes narrowed, clearly trying to look all casual, unworried.

'Maurice says the punters don't want it. But I'm not at all sure he's right.'

'He said he'll talk to me while you're on.'

'Fingers crossed, then.'

'You're pissed off. I done something?'

'Darling - I'm not pissed off.'

'Yeah, right. Face like a smacked arse but you're smiling on the inside.'

Bloody b, made me laugh.

'You want a drink?' he said. Reaching over, stroking the inside of my wrist for the teeniest moment.

'Get me one now, and I'll have most of it after. Bacardi and Coke. Double.'

Sally's opening chords. She'd be done in seventeen minutes. Sundays were lovely that way: short sets, lots of girls. Almost like not going to work at all.

As Eddie loped over to the bar, I could see some of the women checking him out. With his slightly-too-long-at-the-back hair and the spikes on top softened, a hint of five o'clock shadow, and that jacket, he looked louche, appropriate. As Daddy would say, he had the clothes right. Maurice was mistaken: a bloke performing once or twice a week, regularly, was just what the place needed. Don't suppose Eddie would want to do it for long, but perhaps he could open doors for the next wage slave. Let's face it, everyone was grateful for work these days. You never knew when you'd be out on your ear.

'There you go.' Eddie put the drinks on the table, and moved his chair a little closer to mine. 'You think Maurice'll give us a go, then?'

'I really don't know,' I said. 'Must help that you're on as a favour to Daddy.'

'And to you.'

'Trust me, I don't count.'

'You reckon?' He picked up his scotch, held the glass to his lips for a second, then took a sip, his gaze never leaving my face. Even though I knew he was a player, I felt my cheeks get hot.

'Eddie, how did you pick your songs?'

'Your old man helped. He suggested two of them, and I went with the other one to match, type of deal. Why, something wrong with them? He stitch me up?'

'No, nothing was wrong. Which one did you choose yourself?'

'Cheesy, I know, but 'Makin' Whoopee'. Was it a pile of crap, then?'

'No.' So Daddy had suggested 'As Time Goes By'. What the hell was the *matter* with my family? Did every member go round *stitching up* every other member? My life was full of mini-betrayals, and I'm bloody sure Lesley and maybe even Dee could say the same.

'Oh man, knew I should've gone with something else.' Eddie was chewing the side of his thumb; his cigarette had burned to a long roll of ash, where he'd put it down before going to the bar. Very different effect from the slow smoke drifting up from the unsmoked cig in the ashtray during his act. Suppose roll-up smokers forget that tailor-mades don't simply go gently out, to be re-lit whenever you needed to.

'Need to have a quick word with Mickey when Sally's done,' I said. 'I need to change my set slightly.'

'Yeah? Reckon Maurice'll wait for you to start before he moseys over. Won't want to look keen. Which he's probably not.'

'People in the profession should have more curiosity than that,' I said. Eddie ruined my act and didn't give a tinker's damn, as our great-nan apparently used to say. Thinking about it, though, Daddy couldn't have known Eddie would go on before me, so perhaps the sabotage was directed elsewhere, or maybe he didn't much mind who it took down. Perhaps I was the risk he had to take, to get a shot at Eddie.

I took a gulp of my Bacardi.

'She's closing, that's my exit,' I said.

Maybe because it had to be fresh, or perhaps it was fuelled by how bloody hacked off I was, the set went well; I was better than I'd been in ages. Mixing it up, leaving out my signature, forced me to listen to what I was singing, to mean it, to give a truthful performance. Daddy always says if you get bored with a long-running part, the audience will too, so you have to find tricks to freshen it up. The old sod's quite capable of claiming that's what he'd intended for me, if I called him on what happened with Eddie's songs.

And thanks for the trouble you took from her eyes
I thought it was there for good, so I never really tried

I hadn't done 'Famous Blue Raincoat' in months and months - even a couple of years. Maurice didn't feel it was a Basement number, though Mickey and I did a fair version and tonight it felt like a Leonard Cohen night. For the first time in a long time, I hadn't feared I'd have the urge to shout 'Bum!' in the middle of a lyric, either. Must be how Dee's friend Tom feels. Not that I'd actually had the urge, but the dread that I *might* usually brought me out in a sweat at least once during my spot. Maybe having to concentrate removed idle worries, replaced them with real ones, the danger of performing half-forgotten words.

When I got back to the table, via many more kisses and arm pats than I'd had in a while, though no bouquets thrown on the stage, Eddie was grinning. He raised his glass.

'Got the gig,' he said. 'Wednesdays and Fridays for six weeks. Cash in hand, though on the books if he wants me after that, he says. And you,' he added, standing up, 'were fucking great. Didn't have a Scooby you could pull something like that off. Didn't manage to catch you last time I came here.' He hugged me. I could feel his heart against my chest.

'Thanks,' I said, pulling away. 'But do me a favour, okay? Drop 'As Time Goes By', will you?'

Eddie looked at me, hard.

'Not a criticism, right?'

'Right.'

'So that's what Maurice meant when he said I was a cheeky bastard.' He hit himself on the forehead. 'Fucker's yours. You sing it.'

'Don't know anymore. But it's certainly not yours.'

'Your old man's one sick—'

'Congratulations on the gig,' I said, and kissed his cheek. I felt his stubble against my lips.

'Fair enough.' He rubbed the back of his hand on the side of my face. 'Want to go on somewhere, celebrate?'

'Don't you want to ring Dee?'

'Out of 10ps.'

'Sid at the bar will give you some.'

'Lost the use of me legs.' His face too close to mine.

'Want me to ring for you?' My mouth suddenly dry.

'Nope.' He smiled, touched my cheek again. 'Need to see how she takes it when I tell her. Part of the buzz, man.'

'We could go there now.'

'She's an early bird. I'll tell her in the morning. Not like it's that big a deal. She's known me get jobs before, way bigger.'

'Why am I even having this conversation?'

'You tell me.'

'You're an unscrupulous chancer, Mr Muir.'

'Want me to get your coat?' He'd put a laugh in his eyes; an easy trick, one I'd known since I was young and used to rehearse in front of the mirror to impress Ronnie Pettifor. Later, it was useful in the ring, when the audience wanted to have their picture taken with you next to the elephant. But Eddie looked so cheerful, so in need of immediate celebration, so pleased with this new string to his bow, however thin, that I wanted to be part of it, just for one night. I wanted to see how it ended.

'No, don't. I've had enough music for one night.'

'Sure. Okay.' He slipped my copy of *Songs of Love and Hate* back into its sleeve, put it at the front of the record stack, and took the coffee I was holding out. 'Thanks. Probably a bad idea – might keep me awake.'

'Don't drink it, then. Go and get the night bus now.'

'I'll chance it.'

Eddie had switched on the lamps, turned the main light out. I'd noticed while I was making the Nescaff, but it seemed a bigger deal after taking the four steps to the living room part of the room. He put his mug on the floor, pulled over my big cushion, patted it.

'I'm all right on the sofa, thanks,' I said. Sounding horribly prissy.

'Oh come on, bird, don't be like that. I'll put one together.'

'*Bird?*'

'Don't tell me you burn your bra. Come off it.'

'Of course not, but that sounds perfectly ridiculous.' To cover my awkwardness, I did go over to him and sat on the floor, propping myself up on my elbow against the cushion. I'd been comfier, frankly. Tugged at my dress to make sure it covered my too-hefty thighs. Wished I'd changed when we got in.

Raquel Elizabeth O'Leary, what the hell do you think you're doing?

Eddie was rolling a joint, his fingers swift, practised, reminding me of a chef making slim pastries in some French film. He lit it, then rolled onto his back, his head on the cushion, and inhaled. From that angle, I must look all chins and thighs. I took the joint from him, mirrored his action, so that we were lying as if we were two children looking up at the sky. Only it wasn't innocent, was it? We both knew that. There were webs in the corners, thick with abandonment. My surfaces were always spotless, but somehow I never looked up as a rule. That's something Dee and I have in common: we prefer ground level, although I like eye contact and she hates it, especially if it goes on. *It burns me, Raquel.* I imagined that Eddie and Dee-Dee didn't spend much time gazing into each other's eyes.

'Ta.' Eddie took the joint back, toked on it, hard. Still holding in the smoke, he said, 'You missing the dosh?' and exhaled.

'What?' Maybe he wasn't here for some duplicitous liaison after all. Maybe he was here to discuss how we might get Daddy to change his mind. Well, of course, why would he want to mess up what he had with Dee for a night with me? I wasn't exactly the kind of woman men fight over. Yes, I was okay, not at all bad for mid-thirties (probably because I didn't have children), but no one was going to risk everything for my sake. I felt a total idiot.

'It's going to take a while to adjust,' I said. The dope was making my heart beat a little too fast, and I wanted a wee but couldn't quite see how I was going to move. 'But I'll cope. Are you missing it, then?'

'Ouch,' he said, passing the joint back to me. 'One to the solar plexus, that.'

'You'd hardly mention it if you didn't feel personally involved.' Taking a long drag on the joint, I rolled onto my side and propped myself up on my elbow again. 'Imagine that's why you're here.'

'Because I feel personally involved?' He caught my gaze, held it. 'Something like that.'

'Let's get one thing clear, Eddie.' I put the joint between his lips. 'I could get Daddy to talk to you about work, but there's no way I can do anything about the money.' I could feel how hard he was listening, his eyes never leaving mine, even as they narrowed against the smoke. 'Uncle Glen—Glen's always been his first priority, always. Financially at least and maybe even in other ways. He's not about to go short himself, especially the way things are out there, and he's not going to let Glen suffer. End of story.'

'Can't stop him suffering, can he?'

'You know what I mean. Anyway, none of us can know that.'

'Come off it, you wouldn't wish it on a dog.'

'Put down the lame, you mean?' I sat up, my heart apparently in my neck now. Didn't have to look behind me to know that would have hit home. I grabbed my mug, pressed my hands against the lukewarm sides.

'You fucking bitch,' he said. But quietly.

'He's my uncle.'

'Took you to the pictures, did he? Bought you sweets? Made you laugh?' He pulled, audibly, on the joint. 'Didn't think so.'

'It's a relationship, not a role.'

'Could sling that one right back to you.' His voice was hard, thin, dry, as though he hadn't warmed it up. 'I saw him, Raquel. Went up to that home and I saw him, and he never saw me, my *life* he never. Weren't even on his radar.'

'You did *what?*'

'Had to see for myself, didn't I, what Ken was spending Dee's money on. Oh man, was worse than I thought.'

'Jesus Christ, are you mental?' I turned to look down at him. He had his eyes squeezed tight shut. 'Does Dee know?'

'Do me a favour. How'd I explain that to her? She'd just take it fine and wouldn't understand a fucking thing.' He licked his cracked lips. 'Wouldn't even know there's something to get pissed off about.'

He was quite right, of course. Dee seemed in equal measure

baffled by and composed about the vagaries of the world. The normal was as strange to her as the bizarre was straightforward. Yes, Eddie had the measure of her, had to give him that.

'What did they call you at school, Eddie? Come on, what did they call you?'

'What—' His eyes opened.

'No, come on, you know perfectly well what I mean. What did they call you?'

He sat up, quickly, then put his hand to his forehead. 'Whoa, head rush.'

'What did they call you?'

'Steady Eddie,' he said. 'And Sir Limpalot. And Fucking Useless Crip.' His voice even, soft, low.

'Right.' Gently, I removed the joint from his fingers, took the last toke into the cardboard, leaving a horrid bonfire taste in my mouth, ground the roach into the ashtray. My head was swimmy, but I was feeling no pain. Eddie put his hand on my shoulder, rubbed it, moving up to the back of my neck. 'This is ridiculous,' I said.

'It's nothing.'

'No, it can never be nothing.'

He pulled my head nearer to his. 'It can if we say it can.'

'I'm practically her mother.'

'No, you're really not.'

'I love her, Eddie.'

'Me an' all. So? She's—'

'Doesn't make it right.' So close, we were talking into each other's mouths. 'It's the dope. Always used to do this to me.' A disinhibiter, my poly lecturer boyfriend told me. Hadn't smoked it since. Took all the glamour away.

'No it's not.' He brushed my lips with his, barely touching them. 'We're the same, me and you,' he said.

'How do you make that one out?'

'Reckon you get a fair deal, do you?' Kissing a corner of my mouth. 'Odds ever gone your way?' Kissing the other.

'No.'

'Had the breaks? Course not.'

'That doesn't justify anything. It's pathetic.' Why shouldn't I do this, something just for me, that didn't for once in my life take Delia into account, or Daddy, or keeping body and soul together. Just for once. 'If you breathe a word of this to her, I'll kill you,' I said.

'You would an' all.'

'Believe it.' But would I be able to face her, that was what worried me. Darling little Dee, with her funny ways, so innocent, so true, so damn irritating.

'Could tell you you're beautiful, all that old shit, but you want the truth?'

'I do, yes.' No, not really. Disappointment lurched in my stomach.

'This thing between us won't fuck off on its own.' He rubbed his thumb over my mouth, a little too hard. 'It's fate. That weren't random, me being at the club, it was meant.' He must have said that before, to other women, but it sounded sincere. 'I look at you and I see me. You look at me and see yourself. Even if we don't like what we see, it's there. And it's a fucking turn on.'

'Steady Eddie,' I said, 'Narcissus wasted away, gazing at his own reflection.'

'That's because he didn't just fuck it.'

I wished he'd said make love to it: he slightly broke through the hypnotic, doped freedom. But then he kissed me, and I couldn't tear myself away.

'Good God, woman, you going to leave a man hanging all night?'

'Sorry Daddy, we had the records on.' Oh God. *God.*

'We? *We?* Well, well, well.'

'Nothing like that. For God's sake, it's only Eddie come back to talk about the club.' I was still blocking his way into the hall. 'We were playing some songs to get a few ideas for numbers.'

'Were you now?'

'It's very late, Daddy.'

'I could say the same to you.'

'Club hours.' But I knew when I was beaten. I stood aside, and he strode into the flat.

Sweet heaven, it had to be him. And now. My heart was going about a squillion to the dozen, and I just prayed Eddie was playing it cool. I followed Daddy into the living room – now brightly lit from the central bulb, all lamps switched off – where Eddie was wearing his tee-shirt and jeans, jacket slung across the settee. He was smoking an ordinary roll-up and leafing through the records. A tattered little notebook was lying open on the floor beside him, with a pencil across it, and what looked like a list scrawled down one page. He looked up, surprise on his face, and took a mouthful of what must have been stone-cold coffee. It would have looked entirely natural if his feet hadn't been bare.

'Hi Ken,' he said. 'You always visit this time of night?'

'I might ask the same of you.' Daddy swung round to look at me, his eyebrows raised, then turned back to Eddie.

'Working – you know how it is.'

'I believe I do.' Daddy sniffed the air, louder than anyone actually needed to sniff. 'Very 1960's,' he said. But I wasn't about to start apologizing for the dope. My God, if I did that, I'd really look guilty.

'He's an old-fashioned guy,' I said. With an attempt at a laugh.

'Is he now? *Is* he? Is *he*?' He threw himself onto the sofa. Shook his head, too sadly. 'Anything to drink around here?'

'We were just having a coffee,' I said.

'So I see. But d'you have any booze on the premises?'

'Think there's some Southern Comfort from a hundred years ago.'

'Yes, whatever you have. Joining me?'

'Not for me, ta,' said Eddie. 'Had that little one-skinner before. Want to get going soon.' That was good: acknowledging the dope, not rushing off too quickly, sounding casual. For the first time, I believed he might be capable of great roles. 'Got to be up Dee's first thing,' he added. That was inspired, mentioning her name.

We'd been so stupid. Utterly uncharacteristic of me, but probably not of him. Well, we wouldn't be going there again. At least those moments of real intimacy, the talk in each other's arms, the telling one another why this was important, the making it so, had been denied us by Daddy's drug-busting knock. It was fate.

I found the Southern Comfort – Peter's drink – at the back of my bleach cupboard. Over half a bottle left, the top sticky with old times. Ugh.

'Ah, thank you dearheart. *I would give all my fame for a pot of ale.*' Daddy lifted the glass to the light, squinted at it, then downed half of it in a gulp. 'No guesses?' he said to Eddie.

'Not a Scooby.' Too cheerfully for such a competitive man. Still, his voice sounded light enough to be plausible.

'*Henry V*, boy. You gave that up faaaar too easily.' Taking a small sip this time. 'It's not Henry's line but it ought to recall the Hal he'd once been. Boozing it up with old Falstaff, chasing the skirt. Respectability and power came at a price.'

'*I know thee not, old man*,' Eddie said.

'Well, quite.' Looking ever-so-slightly discomfited. 'I never played Falstaff.'

'You should've done,' said Eddie.

'I should.'

I went back to the kitchen part to pour myself a small drink. Time for Eddie to go, surely. We'd demonstrated being beyond reproach, now time to vamoosh.

'Why are you here, Daddy?' I sat on the armchair, nursing my too-sweet drink. Were there any cigs left?

'Ah yes, why am I here. Why is any of us here? The immortal question.'

'Daddy...' Sometimes I could smack him, I really could. I reached over to get the cigarette packet. Fortunately, there was one in there.

'Bumped into an old acquaintance. We ended up in a place round the corner.'

Of course, I didn't believe that for a moment. But nor did I think he'd actually come here to spy. I got the impression he really hadn't expected to see Eddie here, and why would he?

Another knock. We all looked at one another, a feeling of panic in the air. That couldn't be Dee, could it? Surely to God she hadn't suddenly become galvanized by the need to do something. She could just be on one of her walks, though; it wasn't entirely unknown for her to turn up in the middle of the night, unaware of the time, not registering that others might have particular things to get up for. She could be a selfish little b at times.

'You going to get that?' Eddie asked. 'Want me to?'

'It's okay, I've got a spyhole.'

Crossing over to the hall door, I felt as though I'd forgotten how to move naturally, that I was wiggling my bum too much, planting my feet too hard. I looked through the fish-eye glass, but saw nothing. Another knock, though, told me someone was there. Then I caught a glimpse of the top of someone's head. A child? I opened the door.

My gaze travelled down. A large hat was removed from a low head, and a battered, baggy face looked up at me, the wicked dwarf personified.

'Hello, Raquel,' he said. 'Lovely as always. Is your father in? He's expecting me.' He put his head on one side, the flesh sliding onto his shoulder. 'I see you aren't, though.'

'Hello MB,' I said. Losing the moment to say *Fuck off* and have him out of our lives forever.

Delia

I never knew what happened, really. Still don't. Raquel's explained a bit but she says she doesn't know much more than I do. Sometimes people say that and it's not true but I think maybe this time it is true.

Babies are interesting. And nice, they're properly nice, giving you a warm feeling like custard. She was a lovely baby. Fat face, wet mouth, eyes that looked as if they were trying to make sense of the world. Like mine in the mirror. They showed her to me and I loved her and I said I'd always look after her. Everyone laughed then. Suppose it was funny, the idea that little Dee-Dee could look after anyone.

Not sure how old she was. Not a newborn, bigger than that. But not old enough to talk. Her skin was darker than ours, like a Caramac bar. Molly. We called her Milly-Molly-Mandy, Raquel and I. But Raquel preferred going out with her friends to looking at the baby. I always felt that the baby was specially mine.

They took the baby away. They just came and took her. One day I went to the cot and she was gone and then the next day so was the cot. Gone. But you can't take her, she's mine, I said. No she's not, they said. She's not anyone's, it was a mistake, it didn't work out.

She wasn't a mistake. Not to me, she wasn't. She was

mine and I loved her. But they took her away and a little while later, only weeks I think, Mummy went too. Perhaps she was sad. Raquel says the baby was probably a last-ditch attempt to save the marriage. But I think she got in the way of Mummy leaving. When Mummy went, I was sad but it was just more sadness on top, like being given your seconds before you've finished your firsts. It was the baby I missed. Raquel kept doing all the things she'd always done for me, right until she went away to the circus, even after whenever I went to see her, but no one could take the place of the baby.

Sometimes, I'm frightened that if me and Eddie have a baby, I won't love it as much as Milly-Molly-Mandy. Though I've told Eddie that if we had a girl, I'd like to call her Molly. Don't think he was bothered. But when I said I might like to call a boy Glen instead of Larry, he was angry, shouted that I must be mad for wanting to commemorate that. *Him*, I said. *Him*. But he was too worked-up to hear me.

I go to see Uncle Glen-Glen sometimes. When I'm out on one of my walks, and it's daytime, I pop in. I never stay long. But he likes me visiting, I know he does. He watches my mouth when I talk, not that I talk much, I don't have to, he's happy without. We have a bit of a sit. And when I give him chocolate, he breaks it and gives me back half. I even eat it. Would be so rude not to. I know what everyone thinks - they worry that I'll turn out like my uncle. They think I don't know they believe that, but I can see it in the way they try to keep us apart, and by the way they sound when we do get together, all high pitched and formal and panicky-yellow.

But there's something they don't realize: if they don't want me to be like Uncle Glen-Glen, then they must think how he is isn't worth anything. Maybe they don't know they believe it, but they do. Even Daddy must think that, and he loves Uncle Glen-Glen more than anything. Sometimes people can believe things when they don't know they believe them, like Mrs Harris saying she's not a racialist but not wanting Debbie to marry Ahmed *cause of the kiddies*. But *I* don't believe it. Glen just lives differently from them, that's all. They don't know what's in his head, they can't. It's funny: they spent years trying to get me to understand we don't all think the same, but they don't really understand that themselves. Not one bit.

It must have been lovely for Nan, having two babies at once. Then it was lovely all over again, having Lesley so much later. Nan never looked as though she thought anything was lovely, though – her face was little and sour and whiskery like a gooseberry. But she must have thought so once, otherwise how would Daddy and Auntie Lesley have known how to? You have to copy people to make sense of things. Probably Uncle Glen-Glen knows too, though I can't pretend to be sure, as if he's some giant vent dummy.

Wonder if Daddy misses Molly? Raquel said he barely noticed, but she was in a spiteful mood that day.

Raquel hasn't been round in days and days. Hasn't even rung up. That's not like her at all. I've picked away most of the skin on the side of my thumb, and I haven't done that for ages. She'll be cross when she sees it. Shiny and cross. Maybe she'll come today. She'll come and bleach all my kitchen surfaces, I think, and make me a chicken salad. I'll just polish a few of my precious gems and my two new pebbles to show her, and then she'll be here and I can ask her all the things that have been piling up. Can't remember now what they were, but I think I will, when she comes. One of the pebbles is dark grey but it'll be nearly black when it's shined up. In this light, it'll look like jet.

'Fuck, nearly spilt that then.' Eddie was balancing three of my tea mugs from this morning. There was quite a lot left in at least two, my Charles and Diana one and my Winnie-the-Pooh.

'Oh sorry, yeah,' I said. 'You see, what happened was, I didn't finish my tea.'

'And?' Eddie did that look people do when they're expecting you to say something else, like you haven't made sense. Sort of *Come on* with the eyebrows and the way they move their heads. It always panics me.

'What?'

'What happened was, you didn't finish your tea, and…'

'What?'

'What happened was, you didn't finish your tea, and…'

'Oh. No, that's it.'

'That's the punchline, the big payoff, is it? There's tea in your cups because you never finished them.'

'What?'

'For God's sake. You say *what happened was* like there's going to be a story, then *I never finished it.*'

'What? I was telling you.'

'Sometimes, Dee, I think you must be a bit mental.'

'Don't say that.' But I think I must have spoken too quietly – people tell me I often do – because he took the cups out without answering.

He'd been irritated a lot with me lately. It must have something to do with the money, I think, because he mentioned our not having any a lot. But we didn't need more than we had. I didn't, and I couldn't see that he really did. Tom said Eddie probably wanted to move in here and give up renting his place, but I'm not sure that's right. Anyway, every time I tried to ask him to do that, the words stuck in my throat like cold roast potatoes. Maybe we'd wait until we're married. He was here a lot of the time, that must save tons on food and heating, things like that.

'I'm going now,' he said as he came back through.

'Bye,' I said. Putting my face up for a kiss. He ignored it.

'Don't you want to know why I'm going?'

'Yes?' It was horrible when he got like this: interrogating me as though he was a policeman. The Word Police. He'd told me he was going, I'd said goodbye, why was I expected to want to know about his reasons? If they were interesting, I'd assume he'd tell me. If not, he'd just be going home or wherever. It wasn't the kind of thing that mattered. I rattled my pebbles in their saucer.

'Fuck's sake, Dee. Sometimes it don't seem like you care about me at all.'

'Of course I do.' How on earth had he made that connection? Hopscotch. I loved him, we were going to get married, of course I cared.

'So I could leave here, rob a bank, shag the woman behind the counter, spend all the dough on smack and you'd be fine with that, would you?'

'But you wouldn't do those things.'

'Shit.' But he laughed. Ruffled my hair, like Daddy always did. Kissed me on the mouth, but quickly, as though he was already half gone. 'Love you,' he said.

'Are you coming back later?'

'*By Jove, I think she's got it.* Not sure. Give you a bell, okay?'

'I might not be in.'

'No. Well, might see you later then.'

I heard him open the front door, then he gave a sort of yelp. 'Don't do that to me!' he said. Muttered voices from outside, a man and a woman, some laughter. Before I had time to wonder what the matter was, Auntie Lesley and Tom walked in. Which was odd, as they only met twice and they didn't seem to take to each other.

'We met on the doorstep,' Auntie Lesley said, hugging me. I patted her on the back, because she hates it when I just stand there, taking the hug.

'You usually ring first,' I said to her.

'Yeah, well, this time I never.'

'FUCKING SPY. Hi Dee.' Tom kissed my cheek.

'I'm no such thing.' Auntie Lesley swung round to stare at him.

'You can't listen to the words when he shouts,' I said. 'They haven't got any meaning. Think of them as sounds.' I told her that the last two times, as well. Maybe her memory was going. Though it seemed more that she didn't believe me. I looked at Tom, in case he was upset, but he gave me a faint wink so I thought he was probably okay. Twitch, gape, shudder.

'Shall I make FUH-FUH tea?' he said.

'Two sugars, plenty of milk,' said Auntie, 'but that don't mean I want it like dishwater. Nice and strong, please.' She took her coat off, sat down. 'See he makes hisself at home,' she said.

'Did Raquel send you?' I asked. Sitting across from her.

'What? No, course she never. What made you think that?' Lowering her voice, she added, 'Nanti with that one, Dee lovely. He's not as stupid as he makes out. Trust me.'

'Who, Tom? He's not stupid at all, and he doesn't pretend he is.' This was odd. For once, it wasn't me making the quick mistake here. 'What do you mean?'

'Nothing. What made you think Raquel sent me?'

'Not seen her. Is she ill?'

'Not as far as I know. Be quite truthful, I've not seen much of her, neither.'

'Think I'll go round.'

'Well, *I* would. No sense sitting here, worrying yourself about nothing.' She tucked her blouse in. So tiny. I wished I was that small. She took after Nan, but I didn't and nor did Raquel. 'He's proud, mark my words,' she said.

'What?'

'That Tom.' She patted her hair. She was always doing that, even though I'd never once seen a single hair out of place. Daddy says it wouldn't dare. 'He's proud and he's a taker. That act – well, he's good, give him that.'

'Didn't know you'd been to see him.' This was puzzling. I'd never known Auntie Lesley go to a comedy club before.

'What? Sometimes, Dee, not got the faintest what you're on about.'

'I've been hearing that a lot lately,' I said. 'And you're wrong about Tom. He's a giver.' Sometimes, just lately, I looked at my list and it seemed Tom might replace something bigger than The Tomorrow People. Maybe even something that took up as much space as an Eddie did.

As I said that, and as I thought that, Tom came through with three mugs.

'FUH-FUH-Fucking hell,' he said. His arm jerked and the tea sloshed nearly over the top. I jumped up and took them from him. 'Close one,' he said, grinning.

'There you go, Auntie,' I said. 'A giver.'

'On rations, are we? There's only half a cup here.'

'Three-quarters. Tom never fills it right up in case he jerks.'

'HARD COW. And the proof of the pudding,' said Tom, sitting down, 'is that I just did.'

'You must get knackered, really and truly,' said Auntie Lesley.

'Yeah, I do.'

'Look, this is a bit awkward.' Auntie sat forward, patted Tom on the knee. It jerked away. 'I've come here to discuss a bit of family business with Dee. Not being funny, but…'

'Oh, right, yeah, course, I'll be off.' Tom put his mug on the floor, stood up.

'No, sit down,' I said. 'Auntie Lesley, unless you're going to tell me Daddy's a murderer or something like that, I want Tom to stay. Everybody goes, lately. Or they don't come in the first place.'

'It's about me.'

'I want him to stay.' Suddenly, I was all panicky. If people went, they might not come back. They might never come back. And that was true.

'Dee, WHORE LICKER I'm happy to go.'

'Don't say that.'

'Oh for Christ's sake,' said Auntie. 'Blimming sit down then if you're sitting. Just wanted to tell *my niece* that MB's back.'

'Back where?'

'Back in London, where'd you think? Certainly never meant *back* back.'

'How—'

'Your bloody father's been buying him drinks and all sorts.'

'*Daddy* has? Are you sure?'

'Couldn't believe it meself. Tell you, I'm that wild with him. Ken, that is. Don't want him anywhere near me at the minute.'

'But what's he doing back?'

'Something he shouldn't be, tell you that much for nothing. Don't know, Dee, but I don't like it.' Turning to Tom, she added, 'My ex-husband.'

'Ah, right. MAD CUNT. Sorry, I shouldn't be here for this.'

'No, Dee's right, it don't make no difference. Hardly a state secret.' She took a packet of cigarettes from her bag. 'Want one, Tom?'

'Thanks.'

'He's horrible,' I told Tom as they lit their cigarettes. 'Properly horrible, like… What's that stuff you put in gin?'

'Bitters?' said Auntie Lesley.

'That's it. Though bitter lemon's lovely – but I don't suppose that's the same thing at all. They've been divorced for years and years, haven't you?'

'Since 1975. Nine year, that makes it. Bli, time flies when you're not tied to some bastard, excuse my French.' She puffed hard on her cigarette. 'Don't normally like language, but there's times you got to.'

'FUCK IT. Times I've got to, anyway,' Tom said, smiling at her. His smile went right up to his eyes and back to his mouth again, as if he had a kind bulb inside. Auntie Lesley would have to see she was wrong about him.

'I'm normally nicer than this,' she said. That was true, actually. Mostly.

'I'm sure you are. FUH—'

'We met at the circus. Did Delia tell you I used to have an aerial silk act?'

'No,' he said. 'I don't know what that is.'

'Yeah. It's hanging off a bit of material, basically, doing acrobatics off it. Climbs, wraps, drops. Making lovely shapes. Beautiful thing, it is.'

'It's really lovely,' I told him. 'Like a human butterfly.'

I remember when Raquel first sent me a ticket, said I had to see it. Daddy wouldn't come with me even though I was only eleven, but he did take me on the train then went to the pub while I went to the circus. The Anchor. I didn't know how to find a seat, but I did what everyone else did and ended up sitting near the ring because I had an expensive ticket, apparently. Daddy said they'd be looking out for me, but I don't think that was true. The clowns soaked me with their water, splashed me anyway, and I slipped my fingers into my ears. A little boy near me was crying and I wanted to cry too but there was no one to cry for. Raquel came on but I didn't like that much: she was too different, like she couldn't see me, and it was funny to watch someone juggling with their feet. Strange funny – it didn't make me laugh.

But then Auntie Lesley came on, only she wasn't Auntie Lesley, she was this glittery airy creature, and even though I didn't much like looking up – like it even less now, since I started getting Delia's Special Colds – I couldn't look away. After that, I went as often as Daddy would let me. I'd sleep in Raquel's van, cosy and small, like indoor rain. Sometimes, when I can't sleep, I can still see the silk and it sparkles for me when the night's too dark.

'I done aerial dance mostly in the ring,' Auntie Lesley was saying, 'but I did do a bit of circus, didn't I, Dee?' She waited. I realized she wanted me to nod or something, so I did, a bit too energetically. 'Contortion, that means,' she said, 'much harder, but to be right good you got to train from birth. Hard that, in Bow Road.' She laughed. Sat back and crossed her legs. 'I was best at wraps, had some lovely poses I did. Good enough for Girelli's anyway. Was hardly Chipperfield's.'

'It's very dangerous,' I said. 'They don't use safety wires.'

'Well, you got the material for that, in fairness.'

'BORING COW. That's FUH-FUH-fascinating.' Tom slapped his own cheek, hard. 'That one hurt,' he said, quietly.

'That's how she met MB.'

'Yeah, that's how I met him. Swept me off me feet, he did.'

'He was a clown,' I said.

'A Joey,' said Auntie, rolling her eyes at me. I never could remember. 'And a right good one. Could've worked anywhere, he could.'

'If he hadn't had sex with all the circus girls.'

'Yeah, if he never done that.' Auntie Lesley put out her cig and immediately lit another. It was very rare for her, chainsmoking. 'That's how he ended up in Girelli's – he'd had them all everywhere else, and some of the daddies and brothers and hubbies *wasn't* best pleased with him.' She laughed, but I didn't think that was funny. It sounded as though she still liked him, though I knew she didn't. 'Raquel was there by that point, and I thought he might've gone for her or one of the other girls, but it was me he wanted. Thirty I was, then. Near enough.'

'Did you know he was a bit of WHOREFUCKER lad?'

'Oh yeah, I knew. But we all love a bad boy.'

'Yeah, FUCKING IDIOTS I realize that.'

'You're right, we *are* idiots when it comes to men.'

'He didn't mean that,' I said.

'I forgot.' Auntie Lesley leaned forward to pat him again. 'Sorry, love.' She put her head on one side, like a bird. 'Must make my troubles seem piddling,' she said.

'FUCK OFF No, don't be daft.'

'How the hell did you cope, growing up?'

Tom looked at me, but I didn't know what he meant. His long nose had gone brighter red so it looked like a hot-dog sausage.

'People don't normally...I was a FUCKING NOSY BINT punk when I was nineteen. That helped.' Twitch, gape, shudder. 'Had its uses there.'

They both laughed. I was glad Tom wasn't a punk now. He'd still been a bit of one when I met him, though he'd said he used to have a safety pin through his ear and nose and wore a bin bag before when he really was one. Not sure if that was really true or a joke. He had tattoos from then, though, and I liked them. They didn't go with his hair now or his face and I liked that too – people shouldn't all match as if they bought themselves bit by bit from the same shop. I sometimes wanted to have a tattoo myself, a long mazey one that I could trace with my fingers. Always liked mazes in puzzle books, though I'd never been in one in real life.

'Did you know our little Dee used to be a model?'

'I was only four.'

'Still. You always was pretty.'

By the time I was eight I couldn't smile in the way they wanted any more. I could read though, but no one knew that for years. When I was eleven, I was late for history once because of Special English, so the teacher with the glittery-hard eyes and egg in his beard told me pencil-sharp to read out loud from *Tudors and Stuarts*. Then for the first time, I read in front of people. The whole page. They took me out of Special English after that.

'I liked reading better than being pretty,' I said.

'And you're a comic?' said Auntie Lesley to Tom. Maybe I hadn't spoken aloud. You don't always know, not for sure.

'Comedian. Started as Tom Tit, but – FUH FUH – just go on as Tom Allen now.' He stood up. 'Anyone want more FREELOADERS tea?'

Almost before he'd left the room, Auntie said, 'Never upset him, did I?'

'Don't think so.' Strange question, but people often seemed to go in for questions to which there were no possible answers. Talking to hear a voice, I think.

'Sorry love, I'm all over the show today. It's Her Jillpots. You know, whatsaname. Shock to the system, MB coming back.'

'He might not try to see you.'

'Yeah, and pigs might have a go on the trapeze. No lovely, he's after something. He's out of luck if it's money he wants – business is right iffy.' She patted her hair. 'Not got a brandy on hand, have you?'

'No.'

'Nothing stronger than tea?'

'No. Not unless Eddie's left a can of lager in the fridge.'

'You know how fattening them things are? Still, you've no need to worry – lovely and slim still.' Auntie Lesley was the only one who never nagged me about food, not unless she was the one who'd done the cooking, and I suppose I can understand that.

'I don't drink,' I said.

'No, know you don't. Sensible girl.'

Someone else knocked on the door. Tom would get it.

'Are you going back to work soon?' I said. 'I want to go and see Raquel.'

'Say what you mean, why don't you.' But though the words might be cross, she laughed. I laughed too, though I'd no idea why, just that I ought.

Tom came in, but without the tea. He crouched down in the space between the sofa and the chair, put his hand on my leg.

'There's someone at the door, says he wants to speak to you,' he whispered.

'Who?'

'He wouldn't say, but he's – FUH- FUH –FUH A FUCKING MIDGET.'

Eddie

Man, screwing two sisters is the stuff of fantasy, but, be truthful, never of mine. I'm practical. Sorted. Know where I'm going and shit. This was quite possibly the most stupid cunting thing I'd done in a good old while. Chekov meets Joe Orton. Even Stanislavsky's seven questions make no sense here.

Who am I? (a stupid cunt)

Where am I? (in a fucking mess)

When? (every fucking day)

What do I want? (fuck knows)

Why do I want this? (fuck knows)

How will I achieve my goal? (what fucking goal)

What must I overcome? (me. Just me)

Was never meant to go this far. Been keeping her sweet for weeks, bit of a flirt, make her feel good. Not like she was a kid, and older women like all that, they need it after a while. Not that she's older than me, though she don't know that - women and blokes age different. But she sang that Cohen thing, and I was on a bit of a buzz, and she looked well hot in that dress, all tits and arse, so different from Dee's bones, and then there was all the subtle looks and sub-text. Dee wouldn't know sub-text if it put on a tee-shirt saying *I'm Sub-Text* and tried to snog her in Sainsbury's by the yoghurts. Raquel was a relief, in a way, a space to breathe. It weren't meant to get her into bed.

Fuck it, no point sitting round analyzing all day, like I was swotting for a part. Yeah, playing myself, which no actor wants to do.

Still, it was hot, can't deny it. She'd been around, but not for a while I reckon, so she was gagging for it. Never rushed, though. Made me go right through the box of tricks. She was wet as a warm bath when I got in there. Had a job not coming off too early, Jesus. But then when her old man pitched up with that midge in tow, well that just about finished me for good. No one'd take me for under thirty after that. Surprised the hair never went white overnight. No way was it worth it.

So what the hell I was doing going back there a couple of days later, was anyone's guess.

She looked right through me.

'You going to let me in?'

'What for?'

'Just let me in, Raquel.'

I followed her through to the bleachy living room. She sat on the chair, her knees clamped together. Said nothing at all, just watched me, as if she was playing a psychiatrist in an old American movie. But this was no time for confession. Business-like, that was the way to play this. Cool, man. Sweet. Laid-back.

'How are you?' I said, sitting on the settee.

She raised one eyebrow, much as to say, *You're a dickhead, Muir.*

'You're not going to tell her, are you?' I asked. She'd respect that a lot more than piss-arsing about. I pulled my baccy out, started to roll a fag.

'You could have asked me that on the phone.' She

reached for the packet of straights on the table next to her, shook one out, lit it before I could offer. There was a load of butts in the ashtray.

'Yeah, shit.' *Shit.* Tapped my finger hard on my forehead a couple of times. 'Suppose it was a risk, coming here.' Heart went over at the stupidity. *You never think* - could hear Mum now. 'Didn't think.'

'Oh for... No, of course I'm not going to tell her. You really believe what we did was so important to me that I'd want to ruin the relationship with my sister? *My* relationship. Don't give a toss about yours. She deserves better, quite frankly.'

'Yeah she does. Got to make you right there.' But it was a bit rich, really. Okay, maybe I shouldn't've got her sister into bed, but not too many blokes would put up with Dee's *Deeness* past a few – admittedly amazing – shags.

'What is it you want, Eddie? A signed guarantee?' Even the drag on her fag sounded pissed off. 'You'll just have to take my word for it, I'm afraid.'

'Yeah, course, whatever.' I re-lit my roly. 'Just checking how the land was.'

'Checking I wasn't going to dump you in the poo.'

'Come on, that's got to be fair enough, yeah?' No point bullshitting now.

'Well, I can see why you'd feel the need, yes.' She pushed her heavy hair off her face. Dee's was so light, so thin, every breeze lifted it. I remembered the weight of Raquel's mane in my hands, on my neck.

'And it does take two,' I said.

'Oh for Christ's sake, I do know that.' Rolling her big, big eyes. But then, 'It's more my fault. I owe her more.' Theatrical sigh. 'Let's just forget it, okay?'

'So we can still be—'

'Eddie Muir, if you say we can still be friends, swear I'll swing for you.' She shook her head at me, but there was a hint of something like a laugh in her eyes now. Didn't want to shove too hard on my luck, though, so I just smiled and held my hands up. Glanced along her bookshelf, getting the old fix for comfort. Clocked *Memoirs of a Midget*.

'Who was the dwarf?' I asked. And be fair, I wanted to know.

'My aunt's ex-husband. He's a dangerous bastard, quite truthfully. God knows what Daddy was doing with him. Daddy's been...less predictable lately.'

'Your aunt married a midge? Bloody hell.'

'He's very charismatic.' Then she laughed for real, ground her fag into the ashtray. 'And he's got a big dick,' she said. 'Trust me, I walked in on him in the loo once.' She lifted her hands to show me, like the fisherman's one that got away.

'Fuck me.' I laughed an' all. 'He in the business?'

'Sort of.' She shrugged, then looked hard at me. Cheeks a bit pink, but otherwise you'd never guess there was anything weird gone on. 'Okay, this is the deal. We have to make this work. You're marrying my sister, for heaven's sake, *and* we'll be working together. I don't want this to go pear-shaped any more than you.'

'Yeah, I know, that's why—'

'Look, it's my day off so I'm going to have a glass of Mateus Rosé and some cheese and biscuits. Went and bought a nice bottle this morning, treated myself.' Pushed herself to the edge of the seat, like she was going to stand. 'Though God knows I shouldn't be flinging money around. *Don't* read anything into it, but you want to join me?'

Looked at my watch. Five-and-twenty to six. I'd assumed she'd be off to work soonish. 'Sure, why not?' I said. 'Long as you promise not to take advantage.'

'Don't push it, barrow boy.'

But it was sweet, I was safe. Dee would never know, and I'd still be able to have a little flirt with the sister, only even better, with us having that memory to add something. We'd always have Paris. Weren't nothing to get worked up about after all. She was a big girl, she knew the score. Done right to come here.

'You always drink on your own?' I asked her, going over to lean on the work surface that separated the living room from the kitchen.

'Yep. Sad old lush, that's me. You've said something like that before. Bitter spinster, sipping sherry all day.'

'Do me a favour.'

'Well, I didn't have you down as so conventional, darling. If I want a drink, I have one. If I don't, I don't. Doesn't matter who's with me either way.'

'Want me to open that for you?' Expert, I was. Played a barman in that hotel for eighteen months once.

'With all this solo drinking, I shouldn't need help.' But she passed me the bottle and the corkscrew, started putting crispbread on a plate with the Edam. 'Sorry, I haven't got any cheddar,' she said, patting her stomach. 'Slimming. But I've got some Branston somewhere.'

'Hate all that diet shit,' I said. 'Man, it's boring to eat with someone who hates food. Puts you right off, more ways than one.'

'She can't help it.' Gentle, reminding me rather than having a pop.

'Didn't mean…Sorry. Weren't thinking.' The cork eased out the bottle. 'Edam's fine. Whatever. Not exactly a fussy eater.'

She'd got the glasses out, big solid greenish things with spiral stems, one twisted greens, one reds, so I poured for us and gave her the bottle to put back in the fridge. Never once had an evening like this with Dee - drink, food, chatting while we got the stuff together. Not one single time. Weren't complaining, not even comparing really, but it was restful, has to be said, not having to explain every single little thing every second of every day. If I did marry Dee, I'd be doing that all the days of my life.

We never sat down, just leaned either side of the work surface, eating rubbery cheese on hard bits of cardboard, smothered in pickle for flavour, and emptying that bottle of over-sweet wine pretty sharpish. Raquel was wearing a low-cut tee-shirt tucked into cropped jeans, wide patent belt, hair just loose, not much slap. She looked like a girl. Tried to forget I knew how she looked when she came.

'When Dee was little, before she could read, we used to play colour I-Spy,' Raquel told me, halfway down the second glass. 'You know, I-Spy with my little eye, something red. But she'd always say, *I-Spy with my little eye, something the colour of Raquel's blouse, and she's wearing it.* I'd have to go through my shoes, my skirt, my bracelet and everything, and only then say my blouse. She'd be giggling away, thrilled to bits how I kept getting it wrong. That sounds mean, it does, but I didn't... Funny little thing, she was.'

'She still is,' I said.

'That's what makes her loveable.'

'That's what makes her loveable.' We looked at each other, then Raquel picked up her crispbread.

'When I joined the circus, I felt I was abandoning her,' she said, with her mouth full.

'But you was just a kid yourself, weren't you?'

'Nearly eighteen. She was only ten. I was all she had, apart from Daddy.'

'Kick off, did she?'

'What do you think? She just…went in on herself even more.' Raquel took a big swig of her drink. 'But once she started coming to see me, it was better. Some holidays, she was with me all the time.' Looking past me, like she was seeing it again. 'She loved it, being around the animals and watching the acts. She was still turning up for weeks at a time just before I left, ten years later. Darling Dee misses it more than I do, I think.'

'She never talks about it. I've not got a Scooby what it was like.'

'No, she wouldn't, would she? But to be fair, Lesley and I don't much, either. It's… Well, you know. Different. The references.'

'You miss it, then?'

'No, not really. What I miss is the sense of possibility, but that's just missing being young. It's living a mildly disappointed life.' She smiled. 'Chuck my ciggies, would you?'

'Never had you down as much of a smoker.'

'I'm not.'

A mildly disappointed life. That was me, all right. It weren't some big tragedy, nothing was hard, nothing was going to be hard, but it weren't what I'd wanted, what I'd planned, what I'd fucking expected. I was living some other wanker's life and can't say I liked it much. Raquel had most probably wanted the husband, babies, all that. Weren't going to happen for her now.

Raquel had pushed her plate to one side, was using it as an ashtray. My mum would freak out at that, *Dirty little whore, look at her. Disgrace, I call it*, as though dirt really did come from the devil. Not that Mum was going to like Dee any better, *Five pence short of a shilling, that one.* Appreciation weren't one of Mum's talents.

'What'll happen if you don't make it?' she said, blowing smoke across the counter at me. Dee would never ask that. If I said I was going to make it, she'd just accept it. Hardly seemed even to care.

'More of the same,' I said. 'Can't see me giving up, going to get a normal job. I'd still be kidding myself I could make it at sixty, most probably.'

'What would it say on your résumé then?' She tapped her ash on to the plate. 'Actor, fifties, can play 40-65?'

'Probably. *I'm ready for my close-up, Mr De Mille.*'

'*All right, Mr De Mille, I'm ready for my close up,*' she said, firmly. 'And Norma Desmond was a has-been.'

'Instead of a never-was.'

'Well, precisely.' She took a final drag on her cigarette and ground it out. 'It's pretty pitiful, darling.'

'Yeah, like I don't know that.'

'You were right, you know, the other night.' Raquel drained the last of her wine. 'We *are* alike. Thwarted.'

'Least I haven't given up.'

'Meaning I have? Maybe. Who do I meet, doing what I do? I wanted ordinary, Eddie. Looking back, I can see that was never really an option. Deluded.'

'*I'm* not fucking deluded.'

'Okay. Singing in my club's going to make you a film star, I get it.'

'Fuck off.'

'Eat your heart out, Oscar.'

Suddenly, I was so wild I could've smacked her one. Never hit a woman in my life, not even close, but she was giving me a root canal without the anaesthetic. The nerve throbbed, hot-wiring the others. I rolled a fag, my hands shaking with adrenalin, spilling Golden Virginia onto the counter.

'Shit.'

'Doesn't matter.'

I glared at her. 'Don't give a toss whether it matters to you,' I said.

Unexpectedly, she laughed. Then so did I.

'Seem to have left my maturity at home,' I said.

'I was baiting you.' She leaned across, took my roly, had a drag, gave it back, slightly damp from the wine. 'Out of ciggies,' she said. Then, 'It's not you, Eddie.'

'What?'

'The person I'm not going to meet. He's not you.'

'Never thought he was.' Not sure I liked where this was going. We looked at each other, hard.

'He's steady and sweet, with an ordinary job and ordinary expectations. He's a grown-up.' She shook her head. 'And he was married by thirty, two kids by thirty-five. He's long gone. So I'm not looking anymore. All I do now is find distractions.'

'So I was a distraction?'

'An ill-judged one, yes.'

'Thanks a lot, girl.' But I got what she was saying - she didn't want me. She didn't envy her sister. There was no green-eyed monster to mock the food it fed on. I'd been there, that's all. Convenience and loneliness had opened her legs, not passion.

'What about you?' she said. 'Why did you do it? Really?'

'Christ, I don't know. Because I'm a bloke? Because of Dee being Dee?'

'You see? I'm not who you're looking for either.'

'No.' Then I leaned across the counter and kissed her.

'He bloody well died on stage. Probably the only time he's ever died in front of an audience in his life. Couldn't believe it. On television too. Feh, that's one way to go down in history. He always did want to leave his mark.' Ken rubbed his hand over his eyes. 'You can just see the headlines tomorrow, can't you? **JUST LIKE THAT**.'

He sank into Dee's settee, like he'd sunk a bottle or three, but there was no booze smell about him. Something never smelt right, though. Three times he'd told that story in as many minutes.

'Tommy Cooper's dead?' I asked again.

'Don't you ever bloody listen, Ed? Just spent five minutes telling you. Saw it on the telly box, jumped straight in a cab, came here.'

'He's definitely dead?'

'I'd be prepared to bet my last guinea. Delia! Where's that Nescaff?'

'You knew him, then?'

'Knew him, schmoo him. Met the fella a couple of times. Long black curly teeth, walked with a lisp.' He cracked up laughing, ending in a wheeze. 'What was he, sixty-two, sixty-three? Few years older than I am, that's all.'

'He went the way he'd've want—'

'Bollocks. What he wanted was to keep on working.' He looked up as Dee came in with his coffee. Nothing for her or for me. 'They laughed when he collapsed. I was watching at home and *I* laughed. Is that what he wanted? Doubt it, my boy, doubt it very much indeed.' He reached for the mug. 'Thanks, Princess.'

'Was he ill?' Dee asked, sitting on the floor by her ashtray of pebbles, running her fingers through them.

'*We spell away the overhanging night, / We spell away the soldiers and the fright.*' He nodded.

'Robert Graves,' Dee said, but to her old man, not to me. She wouldn't think to let me in on it. Spent half my childhood in a library and she never even realized. Or cared.

'Oh Princess Pea, they all die, trust your daddy, they all die. Twenty years too early. Or they live twenty years too long, dead on their feet.'

'You're not dead,' she pointed out.

'Not yet, my darling girl, not yet.' He took a big swig of his coffee, winced, touched his mouth. 'Bollocks.'

'It's different if they've kept on working,' I said. 'Bound to out-live yourself, you do that.'

'You think people change, do you?' he said, turning to me. 'You think they change? Because I'll tell you one thing for free – no one changes.'

'Don't know—'

'Dee here, and my Raquel, their personalities were set at eighteen months. Dee would sit rocking in her little bed at that age, banging her head on her knees, happy as Larry. Or she'd lay under a tree, looking up at the leaves, for hours. Recognize yourself, Dee? Course you do. And Raquel, she'd be fussing round, picking up this and that, taking care of her dollies, liking her pretty dresses. She'd spin round when she got a new one, so excited, showing off her drawers. Just the same now, show any bugger her drawers if he said he liked her dress. And my…Glen. He's not changed. He's every bit the same as he was, and he always will be.' He put his mug on the floor. 'Got a cigar for me, Princess?'

'No.'

'No, course you haven't, quite right. Kill you in the end, they would.'

He couldn't know. That spiel weren't for me, surely to God. Tommy Cooper's death had hit him hard for some reason. Most probably the age thing. I felt like leaving them to it, but I'd only just got here - even Dee would think that was funny. Well, she might.

'I'm cold,' Dee said.

'Put the heating on,' I said.

'Never have it on after April 14th, not until October 14th. It's my rule.'

'But that's… It's cold, Dee.'

'I'll get a woolly.' But she never moved.

'Cold, Dee-Dee?' Ken ruffled her hair. 'Have my scarf.' But he weren't wearing one, and he didn't move either, like he'd forgot what he'd said the moment he'd spoken.

'Listen, I'll leave you guys to it,' I said, standing up.

'No, I'm off, I'm off.' Ken stood up an all. We was about eye to eye - neither of us would ever play Little John. His gut was a hell of a lot nearer to me than his chest was. I made a note to cut down on the old beer and chips. 'Just called in to give you the news.'

All this way in a cab for Tommy Cooper?

He struggled to do his buttons up.

'*Slanders, sir,*' he said, '*for the satirical rogue says here that old men have grey beards, that their faces are wrinkled, their eyes purging thick amber and plum-tree gum, and that they have a plentiful lack of wit, together with most weak hams; all which, sir, though I most powerfully and potently believe—*'

'*Yet I hold it not honesty to have it thus set down, for yourself, sir, shall grow old as I am, if like a crab you could go backward.*' My voice shook a bit, because let's be fair, it was taking the piss, but I had to show this poxy family I could do it. Nobody might be asking for my Hamlet, but when they did, I'd be ready.

'You shoved me over into Polonius,' Ken said. Indignantly. 'Usurped.'

'*Uneasy lies the head that wears the crown,*' said Delia, unexpectedly. 'Bye Daddy. Thanks for telling us all about Tommy Cooper. It was interesting.'

Swear, every time, every bloody time, I'd thought I must be a mental case for seeing her, she sat there, fragile and nearly beautiful, and said something like that, making me want her all over again.

Then Ken was gone, and it was the two of us, and she smiled at me. Right at me, with no baggage, no tricks, nothing up her sleeve, nothing else in her head apparently except for me. And like a fucking fool, I was gone again.

Just like that.

Ken

Training shoes. Never thought I'd ever own a pair of training shoes. Raquel tells me they're practical for all this walking I've taken to doing, but I don't think they go with Lands' End chino trousers, do you? No? No, quite right. Ought to stick them in the bin, but I don't want to hurt her feelings. So much seems to hurt her feelings these days, better to err on the side of caution. At least you know where you are with Dee – she wouldn't see the point of keeping something that didn't agree with you.

I went home from a party once wearing Cubby Moore's brogues. Haven't the foggiest how. He'd inked his surname in them, like school children do. Got his number from my agent the next day and telephoned him, but he'd gone home barefoot, so Lord knows what happened to my Beatle Boots.

Not funny? Heard it, have you? Feh, everyone's a critic.

Listen, I should have told you this last week, but – well, you knew there was something, didn't you? You always know. Could tell by the way you kept nudging my foot with yours. Had my brown Ballys on then, mind you, nice functional lace-up. I liked that little nudge, made me smile, that's why I didn't realize until afterwards what you meant, you intuitive old devil. You're right, my mind wasn't on the job. Not that you're a job, but you know what I mean. You always know. It's…look, I won't beat about the bush, it's MB. He's turned up again.

Don't look at me like that, wasn't my fault. He telephoned me and asked to meet me for a drink. Since then of course, he's done the rounds, been to see them all. Lesley's none too pleased – we're not on speakers at the moment. She's playing no-speaks with me, anyway. Bollocks to her. But I can't leave it at that, can I? She's our sister. Even if she does only pitch up here a couple of times a year at best, lazy bitch. Damn it to blazes, I'll have to go and see her soon. Gets too easy to let the time go, doesn't it? That's what our father said to me, *To be sure, Kenny boy, it's been a feck of a long time, but it's easy to let the months turn into years.* Remember? I didn't like that *Kenny boy*, not on him, and I absolutely didn't like him talking across you, as if you were deaf or simple. Bet you had a laugh about that one, you sharp beggar.

He wants me to put on a show. MB. To be one of the sponsors, anyway, and do a guest. Variety. Told him, variety's dead in the water, but he thinks if we got a charity attached we'd make a profit *and* look like the good guys. Reminds me of the old Sunday evening benefits for the profession. Remember those? Did a fair old few of them back in the day. Whenever they couldn't get Larry or John they'd get one of the rest of us – I was generally about twentieth in line or some such and fourth on the bill. Speech from *Henry V* usually, or a To be, or a couple of sonnets. They were the easiest, the poems. You feel a bit of a fool, doing proper Shakespeare out of context, but if you remember the emotion has to be massive then the funny old words and those great enormous images seem to fit even without a play surrounding them. You can't paraphrase emotion, y'see – it's its own expression. Well, you know that better than anyone.

December time, it'd be 'The Night Before Christmas' or a bit of *Christmas Carol*, crowd pleasers both of them. Did one once with that Cliff Richard – never seen a fella so clean. Reeked of Imperial Leather.

I know what you'd say – it's not back in the day, and it's not a Sunday nighter. I don't know, Glen-Glen – I told him I'm not risking your money, but the chap's persistent. And something in me... Might even get Raquel a little spot. And Dee's crip. Return of the O'Learys. Don't think we'd ask Dee's nice friend, though – hardly family entertainment.

No, I know, of course I can't do it. If it went wrong, what would happen to you? Don't worry old son, Kenny would never let anything happen to you. Never. Can't deny though, did like throwing those ideas around with the little stoat. Whatever you say about him, chap knows his game. Never seen a better auguste, not in forty years. Even your Erics and your Bernie Winters – close, but no cigar. MB could have made in on the telly-box, if he hadn't been such a deadbeat. His schtick was good enough, and I don't think the other thing would have stopped him, do you? Dwarfs aren't threatening – people don't mind laughing at them. Remember Mr Lawrence, ran the grocer's with his sister? Course you do, they used to give you liquorice bootlaces before you went - no, darling boy, no, Kenny hasn't got bootlaces for you. Let's see – P-p-p-pick up a Penguin? Pack of Penguins do you? That's it. Look, the blue one's second down today. You love the blue one, don't you? Hang on, I'll open – oh, you've got it. Good, good, quite right, you're not helpless. All the kiddies loved Mr Lawrence, and he was no more than three foot ten, *I* know.

Can't do it, can I? No, you're quite right, of course I can't. Better to take one of the VO jobs, only... MB's show would be a one-off, I'd be the draw because it would truly be the only time I'd come out of retirement. More like a Farewell Performance. Still, never mind. Was nice to think about it, got the old mind ticking over a bit, no need actually to go through with it. Feh. MB would end up leaving it all to me anyway. Be far too much with everything else.

Not that there's much of anything else. Do you ever feel like that, Glen-Glen? You sit here, day after day after day, looking at the same two picture books and eating your treats – is it really enough? Is it, my darling boy? Maybe we're both finished, you and I. Maybe the curtain's down on both of us. I wish I could take you away from all this, somewhere you could feel the sun on your skin, see something different, but it's too late now, isn't it? Too late to make changes, you'd never cope with them. Me neither. We're fifty-nine, you and I, trapped in the lives of old, old men. If we don't watch out, we'll be reeking of piss and embalming fluid. Oh Glen-Glen, this isn't what Kenny wanted for you. For either of us.

Mind you, if it did all go wrong, I could take the VOs, come out of retirement. Why not? Then it'd be a comeback instead of a one-off or a bye-bye. Bit premature perhaps, bit premature, but so fucking what. So I'd end up where I hadn't wanted to be – not as though I'm where I want to be at the moment. As long as you were safe, what would it matter if I had to lose a bit of pride? Comes before a prat fall, anyway. Maybe a couple of lines in daytime telly isn't the worst fate in the world after all. I do know I can't go on like this, my old son.

What? Why are you looking at me like that? Stop that. Bollocks, are you judge and jury both, now? Stop it, Glen, stop it this instant or we'll fall out. Look at me, boy. Swear it, I'll make you look. *Look.* I mean it, I can't do with you judging me too, not you. I can't be on trial here of all places, not here.

God, did that hurt your poor chin? I was just trying to make you look – oh Christ. Christ, don't cry, Glen-Glen. Kenny didn't mean it, I'm so sorry. No, darling, don't cry. Or is it me? Sometimes I don't know where you stop and I begin. Oh my dear old chap, don't weep for me, I'm not worth it. And please - don't tell me you're weeping for yourself, or we'll never stop.

Delia

Some people you discover instead of them announcing themselves. Not in our family, not mostly, but here and there are people you sort of stumble across. This one looked like death. Beautiful-still, the way you couldn't picture her being in life. *You look like death* isn't meant to be a compliment but it should be, perhaps. Perhaps it should be. It's missing the point anyway – it can't be confused with anything to do with living. Like it's something dull, a person with the shine-bright rubbed off. Death means you couldn't rely on a person's own version of themselves. You could stare down at a dead body and became…an artist. Not the sort of person our family calls an artist, not an actor, but the sort who paints. No, who sculpts stone or makes things out of clay. Not that I'd ever seen a dead body before. Or since, come to think of it. But seeing that girl made me know that's how death is. I don't think I was guessing, I really don't think that. I just sort of knew.

Her skin was tight and yellow – I had the feeling she was coated in thin plastic but I don't think that can be true. Her mouth was a little bit open, lips bluey-purple as if she was wearing a lipstick Raquel might like. It made you think she'd been in the middle of saying something. Now you could finish that any way you thought of. You could give her words. Sometimes, I feel people do that to me – finish my sentences, but wrong, always wrong. She'd never mind, though. Didn't smell yet or only of soap – maybe Imperial Leather. Made me feel as if someone had washed the body ready. I'm sure I heard somewhere that your hair and nails kept growing after you died. Don't know, though. She didn't look as if she could grow anything.

I never did find out who she was.

That was when MB was still married to Auntie Lesley, of course. He said he'd sort it, said I needn't ever tell the police I found her. Said she was just some prostitute or runaway who nobody cared about. For a long while, I thought MB might have killed her. I even told Auntie Lesley but she said No, he was capable of a lot but not that. He just knew how to deal with the Old Bill, she said. Meaning, I think, that everyone knew Der-der-Delia didn't know how to deal with anything real and hard and true. And after that I tried not to think about it. Seeing that dead cat today reminded me, I think. Or maybe it's because MB's back. Either way, I can see her face, her plastic face, in every face who doesn't just pass by but stops to meet the faces that it meets.

I wonder what people do who don't have others' words in their heads. Wonder how they ever manage to think things through. You might start well enough, but if you didn't have a head full of words, words, words, I should think your odd thought would rattle around. Or perhaps that's just me. Maybe only mine would do that, and everyone else would think just fine. Though not my family. Not us.

'Dolly Daydream.' Eddie patted my head. He never called me that. It wasn't his name for me.

'I'm not a child,' I said.

'Never said you was. Don't start.'

Start what?

He was putting his shoes on. That must mean he was going somewhere.

'I'm off, love.' Another pat. Sometimes, I felt he kept me for a pet. 'All right?' He crouched down, took my face in his hands. 'I said, all right?'

'I'm all right.'

'No – is it all right that I'm going?'

'I'll go round to Tom's.'

'Yeah, that'd be right. Christ.' He pulled away, stood up. 'If that fucker weren't so plug-ugly, I'd get worried, straight up.'

'Worried about what?'

'Come off it, Dee – even you're not that innocent.'

He was right, of course, but it was so stupid, so shiny and stupid, that I couldn't be bothered to unpretend. Tom was the loveliest man in my life, but I wasn't about to do it with him. Didn't even know why, not really, not when Eddie was like this, but I knew I wasn't going to. There was too much…danger. That might be the right word. It scampered about in my head, all alone and scared. *Danger*.

'You know what?' Eddie said, as he shrugged on his jacket. 'Reckon I'm the only one what sees through you. Everyone else buys your little-girl act, but you got it well sussed, girl. It's the rest of us mugs who run round you—'

'Are you coming back tonight?' I said.

'Don't know. That'll keep you on your toes, won't it?'

When he was this stupid, I wasn't sure I was right that I loved him. Just for the odd moment, the odd flash in the pan, I couldn't remember why I wanted him. But then he smiled, and I could see he was just talking himself into being okay with going. If he could make me a little bit cross with him, if he could be a little bit pissed off with me, it wouldn't matter. I stood up, put my arms round him and kissed him on the mouth. He kissed me back, hard. And for a few minutes, I think he nearly didn't go out at all.

But as he turned at the door to say goodnight, see you later, love you, love you, love you, he looked his face into mine and I saw it covered in thin, yellowish plastic. And I had to get rid of all the words in my head. I had to let the space rattle against the space until there was nothing left.

Raquel

When I first went up to the Grammar, I didn't have a best friend. Janice French had been my mate all through Infants and Juniors but she went on to the Secondary Modern and after that, when I saw her in the street, she'd just mumble hello and walk off giggling with her pack of fashionable hairdos, rotten bs. All the other girls in my school were in twos, while I trailed after one particular pair, Helen and Deborah, who each kept me around for someone to whisper about the other to. One day, Helen and Deborah fell out, and Helen said to me, 'You're my best friend now, Raquel.' That was it: I had a bestie just by being in the right place at the right time. By accepting the role. But I never felt comfortable in that friendship, even though it lasted until I joined Girelli's; I always thought one day Helen would move on and announce to someone else that *they* were now her best friend. I've not had a close gal pal since, not really, not outside of work. But I'd always had my Delia. Now she was Eddie's. Funny thing about Helen and Deborah: I can't remember why it was them I chose to follow rather than any other pair. The cool appeal of a non-regulation shoe or a tie worn short became a declared and almost-felt loyalty overnight.

'What we going to do, Raquel?' Eddie was making his

inevitable ciggie, as though the only way he could say anything that mattered was to disguise the thought process with the concentration required for rolling his own. 'Can't go on like this.'

'I know.'

'You want to pack it in?' He licked the Rizla.

'I don't know.' I watched him light the cig. 'Why, do you?'

'Don't know. No, course not, but… This is shit.'

'It's shit.'

The May sunshine pressed through the too-thin bedroom curtains, filling the air with dust motes. There was something about having the curtains shut during the day, mixing up illness with sex, so you weren't sure which you were recovering from. It was like wearing green nail polish: what was divine decadence when you were young was just plain sleazy at thirty-five.

Some people are thinkers. They sit and analyse every single thing they say or do, and come out with a theory explaining it all. Peter was like that. It was fair enough really: he was a psychology lecturer. But it didn't half get on your nerves, as Lesley would say. Did say, in fact. It's just not me; never found myself that interesting, frankly. And if you start all that, where on earth do you stop? You wouldn't be able to butter a bit of toast or pile on the slap of a morning without questioning how you did it. Scary biscuits, frankly. But I'm nobody's fool, and sometimes, you have to look at yourself even if you don't want to. Especially then.

There was only one possible justification for what I was doing: to be in love with Eddie Muir. So that's what I did, I fell in love with him. Well, teetered on the brink in unsuitable heels at least. It wasn't easy, he wasn't a person you could respect or admire or who swept you off your feet with his passion and longing. He wasn't even tall. I concentrated on his looks (good), his company (quite good), his talent (he had some), and on how he made me feel (guilty, excited, desirable, clever). Well, whoopee-doo. Hindsight's marvellous, for sure, but the tragic thing was, I rather knew I was doing it even at the time. My darling, exasperating Dee-Dee was being sold down the river for what I could make myself feel.

My poor thumbs were sore and bloody with the constant inscribing of eights with my nail on the pads, and I was back to turning the bathroom light on and off seventeen times, and stirring my Nescaff clockwise, anti-clockwise, clockwise, anti-clockwise, clockwise, anti-clockwise, clockwise, anti-clockwise, but still I knew something awful was going to happen to me, to Dee, to us.

I go to her flat and she's accidentally electrocuted herself by using her hairdryer in the bath. She's lying there, eyes open in surprise, but there was no pain.

Sometimes, I'd imagine her death, as though killing her was better than her finding out I was betraying her three times a week. *Unthink*, I'd tell myself, *unthink, unthink*, but the thoughts wouldn't stay unthunk, no matter how many times I told myself it was all right, that I was all right. It wasn't and I wasn't and there we were.

I care about you both, he'd said, three times a week for a fortnight so far.

I want you both, he said.

You're stronger than she is, he said.

You're my sanctuary, he said.

We both love her, he said.

Daddy would have said that was all bollocks and it almost certainly was. With a script like that, Eddie already knew the part. And clearly he thrived on the performed passion – but that was a teensy bit true of me too, perhaps. If we were just going out in a regular way, a fortnight would be nothing, far too soon really to care. But in an affairette, the intensity hoiks itself up several notches, and a fortnight is a long way in. Far enough that it's hard to see the end. Who knows, in a month it might seem impossible. Misery loves company.

Maybe I ought to have married Peter. Mind you, realistically, how long can a girl wait for someone's divorce to come through? And a man having a ponytail when he's that thin on top does rather look like desperate compensation. Plus I'm not sure I could have stood those thick yellow nails and his constant use of the word *decoding* and the endless re-writing of a book on the taxonomy of trait-descriptive terms. I never even knew what it bloody meant and I'm not convinced he did either. Dearie dear. Anyway, he wore his pants for two days running.

'You'd better get up,' I said to Eddie, as I watched the dust motes mingle with his smoke. I wanted to say, I think I might love you, stay with me. I wanted to say, Why do you always go so happily. But instead, 'Lesley's coming over for lunch.'

'God help us, don't your family ever give it a rest?'

'What's that supposed to mean?'

'Every poxy day, one of you's seeing another one. Leave each other alone for a bit, for fuck's sake.'

'Just because you don't like your parents—'

'I like my parents, they're fine.' Eddie got out of bed. His lean body, his unselfconsciousness, made me pull the sheet more tightly round me. 'Just don't feel the need to see them every other day.'

'Or at all.'

'It's not about me, Raquel.'

'We're close. Dee and I both lost our mothers, remember.'

'*To lose one parent, Mr Worthing, may be regarded as a misfortune; to lose both looks like carelessness.*' Eddie gave a nasty little laugh and scratched his chest hard, as though trying to make the little patch of hair grow. 'You never lost them – you misplaced them.' But he had a thick black line of hair from his belly button down; suddenly, I wanted to run my fingers along it. I reached for my cigs.

'They misplaced us, anyway,' I said. 'And no, we don't think it's our fault and no, we're not compensating.' I'd heard *that* before. 'You don't know what it's like to have a brother or sister.'

'I know loads of people with brothers and sisters. They don't all live in each other's pockets. Not to mention aunts and dads and Uncle Tom Cobbleys an all.'

'Well, good for you. But right now, I need you to get dressed and go home to your fiancée.'

'Girlfriend.'

'Girlfriend. Whatever, I'm not it, so Lesley can't see you here.'

'Fair enough.' He tossed his cig into the ashtray and pulled on his pants and jeans. 'Where's my— No, it's all right.' He picked his tee-shirt up from the floor, pulled it over his head. No one got dressed more quickly than Eddie. I reached for my dressing gown, struggled into it under the sheet.

'What you come as, Miss Bathing Beauty 1884?'

'I'd best have a quick wash,' I said, sliding my legs out of bed. 'Come on, Ed, don't forget your socks.'

When I came out of the bathroom, dressed, fragrant around my bits and pieces, and with my nose powdered, he was still there. I checked my watch.

'Chop-chop, get a wiggle on.'

'Can't be as urgent as all that.' He shot me one of his

insolent looks, as though he didn't give a tinker's damn who saw him, as though I was his headmistress and he the school bad boy – although he never played that one out in bed. But I knew it was all bravado; he cared all right. Whatever might happen in the future, I knew he wasn't ready to leave Dee, and I certainly wasn't ready for him to abandon her yet.

'Time's getting on. Please, Eddie.'

'I'm gone.' He held his hands up. 'What's your night off this week?'

'Wednesday, but you're working.'

'Maybe see you Thursday, during the day, then. Give you a bell.' He kissed me on the cheek: Dee's sister, his future in-law.

'We can't go on like this.'

'I know, it's shit.' Then, 'Love you,' as though it was the most natural, casual thing in the world. But one little pronoun makes all the difference, doesn't it, as though you don't have to own what you're saying. I didn't say it back.

'Phew, it's stuffy in here.' Lesley shook out three cushions, dislodging a sequin which flew across the room, then she reached up to open my little top window. 'That's better. Lovely day out there, it is – more like June than May. Weather man says we're having a storm later, but I can't see it myself. You can't feel it in the air, can you? Radio always gets things wrong.'

'I've just made us a sandwich,' I said. 'With a few crisps.'

'Corn beef and pickle?'

'Yep. And it's crusty bread. A bloomer.'

'Well, long as the crisps are plain, anything'll do me.' Lesley brushed imaginary crumbs from the settee and sat down, shrugging off her jacket, which she smoothed and placed carefully over the back. 'Got the kettle on, have you?'

I busied myself making tea, bringing through the plates

and bits of kitchen roll. It was pretty clear what this was going to be about. Eddie was right: my family never let anyone alone, never gave any space to breathe.

'You've lost weight,' Lesley said, just as I took a big bite of my sandwich.

'Few pounds,' I said, through the buttery bread.

'Suits you. Man, is it?'

'No, just wanted to be a bit more comfortable in my clothes.'

'Right.' Lesley pulled a little piece of corn beef out of her bread, popped it into her mouth. 'We've not seen much of you, so I wondered.'

'No.'

'Dee's not seen you in three week, near on.'

There we are: that's what she came for.

'I've rung once or twice,' I said, cramming a handful of crisps into my words.

'That child's used to a lot more than you ringing once or twice.' Lesley put her almost-untouched plate on the floor, fished in her bag for her cigarettes. 'She's... Well, you'd notice the difference. Bit more vague.' She lit a cig. 'Got an ashtray? Don't worry, can see one from here.' She got up, and moved over to the windowsill. Picking up the ashtray, she peered into it. 'Taken up rolling your own, have you?' she said, her voice nipped tight.

Shit. Oh buggery shitty buggery bollocks. I'd emptied the one in the bedroom, but I'd totally forgotten that we'd started the morning in here. Keep calm, keep calm, it's all right, you're all right.

'Okay,' I said, 'you got me. There's a man. But it's not serious. His name's Fred and I met him at the club. He smokes rolies. Golden Virginia.'

'Fred. Not a name you come across in a young bloke.'

'Didn't say he was young.' I laughed. 'Beggars can't be choosers,' I said.

Lesley was staring me out, daring me to carry on with the lie. But she couldn't prove anything. Oh come on, she probably didn't even suspect; lots of men smoked roll-ups, and there was no reason to associate me with Eddie, none at all. I smiled at her.

'Can I pinch a cig?' I said, putting my own plate down. It was years since I'd had the self-control to forego the better part of a sandwich, but just lately I'd regularly been leaving half my food untouched.

'Didn't think you smoked at home.'

'Well, you know.' Nosy old witch.

'Anyway, I wanted to ask you whether MB's been back round.'

'Here? No. Only that time with Daddy, and then they didn't stay long.'

'Was such a shock, him turning up at Dee's like that.' She puffed hard on her ciggie, stroking her hipbones with her free hand.

'She said on the phone, yes.'

'Didn't know where to put meself. If I weren't a lady—'

'What does he want?' I took the cigarette packet from the arm of the settee and shook one out. Damned if I was going to ask permission a second time.

'Money, I should think.' Lesley's eyes filled. 'Bastard never really wanted nothing else, did he?'

'Don't. Don't let him do that to you.' I went over to the window. As I moved, my back and my inner thighs reminded me of what I'd been doing this morning. Gently, I rubbed Lesley's shoulder. She always wanted more from me, from Dee, than we could give. Resentment curdled the food in my stomach.

'Think he wants you girls on side,' she said.

'But for what? Must have something to do with Daddy, then.'

'Yeah, most probably.' She ground out her cig, savagely, into the roll-up ends. 'But what kills me is why he thinks my own brother, my own nieces, would take his part against me.'

'He can't think that.'

'Comes to the same thing, though, don't it? He wants something off your dad, he wants to keep you girls sweet about it, which all means forgetting poor old stupid Lesley.' She sniffed, wiped her nose on the back of her hand. Her nail polish was always so perfect; I seldom bothered with mine, it was all chips two hours after I'd done them. 'When he left, I wanted to die,' she said.

'He's so not worth that.' Trying to tone down my impatience. Talk about drama queen.

'You really believe it was about him? Bleeding…grow up, Raquel.'

'But I thought—'

'It was the baby. Couldn't've waited to see the back of him, if it weren't for the baby.'

'Shit.'

'No need for that.'

'Sorry.' Moving a few steps away.

I must have been in my early twenties, with what I thought were years of fertility in front of me, when I found out Lesley couldn't have kids. But after not seeming to care much for a year or two while Lesley grew thinner and more reckless on the silk, MB started to be uncharacteristically great about it, eventually sorting some dodgy adoption from somewhere foreign, another circus probably, and it was all going through, practically signed on the dotted, when suddenly he decided to run off with the tubby tightrope walker's tubbier sister, who was opening her own show on Bournemouth pier. They – whoever they were – wouldn't let Lesley adopt as a single woman, so she never did get her baby.

'I'd met him, an' all.' She signalled for me to throw her the cigarette packet. 'Never told you that, did I? Few times, enough to make it seem... Little boy, called something unpronounceable. Dear little thing, he was, big dark eyes, staring at you like he could see inside your soul. I was going to call him Michael.' She leaned to the flame I held out. 'Maybe he couldn't take it that he'd have a son what was going to be taller than his dad, that's what I thought. Kept trying to make excuses for him, even though I would've cheerfully killed him. But you know what's really awful?' Looking at me, requiring an answer.

'What?'

'Turned out MB had at least three kids running about in tents all over the country, and two of them was normal sized.' Covering her eyes with her hand for a moment. 'Why didn't he tell me, Raq? I'd've loved them an' all. Wouldn't've made no difference to me, whatsoever.' She grabbed my hand. 'You know what I think? I think he never had no intentions of letting me have that baby. Think he was keeping me sweet while he worked out his next move with that fat bird.'

'Oh, Lesley.'

'You all thought he was seeing to the adoption to save my neck, didn't you?'

'You did have a couple of near-misses up there.'

'He wouldn't've cared, lovely. I knew whatever his motives was, that weren't it. But I was too desperate to bother looking for the truth.'

'I hadn't—'

'I *hate* him. Don't want him anywhere near my family, and your dad just won't see it. MB's up to something, you mark my words.' She put out her cigarette, picked one of the roll-ups out of the ashtray. 'Family's everything, Raquel,' she said.

'Mm.' My heart sped up.

'How's Eddie working out at your club?'

'Okay, I think.' They were Fred's roll-ups. Dependable, boring, probably married Fred, who lonely old Raquel was reduced to schtupping. Fred's.

'I hope you tell him that,' she said. 'People should always be told. Your nan used to say, *You got a tongue in your head, use it.*'

'Didn't she say as well that if you can't say anything nice about someone, say nothing at all?'

'Don't remember that one.' Openly eyeing me now. Oh Christ in a basket, she wouldn't. She was clutching her scrawny neck with one of her clawed hands, as if trying to choke back the words. For a split second, I felt like helping her.

'If I never had you girls,' Lesley said, 'I'd've gone mad. But you and Dee, you was always like my own. Her pacifically, what with being that much younger.'

It'll be all right, it'll be all right, everything will be all right.

'It's nothing,' I said. 'Really. Me and Fred, we're… It's over really and it wasn't much in the first place.'

'Sex is overrated, you ask me. All them girls, queuing up for a go of MB. Felt like telling them, There's no mystery, he's just like any other man - but you're more'n welcome to find out.'

'You probably didn't need to tell them,' I said. Which in fairness was unnecessary, but she was talking to me as if she had rights. As if she was my mother.

'Want to tell you something.' Lesley put down the ashtray and went back to the settee, neatly smoothing her skirt as she sat. 'Dee's going to get my things when I'm gone. Not that there's much, other than the flat. Business... Well, let's just say Lou's worried. Won't be nothing much left there, I shouldn't think. But you'll be okay, Raquel. You won't need it. After Ken done what he done about the money, I couldn't bear the thought of her with nothing after I'm gone, so...Mind you, I'm only forty-five so it's not exactly urgent, but thought you should know.'

'We'll get Daddy's and Uncle Glen-Glen's money anyway,' I said. Jesus H Christ, Dee again. Poor little Dee, who nobody could bear to see lift a finger. Peter once said we were enabling her helplessness and I have to say, he was right.

'Yeah, well, you never know what'll be left.'

'Daddy doesn't use the capital.'

'Don't he?' she said, in a tone that made it clear she knew differently. 'Well, that's all right then.' She picked up her mug, took a mouthful of cold tea. 'And there's something else. Before the business folds – and all right, it might not – I want to help with the wedding. Going to tell them later. Not like they'll have a big do, is it? They don't know no one really. I reckon thirty to fifty, max. And I can make the dress meself, or get the girls at work to run it up, and one for you as Maid of Honour. Otherwise I know Dee-Dee, she'll be engaged for ever.'

'They're not engaged.' I had visions of a cheap peach satin. Well, no thank you very much, not this shepherdess.

'There you are, then.' Suddenly she jumped up, grabbed both my hands. 'It's too late for us, love – there's no white knight coming for me or you. Let her have this. We both know it's her only chance.' She smiled then, a weird pulling back of lips over teeth, almost as though she was going to bite me. 'She could have a baby, she's still young enough. Twenty-seven's not so old for a first baby these days.'

Lesley wanted that baby, I could see it. Maybe MB coming back had dragged it all up again, or maybe she'd had this planned all along. She'd certainly been nicer, more welcoming, to Eddie than Daddy or I had been.

'Okay,' I said. 'I'll let her have it.'

But as I spoke, I suddenly knew, beyond any doubt, that I didn't want to turn into Auntie Lesley; Auntie Raquel didn't seem so inevitable after all. Why should it be over for me? There was no clearer reason for me and Eddie to finish than for him and Dee, not really, not based on need. And everything happens for a reason. Maybe Eddie and I were meant to be, maybe he was my escape route, my fate. If only Daddy hadn't stopped our money, maybe Eddie and I could have got away, left the lot of them behind, had a baby of our own. I wasn't stupid, I wasn't deluded: this was less 'What I Did for Love' than 'Send in the Clowns', but surely I deserved more than to be the family's sacrificial cow. Surely I deserved that moment in the night when you awake and know you're not alone. I deserved this last chance to give that to a child who wasn't already fully grown.

It was a long time since I'd been here, three or four years. Daddy gave up trying to make me, especially as Dee goes pretty much every month, I gather. The perfect daughter: docile, family-oriented, delicate; imbecilic, clingy, emaciated. It all depends on your point of view, and right now, mine was centred on me for a change. *Raquel always does exactly as she pleases.* I can remember my mother saying that. I don't have very many memories of her, not really, not significant ones, but I do remember how her red tyre mouth looked as she said that, how then she wrinkled up her nose like I was chopped liver for tea, and turned away from me. I was four, I think, and I'd climbed on to the kitchen worktop to reach the biscuit tin, and eaten the last digestive. But that was it, the rep I've been stuck with all my life since. Raquel does exactly as she pleases: when I joined Girelli's, when I came back, when I took up club singing instead of opening a back-street theatre school for kiddies, whenever I was dating a half-interesting prospect. Funny how it never did please me. Dee-Dee, on the other hand, did what she could. *Bless.*

This place ought to look like a hotel but it didn't, quite: the paint was too clean, without the knocks and scuffs of small children, the curtains too sixties' with no need for updating, the smell institutionalized, disinfectant and boiled cabbage and the kind of lemon polish you never seem to get outside of hospitals and nursing homes. It was too quiet as well, if you ignored the occasional vibrato scream extending to a soprano's operatic high C. It could have been the kind of digs Daddy used to stay in on tour twenty years ago, except that this was on a far bigger scale and you weren't forced to have kippers to your breakfast.

I was told to go up by a bored receptionist with white nails and too much make-up covering how plain she was. It seemed too easy. I could be anybody, she only had my word for it that I was his niece, but I suppose she didn't care. My heart was thumping up to my throat as I followed the fat bottom of the nurse assigned to me, and dearie dear, the sweat, but I don't know what I was nervous about. He wasn't some psychopathic loony, he was just Poor Uncle Glen-Glen, though Daddy never, ever called him that. I really ought to have visited more often. Don't know why I hadn't. Certainly I was always sympathetic to his cause, but from a

169

distance. Sometimes, it felt as though Daddy and I divvied them up between us, and he took Glen while I had Dee.

Such an ordinary door: handle, keyhole, name plate declaring Glen O'Leary to be inside. The nurse unlocked the door for me but went off without showing me in. I knocked but of course no one told me to enter. What if he was having a private moment? What if he was diddling with his bits or having a bit of a cry? He must be in there, not basket weaving or something in the workshop, or the plain girl would have told me. I assume the hours for that sort of thing must be regular, she must know where the residents are.

He didn't look up. He was sitting on a chair, an unopened book on his lap, twisting his hands together. Should I kiss him? No, not a good idea. Instead, I went over to the window.

'Hello, Uncle Glen-Glen,' I said. 'It's Raquel, remember me?'

He looked up. From a distance, he would have appeared to be looking into my face, but actually, it was just off, to the side. My goodness, he was still an amazing looking man. Sounds rather disloyal, but he was far handsomer than Daddy had ever been. His eyes were such an intense blue that it seemed as though they might burn through whatever they were looking at, but no one would ever say he saw into their soul, as he wouldn't look there.

I rummaged in my bag for the Opal Fruits. He wouldn't take them from me, so I left them on the chest-of-drawers.

'How are you, then?' Suddenly, I realized I didn't have the faintest what to say. Should I tell him about the family? Poor old b, couldn't imagine he cared.

Daddy was paying God knows how much to keep Glen in here, to keep him alive really. And for what? What's he to the world or the world to him? Not to make too fine a point of it, if he was suddenly to pop off, I seriously doubted if anyone would be much the poorer. Dee and I would be considerably richer, in fact; Eddie could choose between us on an equal footing. *Eenie-meenie-minie-mo, Catch a sister by the toe, If she squeals, don't let her go*. No that was mean, it was, it was mean. Take it back, take it back. Glen has as much right as anyone else, of course he does.

'Dee's getting married,' I told my uncle. He looked back at his hands.

Even if I could find a way to convince Eddie, I couldn't leave her. It wasn't so much going off with her man but taking myself away with him. She'd forgive the first, I know she would, but the second would be something she'd never recover from. When I joined Girelli's, she pined away until she saw me, and even then I think she lived from holiday to holiday, school just a place that stood between her and the person who loved her. Me. It was always me. Had I given birth when I was thirteen, they'd have taken the baby away; instead, I was landed with a wild animal not-quite-six and expected to get on with it. I even bought her friends from the ice cream van parked outside the school gates. For a while then she was part of a crowd, until she and the crowd no longer wanted ice cream enough to endure each other's company. Then I was out of strategy. Daddy always did say I was a one-trick pony. He shouldn't have done it to me. Wrong, wrongage, wrong to the nth degree, for Christ's sake. Dee was an ugly duckling. After her mother left, she saw me, and that was it.

'Are you happy, Uncle Glen-Glen?' I asked.

He twisted his hands. Dear God, there but for goodness went Daddy – except he wouldn't be Daddy then and I wouldn't exist.

'What's the bloody point,' I said, softly.

I never did find out if he ate the Opal Fruits. Green ones were always Daddy's favourites. Green Fruit Pastels too, and Fruit Gums. Most people like the red.

I saw him from the window; he was sat on the bench at the edge of the square, right up next to the bin end, where I'd more than once seen a rat. What the buggering hell was he doing? I couldn't be certain from this distance, but it looked as though the silly old b was talking to himself. Reciting something, more like. Wonderful.

Pulling on my big outdoor cardigan as I went, I practically ran down the stairs and over the road.

'Daddy?'

He didn't look at me.

'Good Lord, what madness rules in brainsick men, / When for so slight and frivolous a cause / Such factious emulations shall arise.'

'No idea, you've got me there. One of the Henrys?'

Something wasn't right here. I drew three eights on my thumb, hard, quick.

'You went to see your uncle,' he said. 'And I my sister. What good family members we are, to be sure.' He reached out his hand, and I took it, sat beside him on the bench, trying not to think of the rats. 'Did you speak to him?'

'What?' It was tricky to keep focus, with Daddy so clearly not himself. 'Oh, yes, a bit. It's hard.'

'Yes, must be shockingly hard for *you*,' he said.

'I didn't mean—'

'Of course you did.' He squeezed my hand absently between both of his own then dropped it, suddenly, so it hit the bench. I was *not* best pleased that he'd seen Lesley. She could have told him anything. Not that she had any evidence, granted, but why let proof get in the way of a good drama? And Daddy would remember that night he'd seen Eddie at my place. Remember and blame.

'What are you doing out here, Daddy?' And who knew what Daddy would do with whatever Lesley had babbled. I'd never seen him quite so divorced from himself, so unpresent to me. *It'll be all right. I'll be all right. He'll be all right.*

'Came to see you, but changed my mind.'

'Thanks very much. Want me to go?' But that worried me in and of itself: perhaps he'd come here to confront me and at the last minute had a change of heart.

'I came over here to smoke a cigar.' He pointed to the ground. 'Stepped on a snail. Whoever said smoking kills was right.'

'You could have smoked one in my place. I like the smell, you know that.'

'You think it's pointless, talking to him, don't you? You're quite wrong.' He turned to look at me then; it was as though someone had washed Uncle Glen-Glen's eyes once too often. 'You think of me as a stage actor,' he said. 'But I've done fifty-six films, did you know that? Nearly as many as my years upon this earth. Mostly small parts, a couple of second leads, one British starring role – but that sank without trace, of course. I was good, though. Always got the notices, for anything over a single line or two. It's because I was always aware of the camera.'

'I like your films,' I said, lamely.

'Good God, girl, you haven't seen most of them.'

'Well, no, but I've seen—'

'The camera sees everything, Raquel, and I mean everything.' He gestured in front of him, as though the whole world was represented by the banana skins and Golden Wonder and B&H packets round the bin. 'If something crosses your eyeline when it shouldn't do, even for the briefest moment, you need to ask for a retake. Because trust me, that camera will register your seeing, even if you don't think you've shown it.'

'Okay,' I said. Clearly this wasn't the end. Why tell a story in a few lines when a lengthy speech will do? I brought my hand to my face, surreptitiously touching my tongue to my palm, something I hadn't much done in years.

'I'm that camera,' he said. 'I register his seeing. And he's mine.'

I just didn't know what to say to that. He was deluded, that was pretty clear, but I could hardly point that out. Of course I made some non-committal noise, patted his arm as though I understood, but it seemed to me that he was seeing only what he wanted to see. Glen-Glen didn't even have an adult's name, for heaven's sake. He certainly didn't have an adult's perception. Or maybe any perception at all, beyond the most basic animal instincts.

'You and Dee,' he added, 'aren't like that, I do realize the difference, but my darling girl, you mustn't do anything to spoil what you do have between you.'

My heart turned right over. So Lesley *had* talked. Even with nothing to say.

'Come inside, Daddy,' I said, my hand at my face again.

'No, I won't, thank you. *Time and the hour runs through the roughest day.*'

'*Macbeth.*'

'Just so.' He nodded in the direction of the flats. I took my cue and stood. I wanted to ask him what he thought he knew, whether he was going to see Dee, what the hell was going on in his head, but we seldom say what we really want to, or I don't anyway and I imagine it's the same for most people. My unravelled father sat on, smacking his lips as though preparing for another recitation, and I left him unworded and unkissed.

As I got to the bottom of the flats, I turned. Daddy was bending down to a rat, holding something out to it. And walking up to them, his coat trailing along the ground behind him like a train, was MB.

Eddie

'FUH-FUH-' Tom twitched and shook. 'What shall we talk about tonight? Talk about, walkabout, like saddo Abo, in the Bush, beat about the bush, I wouldn't mind a beat about in the bush, FUH-FUH-FUH walk the walk, talk the talk...but they'll not have it. They look at me YES, YOU, YOU CUNT like I'm mad bad sad had it? Yip, YIP YIP. Never. They're all the WITHOLDING FUCKING CUNT same. Make me fn-fn-pissed, twenty-six and never been kissed, never been missed BITCHES don't talk to me about Mrs T hard-eyed thin-lipped purse-lipped BLOW JOB...You with the FUCKING UGLY MISSUS crop wouldn't, would you? Sucky sucky ME PRIVATISE YOU LONG TIME eh? Eh? Well *I fucking would*, and that's no tic schtick, any port in a storm, any brandy and cigars in blue serge how's-your-father...tell me the old, told Tory. *I would*. Round the back of the House of Commonasmuck fuck bugger up the woolsack, that desperate. It's not easy. My mouth BLOW JOB runs away, deep in the yes and murmur sweet FUCK FUCK RUB ME OFF NOW! nothings. Nothing comes in nothing. Just my little joke. You liked that one, didn't you? Lipstick, hip-stick and I would, you know, I would. DENATIONALISE MY MIGHTY SWORD. By the people, for the people, on your back and die for the

Queen. Di for Queen. You know you love it. Eh? Girls? ...
... ... See. Nothing. Dead as a Frodo.'

The strangled, guilty laughs he got for that silence (three
beats, I reckoned) was more uncomfortable than anything
I'd heard him do before. But maybe that was the context,
maybe I was listening differently.

Had to take the biscuit for a boys' night out. Yeah. Lame
bastard, bloke who said *Cunt* when he meant *What you
having*, has-been actor losing the plot, and malicious bent
dwarf. Talk about the blind leading the blind. Beckett
would've loved us, tell you. Weren't always like this. I've got
friends, real ones, actors and musos, even some Del-boys
from school, just haven't seen them lately, that's all. Don't
when you've got a steady bird, face it. Especially when she's
one you can't well introduce to your mates. So like's drawn
to like.

Thing is, you always got to be ready for your break. Don't
matter if you're meeting a cabbie – his brother might be a
cameraman on the next Spielberg – or a director, you always
got to be prepared to make an impression. Smile, offer a fag,
put your hand in your pocket. That's why having one line in
a telly is such a big deal you can't cock it up - never know
who's going to see it. That said, I had a chunky old part in
Purple Sky and no fucker saw that. Do get recognized from
the Vosene ad, though, well, couple or three times, and
Cadbury's might do something when it comes out.

'Nice one, Tom,' I said, as he come over, dripping in
sweat. 'Pint there.'

'Quite extraordinary,' said MB. 'What d'you think,
Kenneth? Dare we?'

'Nothing to dare yet,' Ken said, picking up his G&T.
'But I did tell you it was worth seeing. Like women
preaching.'

'That's hardly fair.' MB held a finger up, as if he was shushing a kid. Tom was bright red. Thought he might lay them out. 'To Tom!' MB added, way too loud.

MB was still getting a load of shit, stares and whispers, but be quite truthful, bloke asked for it. Velvet hat, long silk scarf, green velvet jacket, black nail varnish. That's going to show when you're only three foot something, fifty and ugly as fuck. Never seen a bloke with skin that bad, looked grated, swear it did, or a nose that big – comedy wart on it, for fuck's sake - but he did have massive blue eyes and perfect Hollywood teeth, so maybe he thought that was enough to counteract the effect. It weren't. And that posh-queer voice didn't help, just this side of camp. He spoke that bit too slow an' all, like he was weighing every word first before he let you see the colour of them. Shady bastard. Being out with him and Tom, I looked like John Travolta. Christ, even Ken looked like Travolta, despite being near-on sixty and not having shaved in what must've been days. But Dee reckoned MB had screwed half the birds in the Big Top, so what do I know. Maybe he hypnotized them.

'Lively FUCKING THICKO crowd tonight,' said Tom. He took a careful pull on his pint, holding the glass with both hands.

'Thought they were going to lynch you, dear boy.' Ken raised his glass to Tom now, who ducked his head, all false modesty, like he'd forgotten the shit Ken was giving him a couple of minutes ago. Bloke must know he was good, that the crowd loved him, or loved themselves loving him, which comes to the same thing. Felt a stab in my gut, then. Man, a limp was all right for Byron and for getting laid, but it weren't like what Tom had, it didn't have universal appeal. Best you could hope for most of the time was a sickly form of pity.

The next act was starting up, comedy singer with a folk acoustic, ten years out of date. He was tolerated, but I bet he was worried about following Tom.

'Well I thought you were *wonderful*.' MB half-stood and stretched across the table, patted Tom's Piccadilly packet with his lighter. 'So brave.'

'BOLLOCKS.'

'I beg... Oh, I see.'

'No, I meant bollocks,' Tom said, grinning and taking his straights.

Ken gave a great bark of laughter, making the few punters who weren't gawping at MB turn round.

'SHUT YOUR CAKEHOLES-ASSHOLES-CAKEHOLES,' said Tom. 'Shit, bad sometimes after a gig.' He lit a fag, hands shaking. 'Adrenaline,' he said quietly, but not like he was apologizing for himself. Had to give him that.

MB's shoulders was shaking with laughing, his hat bobbing up and down like a sinister black bird in a Hammer Horror. 'Oh, we so must,' he said to Ken.

'I've agreed to nothing.' Ken waved his hand in a stage-king's brush off. 'This singing fella's awful.'

'Yeah, Woodstock via Little and Large,' I said.

'HECKLE HECKLE. FUCKING TALENTLESS CUNT.'

'Price-less.' MB beamed at Tom then raised his eyebrows at Ken.

Like I said, you've always got to be prepared, and I could sense something.

'You two got a project going?' I chanced.

'Possibly, sir, possibly.' MB nodded. 'Depends on some people, not least this one here.' He got up to drape his arm across Ken's shoulders, who shrugged him off.

'UPYOURASS FUH-FUH- My round, I think.' Tom caught the eye of one of the barmen, who was collecting glasses. 'Billy, do us a favour, get the same again? Couple of PONCEY CUNTYCUNTY G&Ts, large, couple of pints of lager.' He turned to MB and Ken. 'I try not to SPASTIC carry drinks,' he said. 'And Billy? Get one for the act. Tell him CAN'T SING TWEET TWEET I do it to all the boys.'

'All right, gentlemen, here's the thing.' MB sat down again, his chin level with the table. 'I'm putting on a show—'

'MICKEY ROONEY. Sorry.'

'I'd always fancied the Judy Garland part,' MB said.

'Pack it in, MB.' Ken leaned back in his seat. 'Chap's more heterosexual than I am, and I've never been a shirt lifter in my life, if we don't count that lady boy when I was in the Concert Party, and *that* was a merry accident.' He waved both his hands at us now. 'And yes, yes, some of my best friends and all that. But really, don't trade on another fella's act.'

'A show,' said MB. 'With His Nibs here as one of the draws.' Sounding a lot less posh all of a sudden.

'And my money as one of the enabling factors.'

'Well surely, but why not?' Appealing to the table. 'I've got half the funding, he knows that. Minimal risk.'

'Because I'd have to come out of retirement to do it. Afterwards, I mean. I don't have those sorts of funds just lying around doing nothing. It wouldn't be a one-off, it'd be a blasted comeback. Not to mention my sister would murder me. Have my balls made into earrings. Feh.'

'KILL KILL KILL KILL FUH-FUH-FUH-FUH...' Tom was purple and jerking all over the place. He bit his lip, then smacked himself in the head, hard. That'd got to hurt. I rolled a fag, watching Tom's floor show and trying not to give away any feeling. Studied blank look, but intelligent. Thoughtful. Reckon I pulled it off, an' all. Always do when it matters. A big gig? Must be, to tempt Ken. Had to be a spot for me, *had* to be - no reason else for Ken to arrange this weird beano. There'd be press interest. If I got that and I did score that tour, the publicity'd be sorted. Might remind some people of *Purple Sky*, that it'd been good, or I'd been good in it. This could be it, Eddie. It could be your turn. Oh man, play it cool, keep it sweet.

'LOONEY TUNES. Shit. DEAD-EYE JOE SHOOT SHOOT BANG BANG.' Poor bastard was throwing himself around in his chair, knocking his forehead on the table. Bit of my Carlsberg sloshed out onto his hair. Weren't clear whether I should say sorry or he should so I never and nor did he.

'Steady on,' said MB.

'Yes, clearly he's behaving that way because he likes it,' said Ken, rolling his eyes. 'It's never wise to do business with a fool.'

'Come on.' MB looked angry, but of course he couldn't let himself say that, not if he wanted Ken's dough.

I screwed my courage to the sticking place.

'*For in such business / Action is eloquence, and the eyes of the ignorant / More learned than the ears,*' I said.

'That, my dear boy, is the woman's part,' said Ken.

'FUH-FUH-FUCKING TRANNY.'

MB clapped his hands, laughing, like some demented gnome. My humiliation had cheered him up no end. 'Superb,' he said.

'I've had better nights,' Tom said to me, his head in his hands now. 'Light us a fag, will you? Flung the one I had. Hope I didn't get anyone.' Smacking me hard in the chest. Had my arm back and my fist clenched before I knew what was happening, but just as quick I relaxed it.

'Yeah, sure.'

'MIDGET FUH-FUH-FUN FOR ALL THE FAMILY.'

He rubbed his eyes. 'Bad one,' he said. 'Sorry, MB.'

'That's quite all right.' But he didn't look none too amused now.

'Might have to go.' Tom knocked on the table.

'Don't be a prat.'

'Knackers me. And look at my forehead.' He pushed back his floppy fringe. Big great bruise was starting to appear, and he had a graze over one eyebrow. 'It's not fair on the other FUCKERS acts.'

'That doesn't sound like you.'

'Well, that's the trouble, mate – couldn't really sound like anyone else, could it?' He smiled and took the fag I was holding out for him. 'Don't mind being the entertainment on stage, but...' His head jerked, and flecks of phlegm flew out the corner of his mouth. Fucking disgusting, you ask me. Poor fucker.

'Where's the lavvy in this establishment?' Ken stood up, and for a second there didn't look none too clever on his feet. 'Whoa boy,' he said. Tom pointed him in the right direction (several wrong ones an' all), and he weaved off.

'Had a few before he come out, did he?' I asked MB.

'How should I know?' Then, changing his tune, smiled and offered me a fag. 'I take it you think the show's a good idea?' Speaking even slower than normal. 'Big theatre,' he said, moving one arm across like he was laying it out, 'on a Sunday night of course, singer top of the bill - Cilla's interested in the charity schtick - then all sorts, vents, comics, and Ken's comeback.' He held his hands up. 'I know technically it's a bit soon to be thinking of comebacks, he'd be laughed off the stage, but it'll take six months to put it together. More, if I can't co-ordinate the acts in time. Most will be working elsewhere, of course. Though maybe not you.'

Cheeky bastard. But my heart sped up a bit. 'Me?'

'You'd have a spot, naturally. Provided you keep Ken onside. I should be able to talk the lovely Lesley round.' Actually smacked his lips, a miniature Leslie himself. Leslie bloody Phillips. 'Ask no questions, you'll be told no lies, I saw a Chinaman doing up his flies. No project if I don't. We could get some telly coverage, you know. Channel 4's very interested in highlights, that I can assure you.' He shrugged. 'Have to get some of the alternative bods on though.'

'KILL THE NIGGER.'

'He won't take no risks,' I warned MB. 'His daughter told me that in no uncertain terms.' Didn't need to mention it was Raquel and not Dee. 'It's his brother he's thinking about. The one who's in that place.'

'BANG BANG YOU'RE DEAD.' Tom looked at MB. 'I'm probably going to do a film about stand-ups,' he said. 'Including ME me. Any use to you?'

'What film?' I turned to him.

'Docu-drama. Stand-ups with a difference. Short arms. Wheelchair. Sikh. Me. You know the drill.'

Just then, I could've killed the cunt. Stone dead. Bang, bang.

'Congratulations, mate. Man, that's cool, really is.'

'I'm definitely interested,' said MB. 'And if Channel 4 does come through, they're not going to mind… It's still desperate to shock.'

'They can edit me, I'm told.'

'Surely. But not too heavily, I imagine.'

'An editette,' I said, sounding like Raquel. Least I'd kept the bitterness indoors. A limp was as much fucking use as nothing. Might as well have been the ump for all the visibility it gave me. All the disadvantages, none of the advantages. Even if I was a stand-up…don't show when I'm standing still. Tom had it made.

'But we need Ken, right?' said Tom. 'You talked to his agent?'

'Not yet, bit premature. None of this happens without Ken's input.' MB sat back in his chair, his little legs dangling. 'And I think we all need this project too much to let it go easily.'

'FUCK OFF.'

She was nearly beautiful when she was asleep. I stroked her spine, gently. She didn't move. So tiny, every bone showing through transparent skin. This was the girl who'd decided to marry me. This was the girl I couldn't say no to. My girl.

The thing with Raquel was mad, man. Really heavy shit. Shouldn't've done it, should've left well alone, but we all think with our dicks sometimes. No, come off it, was more than that. Dee's my girl but she's bloody hard work, face it. And when I met her, I weren't looking for a nursing job. Still not as it happens, but when she curls up like a skinned rat, she breaks my heart. God knows how much more Raquel must feel about it. I got to stop it, man, before it fucks us all up and shit - Dee, Raquel, me. And my so-called career. Raquel will understand. Couple of weeks of losing it, that's all it was. She's most probably at home now, working out how to finish with me, and if she's not, she ought to be. Not like I was her boyfriend. I was just a convenient shag and someone to chat to. We can still be mates. She can still be useful. I'd lay money she'd never risk losing Dee.

Didn't get to sleep for a long time. Was I putting too much on this show? I'd been in shows before, loads of them. But this one felt different, special. Even Tom was falling over himself, going on and on about his poxy film, desperate to be establishment for once. Ken might do it or he might not, there was nothing to give a Scooby either way. I wanted to talk to Raquel about it, but really should be talking to her about just being friends. Can you be friends with a bird? A bird with great tits and a killer laugh and who's on to you. Yeah, it'd have to be possible. End of story.

In the morning, it was Dee stroking my back as I woke up.

'I made tea,' she said. 'Do you want sex first?'

'Uh... Heavy night, darling. Give us an hour, all right?'

'One hour. Okay. It's eight o'clock now.' She sat on the mattress, pulling her oversized Charles and Di tee-shirt, that she sometimes wore as a nightie, over her knees. I sat up, reached over to take one of the mugs from the floor.

'This one mine?'

'I wouldn't give you Winnie-the-Pooh, would I? It's my special one.'

'No, course not. Seen my baccy?'

I rolled a fag, watching Dee sip her lemon tea. Never known anyone be able to drink it that hot, though she always lost interest before the end.

'I'm going to see Raquel today,' she volunteered, unusually for her.

'Why?'

'Because she hasn't been to see me. And Auntie Lesley said I ought to get round there if I knew what was good for me.'

'She said that?'

'I just told you. She said I ought to get round there if I knew what was good for me.' She put down her mug. 'Anyway, I want to see her. I miss her.'

'She's probably just been busy.'

'The last time she was just busy, she'd joined the circus.'

'Think she's a bit old to be running off with a clown.'

'I didn't say that.' She clutched at her knees, total

alarmed look on her face. 'She wouldn't run off with a clown. Why? Did MB say something to you?'

'No, nothing like that, don't be daft.'

'He's evil, you know. He might seem nice, but sometimes people pretend to be something different from how they actually are.'

'What? Course they do. Everyone does.'

'Do they? I don't.' Twisting her hair round into a rope. 'Do you?'

'I'm an actor, Dee-Dee. I pretend for a living.'

'Well, you don't really, do you?' She was examining the end of the rope, as though she couldn't quite make out what it was. 'Not for a living.'

I had to laugh, fuck her. 'Sometimes it pays the rent.'

'Suppose it must.' She looked up for a sec, smiled. 'It was good when you got all that chocolate.'

'You only nibble the corners.'

'I like corners. The rest freaks me out.'

Look, I don't make out I'm a candidate for University Challenge, but all of a sudden, my gut turned over at the thought of having conversations like this for the rest of my life. It weren't despair, weren't even resignation, it was the weird thought that if I stayed with Dee, I'd have no chance at normal, ever again. Even if down the line I left her, it'd be too late - the pattern'd be set up and I'd be looking for it in every skinny, wacked-out woman I met. If I stayed now, I was accepting it, settling for it, even choosing it. A very different part from what I'd thought I'd take.

'She's not with MB, is she?' Dee said.

'No, she's *not* with MB, for fuck's sake.' Better not bloody be. No, that's crap, she deserves a life. But not with that clown. 'What does MB stand for?'

'No one knows.' Twisting the rope even tighter. 'He and

Auntie Lesley were Mr and Mrs Banks but I don't think the B is for Banks. She told me it wasn't, anyway, and I don't think she tells lies on purpose. Everyone tells lies by accident, don't they? Like you might say Raquel's not with MB but that might be because you don't know, or it's true when you say it but not the next day.' She did a freaky little clap, one two three. 'Auntie Lesley's had lots of names, three names, even O'Leary now - don't know why, it wasn't her dad's name. That was Jacobs.' Not often Dee put as many words together in one hit. She stuck the end of the hair-rope in her mouth, started sucking it.

'Oh man, don't do that – turns me over.'

'Don't do what?' she said, through the hair. I reached over, took it out of her mouth, tapped her hand, lightly.

'That's disgusting, Dee-Dee.'

'It is? Sorry.' Then, 'You do know I'm not a child, don't you?'

'What you on about?'

'Just want to be sure you know that. I'm really not, you know. Sometimes, I think I never was.'

We let that sit in the silence as I drank my lukewarm tea, finished my roly. Dee stared at her knees, stretching her hands out over them, examining her fingers, totally absorbed in herself. That's what it looked like - for all I knew, though, she could have the miners and the recession and the Cold War going on in there, could be mulling over the rise of the NF and the Anti-Nazi League, could be planning our wedding or how to make the perfect sponge cake the way your grandmother done, could be running all the words to *Jesus Christ, Superstar*, but I doubted it. She'd've been great as an actress in some ways - talk about blank canvas. Though as it goes, she'd have sod-all to draw on. Hard to act a feeling you've never come close to having. Mum once said to me that I couldn't play Romeo, *You don't know what love means, you selfish little bugger.* Stupid cow didn't know a fucking thing about *Romeo and Juliet.* About anything. Never got that part - fucking sure it was her words put the mockers on it. You don't go in confident, you're screwed.

'Sometimes wish I had a mother,' said Dee, still looking at her fingers. 'Well, suppose I've got one, somewhere. But maybe she's not my mother, if she went off. Maybe you're only a mother if you stay.' She put her fingers over her eyes, then swung her hands to the side of her face, quick, repeating it several times like she was playing peek-a-boo with an invisible baby. 'Raquel never went, though I thought she had, for a while. But then I went to Girelli's and I understood. She told me that if I was older, I could have lived with her all the time.' Another long speech, couldn't pretend I liked it, seemed too pointed, but Dee didn't *do* pointed. And Raquel weren't her fucking mother, no matter what either of them said. 'Do you think Daddy's gone mad?' she asked.

'That was left field, weren't it? No, don't think he's gone mad.'

'I think maybe he has,' she said. 'He's so far away now.'

'What d'you mean, far away?'

'People are either here or they're not.' She looked straight at me then, dropped her gaze from my eyes to my lips. 'And if they're not they're either bored or in love or mad. I think.'

'How can you make out if people are here?'

'You feel it. Don't you feel it?'

'Yeah, maybe.' But the person who weren't there far as I was concerned, was Dee. Only when we were shagging, that's the only time she was properly with me. Was going to be a lonely old life, if I stayed.

Don't love either of them, but I'm nearer to it here, in

this flat, than I've ever been in thirty-six years. Trouble is, can't stay in here, can we? There's a world out there, and it's got stages, cameras, action. It's got the Raquels, with their stories, their bit of life. It's got money, which be truthful we could do with more of, now it all goes to some mad old bastard and his idiot brother. If something happened to Glen, Dee would take his place, that's obvious. Nice bit of bunce for those who really needed it. But people like him live forever. Nothing to live for, but nothing to die for either.

'Do you want to come to see Raquel with me?' Dee asked her knees.

'What?' Jesus, sod that for a game of soldiers. 'No love, you go. I'd only be in the way.'

'No you wouldn't. I was going to sign on, then walk over.'

'Walk? Fuck that.'

'It only takes an hour and twenty minutes.'

'No, I got to see a man about a dog.'

But sooner rather than later, I'd have to see them together. Pity we wasn't Mormon or something, could marry them both, compromise on them both. Maybe two wrongs *would* make a right. Weren't beyond the bounds of possibility I'd convince Dee, but never Raquel. She couldn't stand the direct competition.

'You had breakfast?' I asked. 'What you got in?'

'Ski, four flavours – apricot, banana—'

'Get the picture. What else?'

'I think there's some bread, but it might be mouldy. Oh, there's a bit of bacon, that Auntie Lesley gave me yesterday.'

'So you had yoghurt? Jesus, Dee, turn sideways and you'd disappear.'

'No, I wouldn't.' She sounded a bit sorry. 'Shall I get you a Ski then?' She got up without waiting for an answer, which yet again weren't like her.

Hate yoghurt, trendy crap. But I ate it – never know when your next mouthful's coming from, round here – pink and sweet and nothingy, and had never been nowhere near a raspberry or a strawberry. Dee watched every mouthful, spoon to mouth, spoon to mouth. I hated the way she did that, she always did, whatever I ate, in a way that reminded me of my nan. Like she wanted to eat me up.

'Finished?' she said, taking the pot. 'Eddie? Look at the clock. It's nearly nine o'clock.' And I swear to God, unless I was hallucinating, she winked.

Delia

'You're even thinner.' She pulled out of the hug quickly which I liked in one way but didn't in another, because she normally held on too long and that's always been how I know she's pleased to see me.

'No, I'm six stone thirteen exactly, no ounces, same as always.'

'Well, I'm noticing it more then.' Holding my arms at her arms' length, looking me up and down in a way I didn't like.

'That's because you're not used to the way I look any more,' I explained. 'You haven't seen me in weeks.'

'Don't start, Delia.'

'Don't start what?' I hate it when people say things that make no sense. Even Raquel was usually irritated if I tried to ask her about them, so mostly I don't. But Miss Wadsworth told us to talk in complete sentences and although I don't always manage it, others manage even less.

She left it to me to close the door. I liked the smell of Raquel's flat: lavender and bleach and faint traces of her perfume, the one called Femme. I literally couldn't stand to be near heavy perfume but she never put a lot on. *Quick squirt*, she always said. My mother wore too much perfume, I think, but Raquel said I'm probably making it up as she doesn't remember it. But today, there was the smell of cigarette smoke, too. It wasn't often that I smelt smoke here.

'You walked over, then.'

'Yes, I walked. Can I have a drink?'

'Lemonade?'

'Is it low cal?'

'What do *you* think?'

'I think it is.'

I thought she'd sit next to me on the settee as she often does, even hold my hand maybe, but she took the chair. We sipped our lemonade and Raquel lit a Silk Cut cigarette. It seemed funny, to see her smoking in here. At Auntie Lesley's she did, and at the club, but not much in her own flat.

'Your ceiling will go yellow,' I said.

'What? Oh, yes, I know. Was given some Duty Frees, and it's a bit too tempting. Too easy.'

'I don't know why you bother with smoking. Just another thing to remember.'

'You're right. I'm the person who can never manage to take a brolly or gloves or sunglasses.' Raquel smiled then, and it was a nice smile, like clean air. 'Probably the last person who should be smoking. I'll stop soon.'

'Have you been busy? Eddie says you must have been busy.'

'Not really. I've been…' She drank some of her lemonade, then pulled a funny face. 'Sod that, darling, I'm putting some voddy in it. More Duty Free.'

As she got up, I noticed that she was definitely thinner, not me. I would say five to seven pounds. People often do that, I think – say something about you that is really about them. They might say, *Are you a bit down?* Or, *Are you fed with this film?* Or, *You look as though you're loving that chocolate.* And what they mean is that they're low, want to

PRESENTING… THE FABULOUS O'LEARYS

turn over to another side or would like your chocolate. Makes things much more confusing than they need to be, if you forget to notice. But then, most people make up others by looking at themselves, as if other people are really just a great big mirror. They do, I think. So when Raquel sees me, she sees me as her sister, and she understands me by thinking about that and by thinking about what she's like and so what I must be like. Where I'm different from her, she sees that difference instead of what's special about me. I wonder if I do that, too. Suppose you wouldn't notice it about yourself. When I saw myself as fire-fierce, maybe it meant seeing others, seeing Raquel, as ash-cool.

'That's better.' Raquel sat down with her new drink. 'Bit early in the day, but I'm not working tonight so what the hell.'

'I'm going to see Eddie sing tonight,' I said. 'He said I ought to. Suppose I should have thought of it myself, but I didn't. I would have done, I think, but it hadn't occurred to me yet. Is he good?'

'Not bad.' Raquel took a long swallow of her vodka and lemonade. 'Are you going on your own?'

'With Auntie Lesley. She was going to bring Uncle Lou, but he can't make it. Something about the factory.'

'Delia, you're twenty-seven years old. You don't have to call our aunt's friends *Uncle* now.'

'No, I suppose not.' I couldn't understand why Raquel looked a bit glittery-angry now, as though I'd done something wrong. But I don't think I had.

'So how have you been, anyway?' she said.

'What do you mean?'

'For crying out loud, Dee. I was just asking how you are.'

'Oh. Fine.'

But I wasn't fine. I'd been so looking forward to seeing

Raquel but it wasn't right. She was often irritated with me, it wasn't that. It was as if she didn't want me here. I couldn't say why – she looked exactly as she always did, except for being thinner – but I didn't feel we were settled in for the afternoon. It was like one of those afternoon visits in Jane Austen novels, that I could never see the point of. Why would you want to visit someone just to leave a card with your name on? And fifteen minutes was a funny amount of time, too short to do anything but too long just to say hello. That's why stories by Dumas always makes my list and Jane Austen never has. Not as many pointless things.

I started polishing my nails with the bottom of my shirt. I'd dropped my pebble out of my pocket on the way here. It wasn't one I much liked, so perhaps it knew. Not that it really could know, but it did seem that way. It made me feel sad.

'Dolly Daydream?'

'Sorry.' I forced myself to look up and I smiled at her. It was nice to hear her say that – she didn't always mean it nicely but I think today she did. 'So will you be back to seeing me more now?' I said.

'Oh Dee, course I will, darling. I've just not felt myself. To be perfectly frank, I've been seeing a man, but it was nothing and it's over. I think it's over.'

'Are you upset?'

'Only with myself for being such a fool. As per.' She finished her drink in a couple of big gulps. 'I've missed you, Little.'

'That's silly then. You could have come to see me.'

'You're right, very silly.' She balled up a tissue from the box next to her, and threw it at me.

'Should I ask about the man?' She might expect it.

'No darling Dee-Dee, not important. Really. Sometimes

I just want to feel there's a future for me like... Well, that's daft. I'm middle-aged, for heaven's sake.'

'Are you? Suppose you are.'

'What about you?'

'I don't think twenty-seven's middle-aged.'

'No, you numbskull.' She knocked on her forehead with her fist, in a way that reminded me of Tom, but also reminded me of school. 'You and Eddie.'

'Oh. Well, I think we're okay.' But how do you tell the difference between what you want and what is definitely true? 'Not sure, really. He does get very cross with me, so sometimes I think he's fed up with me. Tom says it's just the way Eddie is, but I don't know.'

'So what does he think Eddie's like, then?' She leaned over herself as if she had tummy ache.

'Self-interested, he says. Preoccupied with the Eddie Muir Show.' But I didn't want her to think Tom was the sort of person to say just nasty things. 'He says as well that he's spontaneous and good company and that in a group, he can't stop watching me. Eddie can't, not Tom. I liked that.'

'Yes, you would. Anyone would.' She smiled at me again. It made me feel happy. It's such an easy thing, to make other people happy, that I'm surprised more people don't do it. So easy that they must not do it on purpose.

She wouldn't have not come to see me on purpose. Like the time she pushed me away from the back door to stop me coming in when I was fire-fierce, and I fell over backwards and grazed both my elbows and banged my head on the patio, she swore she'd never, ever hurt me on purpose. *I'd never stamp on a wild flower deliberately darling, but we all tread on them as we walk*, she said. I think the wild flower was meant to be me. She did sometimes call me Bluebell, though not for years now. That was before she went away to the circus, and I don't think there's many wild flowers in the Mile End Road or Leicester Square or Dean Street, and that's pretty much the only places she walked. Suppose it's the thought that counts, as Nan would say, though she used to say it before putting whatever the thoughtful thing was - like some lavender bath salts from me once or some diabetic chocolate from Auntie Lesley - into the cupboard or even the bin.

'What are you wearing tonight?' Raquel asked.

'Wearing? Don't know.' I hadn't realized I was meant to wear something in particular. I've never quite got hold of that. Once, I went to the pub in a long black dress and everyone laughed or asked me where I was going afterwards. Home, I said, and then they laughed too. Another time, I went to a dinner date in jeans, and the restaurant wouldn't let me in, so I went home and the man never rang me again. Raquel said I should have sent the waiter in to tell him. Daddy always helped me when it was something of his I'd to go to, or he got Raquel to help me anyway. How do other people know this stuff? I suppose I could learn it, but it would bore me.

'Let me do your eyes at least, lend you some earrings,' she said.

'All right. If you think Eddie would like it.' I didn't want him to think that I hadn't bothered to make an effort when I should have done.

'Wear your black baggies and the little silver top. And the pretty sandals we got in the sale.'

'All right.'

'We'll use my crimpers. And I'll do your make-up here, then give you some bits to take home to touch it up.'

'You know I'm rubbish at that.'

'Not if you're only touching up what's there. I'll show you. Again.'

When I was little, I was Raquel's dolly, her Milly-Molly-Mandy. She was too old for real dolls, so she made do with me, and I let her dress me up, show me to her friends, paint my nails, until one day the dress itched and itched and itched and she wouldn't listen, wouldn't believe me, and the colours were red and black, darting round my eyes, stabbing at them until I opened my mouth and roared them away and away. Later, there was nail polish dried-dripped down our bedroom wall, and miniscule slivers of glass in the carpet and Raquel said it was me but I disremembered and wouldn't help scrub.

Suddenly, I was so tired I could have curled up on Raquel's carpet and gone to sleep until tomorrow. I didn't want to go to the club, I could hear Eddie sing any old time in the bath, I wanted to stay here. But that's not what real people do, so I didn't do it. I sleepy-blinked my eyes a few times to clear the grit away, and tried to imagine myself in full make-up with crimped hair, because if you can imagine yourself doing something, it's sometimes not as bad when you actually do, as though you've already partly done it, or done it once. Raquel was laying Outdoor Girl and Mary Quant and Max Factor out on the carpet, compacts and tubes and see-through lids over multiple colours. I picked up a lipstick and a little mirror so I could see what I was doing, started applying it. Very strange colour – a sort of beige, and it felt hard and dry.

'For God's sake, darling, that's concealer,' said Raquel.

'Yes,' I said.

'What the bloody hell you come as?' Eddie burst out laughing.

'Leave her alone, she looks lovely,' said Auntie Lesley, fussing with my hair.

'Stop it,' I said, but I think too quietly as she didn't let go, so I tugged it away, pulling at the roots.

'Not missed you, have we?' Auntie pulled out a chair, sat down, took a big mouthful of her drink, in what seemed like a single movement.

'Nope. I'm on in ten minutes.'

'Do you really think I look silly?' I sat as he did, and watched his mouth to see if I could spot a lie.

'No, it's cute. Little girl dressing up.' He winked, got out his tobacco pouch.

I didn't like the feel of all the make-up on my face, sticky, like a fever. But I did like the little crinkles in my hair. Reminded me of when Raquel used to put my hair into lots and lots of tiny plaits when it was wet, and then once it was dried would unravel them into waves. But the elastic bands split the ends, and after a while she wouldn't do it anymore, in case it ruined my lovely hair. Which was odd, because everyone said she'd got the hair in the family.

The club was buzzing in my ears, and someone knocked my chair, jarring me right through my back. It was too full tonight, but I suppose that was good, as it meant money was coming in and Raquel and Eddie wouldn't lose their jobs.

'You all right, Dee-Dee?' asked Auntie Lesley. 'You look a bit lost.'

'How could you tell the difference?' said Eddie, but he smiled in that way people did to show you they weren't being horrible when actually they were.

'Can we go after you've sung?' I said.

'If you like.' But he wasn't smiling now.

'I can take her back, if you got to stay.' Auntie lit a cigarette, held it near her face, so the smoke swirled round her head like dry ice.

'No, you're all right. But that's my cue.' He stood, kissed

me on the top of the head, and limped over to the little stage. Instead of using the steps, he put one hand on it and leapt up sideways, like the boys in the alley next to the flats jumping the bike fence thingies.

'My girl's in tonight,' he said into the mic. 'So this one's for her.'

It had to be you
It had to be you
I wandered around
And finally found
Somebody who...

But it didn't have to be me, did it? It never does have to be just one person. We meet whoever we meet and it seems as though it was inevitable, fate as Raquel calls it, but she's wrong. Turn a different corner that day and it would be someone else right this minute telling me it had to be me, and Eddie telling someone else it had to be them. Daddy always says that it depends when your audition is, whether you get the part. After the casting director's had a nice boozy lunch, you're in. First thing in the day, and there might always be someone better down the line, someone taller or more coloured or a stronger singer or younger or older or just more right.

'Listen lovely, there's something you should know.' Auntie Lesley drained her drink and reached across the table to pat my hand. Why must people paw you? But she didn't look happy – the corners of her mouth were down and she was holding her lips tight, as though she had too many secrets behind them.

'What?' Maybe I should be worried.

'It's...Look, sweetheart, people aren't always what they seem.'

'Oh, it's all right, I know that.' Just a talk about what the world was like, then. That was a relief.

The people on the next table started singing along. It's not really that kind of place, I know that for a fact because of it happening before, but they had fur coats and black ties and champagne on the table, probably on their way somewhere else, so no one told them to be quiet. They'd be paying the wages tonight, Raquel would say.

'Dee-Dee, put your listening ears on, there's a good girl.'

'I'm not a baby.'

'No, course not, sorry love. Listen, you got to hear this.' She patted her hair, over and over again. Then we all clapped Eddie and he started another song.

'Relationships are always complicated, know what I mean?'

'I do, yes.'

'Oh bloody hell, what a performance. I should just tell you.'

'Yes.' I was feeling a bit fluttery-nervy now, in my tummy.

'It's…MB. He'll let on if I don't.'

I waited. Eddie was telling the audience it made him love them. It must be to them, because he was pointing to individual people. They seemed to like it.

'You born with no bloody curiosity or what?' She stubbed out her cigarette, glanced over her shoulder at the stage, lit another straight away. 'I'm a *murderer*.'

I couldn't have heard that right. I often don't.

'No. That's not true,' I said, to check. 'You're not a murderer.' But she just shook her head in a way that like nodding yes. I wanted to pop my fingers into my ears. This was not happening, it wasn't happening. I slipped my pebble from my pocket, unpolished and new, tapped it against my cheek.

'In a manner of speaking I am. You know we split up over the baby? Sort of.'

Gimme gimme gimme gimme what I cry for
You know you got the kind of kisses that I die for

'Yes.'

'Weren't quite so simple as that. Dee love, I'm queer.'

'Do you need a glass of water?'

'Not *queer*, Dee. I'm not ill.'

I didn't want to tell you
I didn't want to tell you

Auntie Lesley shook her head again and gave a funny little laugh. 'I mean I'm a lesbian,' she said. 'MB caught me at it with the new knife thrower's wife and that's why he put the kibosh on me having my baby.' A few tears fell down her face, leaving dirty streaks through her make-up like light rain did on my windows because it's too high up to have a window cleaner. 'Not that he weren't up to no good himself, mind,' she added, fishing in her bag, bringing out a screwed up pink tissue.

'But I know you like women,' I said. I hated this. It was confusing, there was too much coming at me at once. What about the murder? Wasn't that important, all of a sudden? Of course Auntie Lesley was a lesbian. I remembered at Girelli's, seeing her holding hands with Rula, and later at the factory I saw her three times with the buttonhole presser – who I think's on zips as well – having a little kiss. I knew we didn't talk about it but I didn't know it was a *secret*.

She was staring at me as if I was doing something amazing, like juggling with the glasses or singing the harmonies. But I wasn't.

'You stupid daft cow, what d'you mean you know?' she said at last, and banged the table, hard, and wobbled the drinks, just as the applause started up again. The fur coats and black ties must have thought she loved Eddie's performance because they started banging too, and calling out for more. 'You mean to say I been sat here, bleeding agonizing about telling you all, decided to do it one-to-one as it's easier, decided to start with you, with you being the baby... And you bloody well knew. Well, thank you very much, lady. Thank you very much indeed. And stop doing that to your cheek.'

'Sorry.' I put the pebble next to my lemonade.

'Make your poor face sore, doing that. Does Raquel know?'

'I don't know.' Surely she must - she knew all about relationships, could always spot who liked who, when I couldn't see it at all. But then sometimes I assumed the obvious and it turned out not to be obvious at all. Apparently.

'You not spoke about it?'

'Why would we?'

'You come out with some strokes, you do.' She hugged herself. 'So it's still my little secret then.' A sort of laugh then through her nose, a laugh that wasn't a laugh.

'I don't understand,' I said. I've probably said that more than anything else, more than *I love you*, more than *Hello* or *Goodbye*. 'Why do you think MB telling everyone would make a difference? Daddy knows lots and lots of...queers.'

'Yeah, I know that. But it got too late. Mummy would've... It would've been like being proper handicapped for her, something you shut away, shameful—'

'But you shut it away anyway,' I pointed out.

'Always was a good girl,' she said, sounding half-strangled. 'I right need another drink. Look lovely, the thing is, it's not just... You got to listen to this. Was my own fault I lost Michael. My baby. My own bloody fault. He's going to tell everyone *that*, make it sound even worse, like I didn't give a tinker's damn, when it mattered more than anything in the world to me. Loads more than Rula, so why I... Oh bugger it.' She grabbed my hand then, hard. 'He said it was like murder, Dee. Said Michael's real parents was bloody wicked sods and Michael would have no life and it'd be my fault. And if he's right, then I'm a murderer.'

That couldn't be true, it couldn't. Babies didn't get taken away because of how people behaved, when it was nothing to do with the baby.

'But why's he come back to tell us?' I said. 'I don't understand.'

'He hasn't. He wants money. And he's conning your poor old dad out of it right this minute, you mark my words.' She let go of my hand and I sucked my squashed finger. 'This ain't about MB, sweetie, it's about your father.'

She shouldn't have told me first. I wish she hadn't told me first. Raquel should be first, so she could explain it to me. I had absolutely no idea what Auntie Lesley was talking about, and I could feel my insides shiver and shake and the blood move around my body, could feel it skidding by my heart, leaving my head, swirling round my tummy.

'I'll get some more drinks.' Auntie Lesley squeezed past my chair but I didn't think to pull it in until it was too late.

I don't know who Milly-Molly-Mandy went back to, but I don't suppose it was her real parents. An orphanage maybe. And maybe she was treated not nicely, and maybe she cried for us, I'm sure she cried for us, for me, and maybe no one ever loved her like I did again. Maybe she was even dead. I tried to imagine how my auntie must have felt, and it must have been like I did when they took our baby away. Michael's a nice name. Mickey. Mickey Mouse. She might have bought all the little bits and bobs for him – I don't think she knitted bootees and things, I don't think she can knit – and she'd have been looking forward to him coming to live there. She already loved him, had already held him and kissed him and wiped the fat drool from his cheeks, and laughed when he pulled her hair. I could imagine, easily. In English, after they'd realized I didn't need to be in Special English, they always said *Delia O'Leary lacks imagination*. Daddy used to read it out in his special pretend-theatre voice, and tell me I couldn't be his child. Every year, the same, until I left school. But they were wrong. I only lacked imagination when something hadn't happened. When it had, I could sometimes imagine so well that I could feel the pins in my heart and my eyes, and I could cry for the hurting.

Everyone was clapping and Eddie jumped off the stage, half-ran back to the table. 'No drink?' he said.

'Auntie Lesley's gone to get them.'

'How was I...shit.'

'No, you weren't shit.'

'I didn't mean... There's Raquel, look.' He raised his hand. 'She's not working tonight.'

'No, she said she wasn't.' I turned round, saw her as she pushed through the crowd, getting a kiss from some man as she went, and I waved. Oh thank God. Raquel would make everything all right. 'But that's a singing dress.'

'Yeah, you're right, it is. Someone must be off sick, must've called her in.'

'Well this is cosy.' Raquel kissed me on the cheek, then went round the table and kissed Eddie's cheek too. He stood. 'You look surprised, Ed,' she said. 'Didn't Maurice tell you? Louise fell down the stairs, banged her face. That's her story, anyway and no doubt the boyfriend's too.'

Auntie Lesley reappeared. 'Never got one in for you,' she said.

'And hello to you as well, Auntie. Isn't this lovely? Family reunion.'

'You really have to come?' said Auntie Lesley.

'Work. The show must go on. That's what the O'Learys are famous for.'

'Certainly ain't for nothing else,' Auntie said. 'Nanti.'

Who was supposed to watch out? Nanti for what?

'I'll get you a drink, Raquel,' said Eddie. He kept running his hands through his hair, spiking it up more. He didn't like it spiky for the club but I didn't point it out in case that was wrong. 'What d'you have, again?'

'Bacardi and Coke. I'd have thought you'd have remembered that.'

And I knew that everyone was speaking in code and I didn't know if I knew more or less than the rest. Knowledge isn't power, it's crippling. The three of them stood looking down on me, as if they expected something, but I couldn't think what. I didn't know if Auntie Lesley was going to tell Raquel now about being a murderer, if Eddie was allowed to know, I didn't even know *what* there was to know really.

'Sometimes I think this family is too close,' said Auntie Lesley.

And I heard that properly and understood it and agreed with her. But I didn't say anything, I'd only fluff. I just picked my pebble up and started polishing it with my floaty scarf. Might start wearing those regularly. They're useful. But I didn't think I'd be going for the whole look again.

Ken

Are you happy here? You don't look up as much as you used to, old son. The view's really quite lovely at this time of year. London's got the best scenery in the country, can stick your gardens of England up your arse. You're not missing much in not seeing the provinces, my darling boy.

May's always so full of promise, isn't it? Ha – in a way, *that*'s the cruellest month, rather like God putting the feeling of sure and certain hope of salvation into people only so he can turn around on Judgement Day and say, *Sorry, dear, you're all wrong for the part. Exit's over there – take you straight to hell.* Played Calvin in a radio once. Good part for me, but then it went to a telly and suddenly no one believes in me as an ascetic. Fair point, I couldn't have seen me in the part either. Fortunately, it was BBC2, long before the days when anyone watched. '67 I think, or maybe early '68. If I could, I'd pause all our lives at May, and never get to the autumn and the winter with our dreams dashed. Never get to heaven's gates.

Look at that cockscomb down there. Bloody magnificent plant. Always recognize that one, thanks to Percy Thrower. That was when he was on that lunchtime show after me – me, who couldn't spot a tulip from a daff. Still can't.

Remember Dee-Dee saying to me, she can't have been

more than four, 'Why has that lady got a yellow flower, Daddy?' This was after she'd clarified that yellow was her third favourite colour, or was it fourth. I said the lady's lover had probably given it to her. But she wasn't having that. Oh dear me, no. Said, 'Maybe she's taking it home to her children because they're sad, and they will smell it and be happy because spring is here.' I thought then she'd be a poet or a playwright. Was quite a shock to me when she turned out not to have a creative bone in her body.

Tremendous plant, the cockscomb. Wish I knew more about flowers, but I never shall now. *Rosemary, that's for remembrance.* And everyone does remember that line, of course. Hobbies. Feh, load of old bollocks. Look at it, go on. Tremendous.

But you're not looking, Glen-Glen, are you – not these days. You see less and less. Maybe that's because there's less and less to see. Bollocks to it, perhaps you *should* come and live with me. No. No, you'd hate it, of course you'd hate it. Left it far too long for that, but I tell you this much for nothing, old boy – I wish I hadn't. Wish to God I hadn't.

Trouper, that was me. Plates up on sticks, two verses of 'Brown Boots' and off, bugger the encore, in the pub before the curtain call. That's the way. Then we got all serious in the profession, d'you remember, and of course I was young so it affected me too. Wasn't enough to be on speakers with Larry Olivier, I wanted to be him. You're the only person in the whole world who knows that about me, Glen-Glen. I was an ambitious man. Secretly. You forgive me, I know you do, and I'm grateful – but it's a bugger of a thing to try and forgive yourself.

Feh.

Look what Kenny's got you today – little jelly bears. Gummi Bears, they call them. MB got them from some

American chap he knows. No? Because they're from MB? Don't blame you, chap's a cunt. Leave them on the chest here, in case you change your mind. Have a KitKat instead. Got you two – had a feeling you wouldn't appreciate the bears. Not both at... No, right, you go for it, old boy. Who's to say where we'll be tomorrow? Don't know where you put it, though – how's a chap look like an ex-athlete when he seldom leaves his chair? *This* chap – look at me darling, turning face – this chap, your Kenny boy, walks about in his ridiculous training shoes and look at that! That tummy. *All bought and paid for*, that's what our father said when he showed up. Not by you, I told him. That shut the bastard's trap. You'd have laughed. Naughty of me, but you've always appreciated that.

I'm going to do it, Glen-Glen. Going to sign up to MB's ridiculous show and give him the money and I'll have to work then. What else can I do?

There's no business like show business

There's no business I know

Sorry, I know – don't give up the day job. If I don't force myself into this, what's left to me? MB thinks I'm a fool, he does you know, he thinks I believe this is a big chance for me. He thinks he's appealing to my vanity. Feh. He's giving me a way out, that's what he's doing. You know that, I know that, but no other beggar will ever know that. His show will lose my money, but not whatever he's skimmed off for himself. Show will probably never see the light of day even. I can afford to give up my savings – not yours, my dear old chap, never your security – but I can't afford to give up the truth, that I made a mistake in retiring. Can't give it up to anyone but you and you know it already.

You don't need your eyes to see, Glen-Glen, you don't need to look, you can see with your ears. You can see into my heart, where it's black and empty and yearning for the spotlight, if just to show me the way to the grave. Oh Glen-Glen, how's it come to this?

My head hurts. Not just now and again, but all the time. Remember when you used to knock your head against the wall half the night? I think now that was the headache, think you were trying to knock it out. Had a go myself the other evening, but two knocks and I was nearly out cold. I eat asprin like they're Smarties… No, old chap, no Smarties. Next time. Sorry, am I being an old moanio? Don't mean to be. You're kind, to put up with it so patiently. But you always were the kinder of we two.

D'you think Dee-Dee… Listen, old son, do you think Dee-Dee can be left to the mercies of that crip? He's an ambitious sod if ever there was one, makes *me* look contented. Glen-Glen – I've been thinking about it a lot, middle of the night when the headache's bad and I can't sleep and there's no lines to learn – but do you think I took too little care of her? Do you think she's…not like other people? Is she… Fuck it. You can take it, I know you can.

Is she like you?

She is, isn't she? You know it, I can see you do. Maybe *she* should come and live with me. Maybe it's not too late for her, for her and me. Would you mind, Glen-Glen? She'd never take your place, you know – no one could ever do that. But maybe we could make it up to her, you and I, for me not noticing before. *You* noticed, I'm sure of it. Why didn't you tell me until now? Sorry, darling boy, sorry. That was low, blaming you. Mummy always did say I was out for myself. *No one's looking at you, Kenneth, so you can stop that nonsense right now. Out for yourself, you are.* But she was wrong, they *were* looking, and they will again. They'll have to, otherwise how the hell will I know who we are?

Her mother was a lovely creature. Granted, Raquel's mother was a fine woman too, no denying that, but Dee's mother was exquisite. D'you remember? You liked her, you did, she'd bring you peppermint balls and pineapple cubes and other good things out of jars. Never once got it wrong, did she? Thought I was the funniest fella in the country – she was a lovely audience. But that's not enough for them, is it? Being an audience. Can't say as I blame her. No, bollocks to that, of course I blame the bitch. Leaving me I could understand, but leaving Dee? And Raquel, she must have felt it. *Her* mother was flighty, a bolter – that's what you get with actresses, I'm afraid - but she must have thought she had a second chance with Dee-Dee's mummy. I'm lucky she never resented her baby sister, or where would I have been? Stuck at home, that's where. No one can say I've any illusions about myself – well, I couldn't, could I, with you shining back at me.

Damned headache. Oh Glen-Glen old son, feels like the worms are eating my brain before anyone's bothered to bury me. Clangourous railway line through my head, as though I'm wearing cans and some over-enthusiastic Spot's rattling his tins of dried peas too close to the mic.

What's that you want, old chap? Kenny's arm? There you go...What? Oh my darling boy, an elbow rub? *You're* giving *me* an elbow rub? Oh, thank you. Hardly dare breathe. If I die right now, they can have me, hell and...*Ow*, that's a - ow, *bollocks* - darling boy, that's a bit hard...No, ssh, never mind, silly Kenny. Big girl's blouse, I am. Ssh. That's it. I'm quiet now. You keep on. *The rest is silence.*

Raquel

I've never come first with anyone. Not to put too fine a point on it, even my mother couldn't put me first, or not for long. Daddy's never prioritized either of his daughters, and if he did, I wouldn't be first in line there. No one's ever married me first or loved me first or looked to me first. Only Dee has ever needed me to give her my first duty of care, but she'd move on in a heartbeat if she ever felt truly safe anywhere else. It's not me she wants, but my role. My familiarity.

I nearly came first once. Just the once. We were on holiday, the only time we went to a Holimarine camp. Burnham-on-Sea, 1958 or '59. Dee's mummy, Marmie to me (her idea), made me a fairy princess costume of crepe paper for the fancy dress competition, took her hours and hours, and she glued glitter to the inside of a Rice Krispie packet for my crown, and even bought me little ballet slippers because I hadn't thought to pack mine, though Daddy said it was a waste of money. Pink of course. The baby was left to cry for longer than usual because Marmie wanted to get done. I was one of the oldest competing, but I didn't give a tinker's d—, I looked pretty, really pretty. You had to do a song or dance, so I did both – 'Nobody Loves a Fairy When She's Forty' – and it brought the house down coming from a nine or ten year old.

And I nearly won. They announced my name and there was clapping and everything, but just as I was going up the steps to where the fat man in the shiny suit was standing by the mic, some lady with blue hair came rushing over and they said it had been a mistake, I was second, and the boy in his soldier cadet outfit complete with his daddy's medals was the real winner. That wasn't even a costume, not a real one that you made. Mind you, the poor boy who'd come third dressed as a caterpillar was relegated to fourth, and that wasn't a real position at all, it didn't even carry a prize. I got a ten bob postal order, but the winner got another free week at Holimarine. Daddy said he couldn't have spared the time anyway, he was opening at the Thameside Theatre on the Monday. Rattigan, whatever that meant.

So naturally I wasn't surprised this time. It would have been entirely uncharacteristic of my life for it to have been any other way.

'Yes, of course I see that.' I clicked Sweetex into my coffee and pushed his mug across the worktop to him. He had the one with the hairline crack.

'It's not you—'

'If you finish that sentence, swear I'll top myself for ever getting involved with someone that crass.' Forcing mocking amusement into my eyes. God knows, I'd had the practice.

He laughed. 'Was going to say it's the situation. It's her.'

'I know. Just wish you'd let me dump you first.' Seldom been so sincere.

'Was you going to?' He re-lit his roll-up.

'You'll never be sure now. Come to that, neither will I.'

'Pack that in, will you. Say stuff like that and—'

'You'll remember what you'll never have with her, and we'll limp on for another couple of weeks until one of us ends it anyway.' Giving him The Look.

'Yeah. Something like that.'

'For Christ's sake Eddie, I don't know what either of us thought we were doing. Was I some sort of insurance policy?' Tracing a quick eight on my thumb.

'What's that supposed to mean?' He scratched at my work surface as though he was Dee. It was all I could do not to slap his hand away.

'Dee's not as useful as you'd imagined,' I said, 'so let's see what good old Raquel can do? Schtup her, keep her sweet?'

'Leave it out. You don't mean that.'

'Don't I? I don't know, sweetie. And I don't know who I'm more pissed off with – you or me.' I took a mouthful of my coffee, even though it was still hotter than I'd normally chance. Well, this was just perfect: I'd have guilt now for the rest of my life, every time Dee said anything about Eddie, every time she looked to the side of me with those puzzled eyes, every time I held their baby – there would no doubt be a baby – I'd know how I'd betrayed her, how he wasn't good enough. She didn't have much; I'd tarnished what she did have. And for what? For nothing, for a nobody.

Bet he was grateful to me - he'd probably imagined I'd cry, even beg. Leave them wanting more, that's what Daddy always says. No way would I give him the satisfaction. I've done that twice in my life with men, and never again.

'Should thank you as it goes,' Eddie said. 'Made me realize—'

'How much Dee means to you.' More coffee. 'You really should get a better scriptwriter, Eddie. I've heard that one a few too many times.'

'About Dee?' Too quickly. Too suspiciously. Too, God damn him, jealously.

'No, not about Dee.' I shook the last Silk Cut from the

213

packet. 'You know what? I've had it with married men, or nearly-married men. You're all the same.'

'We're not. If me and Dee get married—'

'You'll never cheat on her. Right.' I lit the cig. 'But I tell you one thing for nothing, Eddie Muir – I'll be watching you.'

'What d'you—'

'Just that. I'll be watching you, so you watch your step.' I smiled at him then, my best 100 watt dazzler. 'No one's going to hurt my Dee-Dee.'

'You got some fucking front.'

'Maybe. But I mean *that*.'

His hair was badly receding. Should have noticed that before, but somehow I hadn't really, or not consciously. That's probably why he spiked the front, so it didn't show as much. And his neck was just starting to go - well, in fairness so was mine, but that's where having a little bit of weight did me some favours. He'd look scrawny soon, and every bit his real age. How long did he think he could keep claiming to be just under thirty? Soon, very soon, he'd just look rather pathetic, in his too-tight jeans and his teenage-boy tee-shirts, with his winking and his pointing and his all-lads-together. The limp would seem less romantic than arthritic. Dee deserved better. That nice geography teacher Daddy imagined for her. Or maybe an older man, a widower who was still sad, where her innocence and neediness might bring him back to life. But she'd chosen Eddie, or more probably accepted his choosing of her, and I had to protect her. He was a chancer. I really would have to watch him for the rest of their lives together.

'You might as well go now, Eddie.' I stuck my hand across the work surface, and after a brief hesitation, he shook it. I put my other hand over his. 'Don't worry, I'm not asking you to go so I can cry myself into a stupor with a bottle of gin. Don't even like gin.' Letting go. 'But I can't see the point of dragging it out.'

'No, I get that.'

'And let's face it, I've been rejected. Think I can give myself an hour to lick my wounds and put my face on.'

'You're incredible.' He shook his head and of course did the finger-gun point.

'Yep, that's what they tell me. Just not quite incredible enough.'

He nearly blustered, I could see it coming, but then he looked me in the eye.

'Maybe not,' he said.

So with a kiss on the cheek, he got away lightly, no doubt heaving an enormous sigh of relief as I closed my door on his back. My one consolation was that Dee would never have to know how close I'd come to ruining her life, and how little I'd thought about the reality of that until now.

There wasn't much booze in the place, only a little vodka. I poured that into the remains of my coffee even though it was ten in the morning. Never let it be said that I don't have a sense of drama.

Oh Raquel, you fool. You don't love that excuse for a man, you just wanted to, and for that, you changed the way you'll look at yourself forever.

And there weren't even any bloody buggery cigarettes left.

She may still have a magic power but that is not enough -
They like their bit of magic power from a younger bit of stuff,
When once your silver star has lost its glitter
And you tinsel looks like rust instead of gold,
Fairy days are ending when your wand has started bending,
No one loves a fairy when she's old.

Her eyes were black. Eyes usually so pale were as black as her jet, the way they used to get as a child. She was hitting herself in the head, over and over, over and over, not making screaming sounds but barking like a seal, an injured seal. Clawing at her face then. I tried to grab her hand, but she flailed wildly at me, catching my cheek with her nails, hitting me on the side of the neck, winding me. She backed herself into a corner, still hitting at her head with one hand, but the other was now pushed inside her sleeve, and she was wiping it furiously across her nose.

'No no no no no no no no no no no no,' she said. 'No no no no no.'

'Dee, darling, stop it, please. It's not worth it.'

'No no no no no no.' Still banging at her head. I tried again to get her arm but she snarled at me, baring her teeth. I don't think she knew by that point I was there.

It felt like an hour, but I think it was probably about fifteen minutes. That's long enough to be blind and deaf and mute except for those unearthly scrapings from the throat and the single word repeated again and again. *No. No. No.* I hadn't seen her like this for a decade at least. This had been the soundtrack to the sixties and early seventies for me.

Even as a baby, she'd yelped and moaned. In the night, I sometimes thought she was a ghost.

Marmie in the mornings or late evenings thrusting her at me, begging me to walk her up and down the road. *Please, Raquel sweetheart, please. She'll drive me straight into St Clements, honest to God she will. Just half hour.* The neighbours shouting from their windows,

Can't you keep that brat quiet?

Throw a bucket of water over it.

Once, a man pushed me against a wall and said he'd knock my teeth down my bleeding throat if I didn't choose another street to march about in like I owned it. I think he used to visit Mrs Holdsworth at number 20 when Mr Holdsworth was on shifts, but that might have been some other man.

Marching on, she holding herself straight and rigid, as though she was dead, but no dead thing ever made a racket like that. Daddy said she'd be an opera singer, but Daddy said a lot of silly things, the odd time he was home long enough to hear.

Here we were again. But this time, we were both grown-ups. I knelt near to her, yet not too near, making soothing noises from time to time, helplessly, guiltily, fearfully. It wasn't the meltdown in and of itself that alarmed me, but that I was capable of bringing it on, and maybe there'd been no need. Daddy would be furious, and Auntie Lesley. They might not speak to me ever again. They'd choose her, of course they'd choose her, but would she be damaged? She sounded more like a cow now, or maybe a calf, mooing almost, softly, as if she was running out of steam. 'Ssh,' I said. 'Ssh. It's okay, I'm sorry, it's okay.' It wasn't okay, I was lying, but I *was* sorry.

Crying now. Tears running down her skin-covered skull, like some holy miracle that Nan used to go on about. 'Mm mm mm mm,' she says. 'Mm mm.'

'I didn't mean to hurt you.' Like every bad film I'd ever seen. But I hadn't hurt her, that was ridiculous; I'd turned her back into a child whose anger was too great for them to bear. Eddie had hurt me maybe, my pride anyway; I was killing my sister. I was shaking with the shock of her reaction, visibly shaking, and igloo cold. Hugging myself, I tried to keep my arms still, but still I juddered.

Hand on heart, I truly hadn't gone there to tell her. Heavens, I'd been terrified enough that Lesley would spill the beans, or what she thought were the beans. Otherwise,

I'd believed it would be my sordid little secret for always. Just this morning, just hours ago, sipping vodka-laced coffee, I'd absolutely decided she must never know. And I wasn't pissed, far from it; the booze had taken the edge off, nothing more. It was only about a double, if that, and although that's not nothing first thing in the morning, it's not a bottle. I knew exactly what I was doing. And at first all I was doing was going out to buy cigarettes.

But somehow, I kept on walking. Down the stairs to the tube, up the stairs at the other end. Into the Indian shop on the corner for my ten Silk Cut, no make it twenty, quick word with nice Mrs Kapoor, Yes I was fine, No I hadn't been in for a while, Yes my sister was fine, then along the Mile End Road to the estate, and no way was I chancing that lift, up the piss-smelling stairs, past Tom's door, up another floor and another, to Dee's flat.

And oh Christ, she was so happy to see me. She even hugged me, or sort of, her funny stiff-armed embrace, and half-danced me into the living room. I looked at her and my heart opened as though it was a stubborn nut at Christmas, one of the ones that gets left in the bottom of the bowl because nobody can be bothered to try that hard to crack it. For better or worse, I was all she really had, and she was certainly all I really had. I couldn't let her go on with that poor excuse for a man.

'I've got something to tell you,' I said.

She looked at me, a proper long, slow look. Then she put her hands over her ears. When she was little, three, four, five, she'd walked around for most of the time with her hands over her ears. We never knew if she was shutting out sound or dealing with stress. And now it was back, that exact-same gesture, the same casting the eyes down, the same pressure not to let us in.

'It's Eddie,' I said.

'Dead?'

'No, Christ, no. Not dead. It's... Dee, I've slept with him. More than once.' Trying to control my breathing. 'It's over and it was a mistake, but my darling Dee-Dee, he's not good enough for you. And nor, I suppose, am I.'

'No. No no no no no no no no no.'

That's when her eyes turned black, and her hands came away from her ears only to beat them.

At last, long last, she was just crying, gently, her face in her hands. I was still shaking, but not as violently. Dee was back, thank God, she was back, but how changed, I didn't know.

'I love you, Dee,' I said. To my amazement, she looked up.

'Yes, I know,' she said. 'But you still did it.'

'I still did it. I've always been...Oh Dee, forgive me but I've always been jealous of you.'

'Have you? That's still not a reason.'

'It's a reason, it's just not an excuse.'

'You sound like that boyfriend you had. Peter.'

'Yes.' I rummaged through my bag. Where the hell were those cigarettes? I found them, fumbled with the cellophane and finally lit one. Dee wasn't crying now. She rubbed her eyes with the palms of her hands. 'Can you forgive me?' I asked, blowing smoke into her face. 'Shit, sorry.' I wafted it away with my hand.

'Forgive you? I don't know. I'm not sure I know what that means.'

'No, I'm not sure either.'

'Why did you have to tell me?'

'I don't want him anywhere near you.' But she might forgive him. That hadn't occurred to me. 'Dee – you'll tell him where to get off, won't you? I mean, to leave you alone.'

'I don't know. I can see that you think I should. But I don't know. I'll have to think, I can't think about it straight off the top of my head.'

'Do you want me to make you some lemon tea?'

'No.'

'Do you want me to go?'

'No. I don't want to be on my own.'

'I could go and knock Tom for you, if you don't want me.'

'No. I want you to stay. I don't know about later, I don't know if I'll ever want you here again, but I want you here now.'

She held out her hand to me, like she's almost never done, and I took it, careful not to squeeze. We sat there for at least another quarter of an hour, not speaking, just me smoking and us holding hands. Hers were so old for her age, so tiny and baggy, the veins so prominent through her transparent skin. It was as though I was holding the hand of an ancient lady who was ill or even dying, supporting her with my own plump life. Wasn't even telling myself it would be all right, because clearly it wouldn't be. That's when I really knew: whatever had happened, whatever decision she made, I'd never be free. She was the closest thing I'd ever have to a daughter and although I didn't want her, didn't want to be her mother, I was stuck with loving her now, in my own way. And she, I'm sure, whatever she decided, was stuck with loving me.

Eddie

'Fuck me, everywhere I turn, there you are.'

'Like a naughty sprite?'

'Not quite the image I had in mind as it happens, no.'

'What a pity. I'm guessing I must be the evil leprechaun, then?'

Wanted to tell him to give it a rest, but something about the show that I still believed in held me back. 'Could be one of Father Christmas' elves for all I care,' I said. 'Just want to get a drink. Thought you was meeting me here in half hour.' I pushed open the door of The Owl.

'Ken's come across with the money. It's all systems go, or will be once it's cleared,' MB said to my back. To my arse to be strictly truthful.

Everyone turned, like we was in *Deliverance* or *Teenage Werewolf in London*. MB was right blasé about it, but then I suppose he's had to be. Hard to feel pity for someone as pleased with theirselves as him, though. Hard to feel anything except the urge to slap him round the head.

'G&T?' I asked. Without really waiting for his answer, I pushed my way to the bar – pub weren't that packed, but the punters was curious – and ordered. Carlsberg had gone up to 70 pence, barman told me. What a joke, was 68 last week, I said. That's inflation for you, he said. You're not wrong, I said. You should go back to the bitter, he said. No, it's an old man's drink, I said. Oscar, eat your heart out.

'So the show's going to go on,' I said as we sat down, trying to sound casual.

'Looks that way indeed, provided I can supply a theatre.'

'He handed over the dough before you got a place set up?'

'How else am I to get that place?' He took a sip of his drink and looked round the pub. 'Very East End,' he said.

'That'll be because this *is* the East End.' It was hard not to take a run at the bloke, verbally speaking, but I took a couple of mouthfuls of my lager, swallowed it down. 'Had to walk past some old bill with riot shields before. Thatcher's private army, police are these days.'

'So you're telling me you're a political animal?' He lit a fag, blew the smoke in my direction.

'No, don't give a shit really. Just an observation.'

'And a very original one it is too.'

Cunt. 'So you're sorted then,' I said, counting to ten in my head. 'Ken don't strike me as the type of bloke to give up his cheque book without crossing the i's and dotting the t's.'

'People change.' He examined his painted nails. Bet that was going down a storm with the table behind. One woman was craning her neck so far, she was in danger of coming off her seat.

'Be honest, it sounds a bit... Not being funny, but you sure it's kosher?'

'He's given me the money, I'm looking for a theatre, several acts are interested. I'm not sure how much more kosher you want at this stage.'

'Contacting our – well, anyone's agents?'

'All in good time.'

'But you got contracts with him or what?'

'I think that's our business.'

I did still believe it'd be all right – Ken weren't nobody's fool. He'd been in the business forty years. But there was something about the way MB popped up everyfuckingwhere, the way he looked at us all, the way Lesley was running scared – even Dee said that, or something very like it, in her own way – that smelt wrong. Raquel didn't trust him, knew that much. Couldn't talk it over with Raquel now though, not for a while. Fuck it, wish I'd learnt to keep my dick in my trousers. *You always was a fool for a pretty face*, Mum said. Yeah, well, for a long time pretty faces didn't want nothing to do with me, so you can hardly blame a man for taking it once he could get it.

'So what did you want to talk to me about?' Keeping my cool.

'This and that. Cabbages and kings. What you might want to do in the show.'

But all of a sudden, I knew that weren't it. Nobody, unless they was very bored, would track down someone like me to talk about a spot this far in advance. Can't tell you how much I wish I was big enough fry for that to be likely, but I weren't. He might want me to help keep Ken sweet, granted, but that didn't feel quite right either. Something was well funny here. The hairs on my arms was standing up, and it weren't chilly in the pub.

'Look MB, man, you might as well spill it.' Fronting him out.

'Spill what? I'd rather drink it, thank you.' He lifted his glass. Sitting down, you could see he was short, but it weren't as noticeable as when he stood up. He was swinging his little legs, bang, bang, bang into the table, rattling my pint and the ashtray. I wanted to tell him to pack it in, but I didn't quite dare. He pushed his B&H packet across to me, and I took one. I held my nerve, not saying anything, waiting for him to make the move. MB smiled and smoked and banged and sipped, daring me *not* to make a move. His long scarf was trailing almost on the ground; he scooped it up and tossed it back round his neck, never taking his eyes off me.

'What?' I said at last. *Pillock.*

'Do you know the kind of family you're joining yourself to?' he said.

'Yeah, I guess. Why?'

'The whole lot of them revolve around the one person.'

'Ken's a big figure.'

'Around the person who isn't right in the head.'

'Oh right, course. Yeah, I know.' Not wrong there. That's where all the serious dosh went.

'I wanted my own Big Top,' MB said, leaning forward, flattering me with the intimacy. But I'd played that gesture too many times, pal. 'And I'd have been good, too,' he went on. 'When I met Les, we were ambitious. That's what I saw in her. I thought she was probably Lesley the Lezzer and I was right—'

'*What?*

'Don't be so suburban. How can it possibly matter to you?'

'Well, no, it don't, but—'

'But we liked each other, at first we definitely did, she admired my talent and I thought she was brave, given she had no circus background.' Slowly, he squashed his cigarette butt into the ashtray. 'And we rubbed along well enough in bed, now and again. We could have ignored each other's peccadilloes, looked the other way.' A punter walked too close, knocked his chair. 'Excuse *me*,' MB said, with a flash of proper anger. 'Sorry, where was I? Yes, I was even prepared to get her a baby, to keep her happy. But the only chance we really had of funding was the grandfather's money. He wasn't Lesley's father - you probably know that.'

'Yeah. She's much younger than Ken and—'

'Precisely. But Ken loved his little sister, he'd have helped us get enough to get a deposit and so a loan. I had everything in place, everything.' His face was sort of twisted. He didn't look right in the head himself. 'Would have been smaller than Girelli's – which was small – but it would have been great.'

'But Glen got the dough instead.'

'Oh for sure. No way was the capital going to be touched, because of *Glen*.' Someone put 'Brass in Pocket' on the jukebox. I nearly laughed. 'Then Ken made his own share, which was much smaller, over to the girls,' MB continued, all oblivious. 'But that was never the real problem, the real problem was the bulk of that money was never going anywhere. So I had to move on, no choice, bye bye the lovely Lesley. Ended up with a poxy little show and some fat dolly instead of a Big Top.'

'So what's the score now?'

'Glen everything, the rest of the family, nil. And Ken's losing his grip.'

'But you got his money.'

'Between you and me and the bedpost, it's not enough.'

'You'll never get Glen's off him. No way.' Suddenly, I saw what'd been happening: he'd been going round everyone trying to see a chink where he could ease out Glen's dough, or some of it. Bet you a million pound part that's what it was.

'Not while he's alive, no.'

That sat between us like a sword; he waited to see who'd pick it up.

Didn't want to hear this, no way did I want to hear this.

All right, it might be nothing, it might just be a factual comment, but I didn't like that leer on his battered old mug, didn't like that challenge in his eyes. It's true that he'd hardly been buttering me up, but maybe he was hoping to humiliate me into submission. That weren't a bad technique, as it happens. He was a good people reader, give him that. Shit, I'm sure most of us had wished the bloke dead, but you don't say it out loud, you just don't. Makes it reek of intent. Maybe I'd seen too many films, but then again maybe he had an' all. Hitchcock'd walk by in a moment.

'Bloke's not sixty yet,' I said at last. 'I've seen him. Fit as a butcher's dog.'

'As I said, people change.' Not even blinking.

'Not that much. Not that quickly.' Surely to God I weren't hearing what I thought I was. Got to have called this wrong.

'You'd be very surprised how quickly a life can change,' he said, his lips fat, red, wet, in that grated face. 'As an ambitious man, that should be cheering news, I'd have thought. Want to hear how quickly? I've stories that would make you weep.'

Bastard thought he had me taped, I could see it. He thought I was like him, only not as clever, not as strong. Even if I'd called it wrong, he was getting off on this, tormenting me that I might've called it bang on.

I had a couple or three choices here. 1. I could listen, and let him tell me stuff I maybe weren't up to hearing, stuff that could even get me banged up. 2. I could go over to the phone in the corner, ring Ken or Raquel or even Lesley. 3. I could leave the pub now, take a chance on throwing the spot away, throwing all the contacts it could bring me away, take a chance on this family. Even if I'd be doing that for a reason that turned out to be nothing much at all.

'See you later, MB,' I said. And I got up, walked out the pub without looking back and kept on walking until I got to Dee's flat. It felt good. For once in my life, and most probably against my own interest, I'd done totally the right thing.

'Dee? Babe, it's me.' I went into the living room, and there she was hunched over on the floor. Something was badly wrong. 'What's up, love?'

She didn't look at me, just at her hands.

'Come on, Dee, what's happened?' It must be MB, he must have come out with the same stuff to her. She loved her uncle, she didn't believe anyone behaved like that. Be devastating for her, even to hear that someone hinted at thinking about it. 'Beautiful?' I crouched down and reached out to stroke her hair, slowly, carefully, trying hard not to startle her. Normally, she'd press her head into my hand, but she didn't move. At least she didn't flinch. 'Want me to get someone? Raquel?' Still, no movement. To be truthful, weren't too keen on phoning Raquel unless I had to.

Shit, please don't tell me she was going like her uncle. There was always a fear round that in this family, you could feel it. Be fair, though, however much anyone give it all the flannel about every life being worth the same, mothers of handicapped kids always watched the next one for little signs of the worst thing in the world, and no one wanted to admit to being related to the mad old bat who heard voices and killed herself. Load of bullshit. I've lost parts, loads of them, because of my leg. You don't see young actors rushing out to kneecap theirselves just so they could be like me. Difference is always great and fine and dandy, so long as it's over there. Not in our backyard.

'Dee, baby you're frightening me.'

I couldn't even hear her breathe. If I didn't know better, I'd have thought one of us had died.

'Come on, baby.'

She did move then, shifting her head slightly away from my hand, clasping her own together. But she didn't look at me, and was still weirdly quiet.

Oh Christ, no. 'It's not your uncle, is it? It's not Glen-Glen?'

Finally, she raised her head. 'Uncle Glen-Glen? No,' she said, in a small, cracked voice, as though she hadn't used it in a week.

'Then what?' Oh *shit*. Please God, no. Let it be Glen after all. Not Raquel, please. She wouldn't've. No way.

'What's wrong with me?' she said.

'What d'you mean? Nothing's wrong with you.'

'But there is. You and Raquel, laughing at me, preferring each other.'

'No, no one's laughed at you. What you on about?'

'She told me that you'd slept together. Six times. That's six mistakes, isn't it? Six times it just happened. Six times you didn't know what you were doing.'

I'd never heard her like this. Didn't know she *could* sound like this. Not bitter exactly, not sarcastic, but sure of another person's probable response. Must be from whatever Raquel had said. What the fuck *had* she said? Stupid *bitch*.

'I don't know what to say, Dee. I was an idiot.' My heart was going, my mouth was dry. What if I'd made a choice and it turned out to be no choice at all.

'No.' Clear and calm, through her hair shield. 'I wasn't enough.'

'For fuck's sake, don't blame yourself.'

'I don't.' Shaking her little head, so her face peeped out

from her hair. There was a mark on her forehead, one on her cheekbone. Bruising maybe. 'It's not my fault, how I am,' she said. 'I wish I wasn't, I wish I was normal. But I can't help it.'

'Please don't tell me you want to finish it.' I'd have nothing left. Nothing.

'It's already finished.'

'We could try again.'

'No. It'd happen again. I can't ever change, and you aren't ever going to find the way I am good enough for long enough.' She gave a little smile, sad and sweet. 'Suppose I'll never be enough for anyone. I didn't want to spend my life just me.'

'You don't have to. Come on Dee, I love you.' At that moment, it felt true.

'I don't know what that means.' Pushing her hair right off her face.

'Because of me?'

'No. Because of me. I think so. Because of me.'

She might've been waiting for me to tell her, but I couldn't. I didn't have a Scooby either. Love. Said the word a hundred times, in plays, in life, had even sang it, but I weren't no closer to knowing really what it meant, except in the cracks and the spaces the glimpses between the words, something warm and yet somehow hard, that was mostly hidden from me, maybe forever.

'And what about me?' I said instead. 'What am I meant to do?'

'Do?' She looked amazed. 'I don't know,' she said, finally. 'Is that really what I should be thinking about?'

Knew her well enough to realize this was a genuine question. 'No,' I told her, truthfully, though I wanted to say yes and she'd most probably believe me.

Dee uncurled her legs then, moved away from the corner, gave a little stretch like a baby ferret and reached along the floor for her saucer full of stones. She ran her fingers over them, softly, rhythmically, watching the movement. I didn't know if this was a good or a bad sign.

'What's going to happen?' I asked. Most probably should've waited, but I couldn't watch her disappear back into her own world, leaving me behind, even if the alternative was hearing what I didn't want to hear.

'Nothing, I'd imagine.' Stroke, stroke, stroke over the stone. 'You'll collect any of your things you've left here and go. I'll carry on being me.'

'What about...Raquel?' If that bitch was in and I was out, I'd murder her.

'I don't know yet. I can't see my life without Raquel in it, but I can't think about what she's done. Not yet. It doesn't make any sense.'

'That makes three of us,' I told her. Then, 'What happened to your head?'

'I got burnt,' she said. I didn't ask any more.

A light early summer rain had started some time while we'd been talking. My ear now caught it fluttering like a trapped bird against the filthy windows. I sat on as long as I dared, listening to the rain, knowing this could be the last time we was together like this. But there was three of us still sat here, I had to know that, and each one of us a fool.

Alone in my flat, I went into the bathroom and took off my damp clothes, dried myself on a hand towel. But today, instead of quickly rubbing the left leg without looking at it, I forced myself to proper examine it. Withered, twisted, wasted, the skin puckered as if I'd been burnt and had skin grafts, but I hadn't gone through either. No doubt about it,

I was deformed. Don't think Mum'd ever forgive me that: being born perfect and then mutating into this. Sort of reverse *Frankenstein*. Sometimes, when I was a kid, I could feel her disappointment, even her dislike, boring into my leg, making it throb and seem to shrink further. Dad just ignored it, though I think it pissed him off that I couldn't play football with the other kids, was a bit of a boffin instead. Maybe what happened to me was the reason they never had other kids, but I can't be sure because I never asked. Some things you don't want to hear.

I should've told Dee about MB, though it sounded well mental thinking about it now, away from his evil eyes. After all, bloke'd just said that there wouldn't be more money available while Glen was alive, which was just a statement of fact. Wanted to think he had me over a barrel, most likely the only sort of power he had. Was a nasty bastard, everyone said that from the kick-off. He might've just been playing me, either to get me away or most probably just for his own amusement. Sick, yeah, but it sounded much the most likely now, in my tiny bathroom with the mould round the loose metal window frames and the jokey soap on a rope from Dad hanging from the bath tap.

What would Dee've done, anyway? Run her fingers faster through them poxy stones, most probably. Raquel should know, maybe – if there really was anything to know – but I didn't reckon I'd ever speak to her again. And Ken just weren't a goer. It was finished, all of it. I'd fucked it up and not for the first time. On the too-full bathroom shelf was some baby oil that Dee'd left here, one of the few times she'd stayed round mine. She always preferred her own place. I poured some into my palm. More greasy than I'd expected, not something you'd want to rub into a baby's skin. I made myself start to massage it into my leg, the skin under my hands leathery, dead. Dee had touched that leg though, caressed it even, just that once and I'd let her. It felt good and shaming both, and I never let her do it again. Wish I had now. Just one more time. But that would never earn its place in my story now. Some things, you leave too late.

Delia

I was lost in the fire-fierce and it burned me up. It ate at my face, my lungs, the place where my memory lives and all my other feelings. Consuming me. I know what that means, now.

It had been gone for years, but it was back and I recognized it but I couldn't place it, because my words and my memories went first, licked and quickly covered by the flames. And I let it eat me, love me, want me, and I let it rape me and I think I even wanted it to. It must have been like this when I was a child, a teenager. It must have been but I don't really remember, except the colours and the heat and the force. After it was over, they matched up, like cards in a game of Memory. I'm excellent at Memory, so good no one will play me now. I should ask Tom. He'd play.

After it was over, I was exhausted. My head and my jaw hurt, and I had bruises, marks, but I was coming back into myself. Slowly. For a little while, I wasn't sure all of me was back, but then I checked, carefully and slowly, and there I was. It could have killed me, I think, I do think so, but it didn't. I'm stronger than it is, now. I'm happy about that, but I'm not happy.

Eddie's gone and he won't be back. He'd come back, but I don't want him to. There's no point. I was mistaken in believing that I could love him and have children and be like real people, and I think he was mistaken in believing he could love me and have children with me and pretend I'm like everyone else. But that's no one's fault, that's just a mistake anyone could make.

Raquel though, she'll be back, and I can't stop that because I need her to be back. I'm not sure how I feel about that need, how I feel about her even or about me as she must see me – a bit pathetic. She clings and clings to that view of me perhaps, I think she does, but it's not as simple now. I do know that it's me who's in charge here. That's an odd feeling, rather powerful I think. She doesn't like it, I can see she doesn't, but she keeps coming back so she's stuck with it, the wind having changed.

She doesn't want me to tell Daddy or Auntie Lesley but I don't really know about keeping secrets. I might tell or I might not – I don't want the pressure of having to decide that beforehand, to say *All right, Raquel, I'll keep schtum* and having to stick to it. She likes words like that, like *schtum*. I think they remind her of her mother, not because her mother said them I don't think, but just because they're Jewish. I want to tell or not tell moment by moment. I want not to think about it.

Raquel's eight years older than I am, so she'll probably die before me. I know I'll lose Daddy and Auntie Lesley and Uncle Glen-Glen, and I've lost Eddie, but I don't want to be alone in the world. I don't want it to be just me. When I was little, I thought I'd live with Raquel forever. I told her I would and she said I could and then she ran away to join the circus. But I followed her, even if it was only in the holidays. And she came back, but by then I knew I wasn't going to live with her and for a while the panic in my tummy turned around and around and I couldn't eat at all. But I got used to it, and I started eating again, though Daddy and Raquel and even Tom think I don't eat enough. Auntie Lesley's said lots of times that she'd love my self-control. It's nice, having something that someone else envies and would like for themselves. But it's all been part of knowing I had to live by myself. Not quite the same as being completely alone for always though – that's the thought I can't bear. The world's too big to have just me in it.

For twenty-four hours, I had Delia's special cold, though I'd never have to call it that again. I probably would, though, because it's how I thought of it. The world swam in a comfort-haze – it was a fear I was certain of, that I understood, so even as I hated the dizziness and the sicky feeling and not being able to focus, it blurred the pain. Must be like alcohol, I suppose. I can see now why people drink, though I can't say I was tempted. Always, always better the devil you know, though Raquel says that the next devil might be better looking. Raquel says that.

I sat indoors for three days after the dizziness passed, not answering the door or the phone, but then I knew I had to go out, to feel the world on my flesh or I'd never do it, and they'd find me buried in free newspapers and leaflets about double glazing and loans. I could imagine that and it seemed quite a peaceful life, a peaceful death, but as Auntie Lesley says, *Get off your bum or you'll take root*, and it's them finding me having rooted that scares me.

Tom found me sitting on the little wall outside the Londis, eating the corners off a Chunky Choc Ice. I'd been wondering what to do with the rest of it – I can't bear them once they get melty and gooey and blind.

'Can you eat this for me?'

'There's a LAZY COW bin right there, Dee.'

'Is there? Shall I put it in?'

'No, give it here.' He finished the ice cream in three mouthfuls while I licked my fingers clean. His mouth's wide enough to eat the whole thing at once, I should think. 'You cold?'

'No, it's nice and warm in the sun here. Anyway, you can't help. You can't give a jacket if you're not wearing one. Don't often see your tattoos. I like them.'

'So where've you been?' he asked, sitting next to me, putting his hand, just for a second, on my thigh. 'I've been knocking.'

'Indoors, not answering. Eddie's gone.'

'STUPID CUNT. I know. I saw him in the pub.'

'You'll still see him. I'd not thought of that.'

'No, I won't. He didn't say what had happened exactly, but fn-fn-FUH…'

'He had sex with my sister.'

'Yeah, I gathered from what he didn't UPYOURBUM say.' He took my hand then and I let him. He's easy to be touched by, in some ways. 'Won't tell you what I think about *her* – not on purpose, anyway. But the bloke's an idiot.'

'Thanks, Tom, that's a lovely thing to say. But you don't have to.'

'LOVE fn-fn-fn NIGGERPOOFYIDARSE.'

'So you choose me? If it came to it, and it has come to it, you choose me?'

'Always.' He chucked me under the chin, and he nearly took my head off when it went wrong. I choked a bit, but I was okay really. 'Dee – Oh God, sorry—'

'Do you want to come for a walk with me?' I said when I'd got my breath back. 'Have you got time?'

He nodded and stood up, still holding my hand. Twitch, gape, shudder. He was quite bad today, probably angry for me. Even Auntie Lesley's changed her mind about him, now. *Don't have a bad bone in his body, that one.* So we walked quietly along to Barmy Park, together. Once, he hit himself in the throat with our joined hands, but he didn't mention it.

The paddling pool had no water in it, just broken glass. Maybe they weren't going to fill it this year, or perhaps they were two weeks late for some reason.

'I used to sail paper boats on here when I was little,' I said. 'Daddy made them for me. He was excellent at making paper boats, and planes too but I didn't like the planes so much. Uncle Glen-Glen loved the planes, but he doesn't like them anymore. They scare him now.'

'Can't make anything. Tics and, well, me I USELESS BASTARD suppose.'

'You don't have to make things. It doesn't matter.' I watched a small girl tagging along behind a bigger one. 'When I was three, I didn't really speak. Daddy says I used to say *Would Dee like a biscuit?* Instead of *May I have a biscuit?* because I was just copying what I was hearing. I used to copy Raquel more than anyone, apparently. It was cute. Apparently.'

Raquel's name stood there, as if it had turned into her. Hadn't tripped me up when I was saying it, but straight afterwards she cast a giant shadow, grinding my bones to make her bread. Tom shook my arm.

'Imagine if you'd FUCKING PAEDO known me then,' he said.

'Hm?'

'Copying me MONGOL EYES.'

We both laughed, though it didn't sound very happy, on either of us. 'Not sure that would have been cute,' I said, because I wasn't sure.

He squeezed my hand. 'Are you sad?'

'Oh yes. Very sad.' I smiled up at him. 'But I like this.'

The end of his red nose had a drip on it, and his eyes were rimmed red. He gets hayfever. His hair was all stiff as if he'd sprayed it with Auntie Lesley's hairspray, and his skin was even flakier than usual. If I'd had my pencils, I'd have drawn him then. He looked so Tommish.

'You're WEIRDO DILDO amazing,' he said.

'That doesn't have to be a good thing.' But I touched his arm with my other hand, to show him I didn't mean anything bad or think he meant anything bad. He stopped walking. I traced the tattoos on his bare arm with my fingers. Smooth, just like skin. And such lovely colours – blue, indigo, deep green, dark red.

'FUCK ME. Dee, I…' And he bent right down, let go of my hand, grabbed my shoulders and kissed me. I was so surprised, for the tiniest moment I kissed him back. Maybe 40% kissed him back, then I pulled away.

'Was that a tic?' I asked him.

'No. God, sorry LOVELY CUNTY JUICY GIRLS. Sorry, fn-fn-FUH-FUH-FUCKING fn-fn-fn…' Twitch, gape, shudder. I just let him get over it, not sure what I was supposed to think. My mouth fizzy-tingled.

After at least a few minutes, he managed to say, 'Sorry Dee, I never meant you to know.'

'To know what?' I could still feel his kiss on my lips, all teeth and spit.

'I'm in FUCKMEUPTHEBUM I'm in love with you. I'd marry you in a heartbeat, if you'd have me, but QUASIMODO why would you?'

Oh dear. Oh *no*.

If I'd met him before, then maybe I'd have been able to love him back. But not now. That wasn't how I knew him, wasn't how I thought of him. People can't just be shifted from role to role any old how, as though the tea lady was suddenly in charge of casting, or as if I was. It was too much. That's how everything went wrong. That's how everything burnt up.

'Dee? DEAF COW Did you hear me?'

'Yes, I heard you. Tom – no one wants to marry me. I'm not like other people, you know that. *You* know that.'

'But that's why I love you. STRANGER DANGER.'

'Two strange ones together?' I stood on my tippy-toes and kissed him on the cheek, put my arms round his neck. 'Darling Tom, I'm sort of pleased you want to. Sort of. If someone as special as you wants me, that makes me special. It does. But I can't ever marry you.'

'BOLLOCKS STUPID CUNT. Just tell me – for you it's not the tics, is it?'

'No.' Surely he couldn't be serious. Would some people really care enough about that to lose the chance of a lovely, lovely, lovely man, the loveliest man of all? 'I hardly notice them now. Unless you hurt one of us. Me or you. Then I notice.'

'Then – is it Eddie? I should've waited, shouldn't I?'

'Not really. Not like you mean. You're my friend, Tom. My only friend.'

'So that's where I'll PISS BOLLOCKS UGLY stay.' He laughed then, stroked the side of my face. 'Yeah, I get it. I do.' He kept on stroking, and it felt so nice that I didn't want him to speak. He did, though. 'It's not even that you don't want to ruin our friendship, is it? I'm your friend, so that's who I am. It breaks my heart SENTIMENTAL SHIT BUMBUM FEED THE DUCKS FUCK but what can I do? Categories and timing.'

I loved him so much then.

'Categories and timing,' I agreed. 'It's too late. Forever. I think forever.'

'I think forever too.' His eyes filled with tears, so I touched the edge of each one, gently, to see if I could stop them falling.

He pressed me into him, and we stood there in Barmy Park, two friends holding each other forever. The world, just for those minutes, the exact right size. For me. I think maybe not for poor Tom.

'Tell me, daughter Delia, how stands your disposition to be married?'

'Don't think it's going to be *Romeo and Juliet*, Daddy.' Did he know or didn't he? It was impossible to tell.

'No? *Men were deceivers ever.* Darling darling darling Dee-Dee, pretty Princess Pea, shall Daddy challenge him to a duel?' He kissed me on the top of my head. A bit hard, but nice all the same.

'Are you drunk?'

'Drunk? *I'm drunk, as I live, boys, drunk.* Poet in Purcell. Damn it, wish I'd had a voice. Glen-Glen probably got the voice. Now wouldn't that be just delicious?' Daddy almost fell into my hallway. 'Raquel can sing, after a fashion. But she hasn't got what I'd call a voice. Nor did her mother, though she could put a song across. Sexy piece she was, but not a patch on *your* mother.'

'Do you want a coffee?' You were supposed to offer drunk people coffee. But I wasn't really sure Daddy was drunk. He'd had a drink, I could smell it, whiskery-leather, but he didn't usually behave quite like this when he was drunk.

'Nope. Came with an offer – do you want to live with your Daddy?'

'Do I want to live with you? No.' I can't think fast like that, no idea how other people do it, but something told me that no was the right answer. He couldn't possibly be serious. He hadn't wanted me to live at home since I was twenty-one. Helped me find a place, just so I wouldn't live at home *Until you're a dotty old spinster with seventeen cats pissing all over my furniture. Get out there, get a life.*

'But Daddy has to help you,' he said, sitting down on the sofa with a great thump. He was getting fatter. Definitely. 'You need help,' he added.

'Do I? Daddy, what's wrong?' I didn't like this, not one little bit. My tummy was going over and over, and there were little black dots in front of my eyes, little eye-midge-biters. Nothing was as it should be this week. Nothing. It was all crumbling like dry sandcastles. You have to put water on them and in them or they disappear into the beach they came from as if they'd never been.

I knelt in front of his chair.

'Wrong, Princess Pea? Nothing's wrong. I've found you again, that's all.' He put his hand on my head. 'But what of this young man? This crippled bastard. Has he really hurt my baby?'

'Yes, Daddy.' There was a lump in my throat and I was close to crying. When I was younger, I hadn't understood when people said they felt like crying – if you felt like it then you did cry, I thought. But lately, I understood.

'Some floozy, was it?' Daddy's slightly jowly face looked right at me. I ducked my head away, just a little, hoping he wouldn't notice.

At that moment, I knew I had to be worthy of the love and trust so many people had put in me: Daddy, Auntie Lesley, Uncle Glen-Glen, lovely Tom, and Raquel. *And* Raquel. And *Raquel.*

'Someone at the club,' I said. I slid a gemstone out of my pocket. Purple quartz, lovely but spiky to hold. 'It doesn't matter. It really doesn't. He's...what does Raquel say? He's history.'

And perhaps it *didn't* matter. Or wouldn't matter, sometime. It'd have not to matter sometime, I think.

'That's him out of the show, then.' He laughed, a big, proper belly laugh. 'Show. Does MB really think I believe in a show?'

'Don't you? I thought there was going to be—'

'A no-show. My darling girl, I've given him nearly all my money in the sure and certain knowledge that it was all BS and wishful thinking.'

'What do you mean? Uncle Glen-Glen's money?'

'No. What d'you take me for?' Glittery-angry, but it flashed past. 'My own money. No contracts even, all done on a gentleman's agreement. A handshake.' He beamed at me. If a gentleman's word is his bond, I'm fucked – that crapulous toad's no gent. Delia Dee, your old Daddy will have to go back to work.'

'Oh, is that all? You'll like that.'

'I will. I'll like that. I'll hate looking a fool, but feh, better an amiable dupe out to help a friend, than a sad old sod who can't handle retirement.'

'Okay.' I didn't understand anything in that, but it was good that Daddy was going back to work. I wasn't sure he should have given away his money, but it didn't actually concern me much. 'I don't like MB.'

'Nobody *likes* MB, darling girl.'

'He gave me an ice lolly once. On purpose. He knew.'

'You never told me that.' Daddy looked serious then. 'The swine. Really. Bollocking swine.'

He'd held it out to me, unwrapped, orange and dripping

down the horrid sticky stick. I screamed, long and loud and purple-feared. He'd smiled and kept holding it out, me frozen in the scream, until the juice started to run up his arm. Then he threw it in a nearby bin, smiled, and said, 'You don't want it? What a pity. Rather a waste.'

'I wouldn't have given him the money,' I said. 'You could have given it to someone who really needed it.'

'No, I really couldn't. But I do take the point. He'll benefit from my need to work. Not ideal.'

'He told Auntie Lesley that the baby, little Michael, would be killed from neglect because she wasn't fit to have him.'

'Don't.' Daddy covered his ears. 'Don't tell me, I can't hear it. I made my decision, and it's done. Finished.'

'How long does the pain last, Daddy?'

'Got me, sweetheart.' He turned his palms up, in the exact same gesture he did when he was playing Shylock. 'Not sure I felt enough pain when either of your mothers went. But Les – she's still grieving for that baby, after all these years.'

'It hurts in my heart, Daddy.'

'You'll meet someone else, Princess Pea. Someone more *appropriate*.'

'I don't want appropriate. What's appropriate, anyway? Someone you think won't run off and leave me or have sex with…someone else?'

Daddy raised his eyebrows. Both of them, not one like Eddie. Like Raquel.

'The worm turns,' he said.

There was a knock at the door. I recognized it the second time – Auntie Lesley. I got to my feet and went to let her in.

She looked awful, white, with black mascara all round her eyes. She must have been crying.

'Is it MB?' I asked.

'No. Is your dad here?'

'Yes. Do you want to come in?'

'Of course I bloody want to come in! What's the *matter* with you, girl?' Then she scooped me into a too-tight hug. 'Sorry love, sorry. But I need to see him.'

I followed her down the hallway, into the living room. Daddy looked up, and all the colour went out of his face.

'What?' he said. '*Tell me.*'

'Oh Kenny, I don't know how.'

'Tell me. Now.' He stood, towering over her.

'It's—'

'It's my Glen-Glen, isn't it? Speak, woman.'

'Kenny – he's gone.'

'Disappeared?' I asked, but neither of them took any notice. I didn't like this. My heart was going far too fast, and I could hardly catch their words as they past.

'Gone?' he said.

'Glen-Glen's dead.'

Daddy stared at her for what felt like a long time, a minute even, then he lifted his face to the ceiling, and roared.

'Noooooooooooooooo,' he howled. No person ever sounded like that, I think, howling at the light bulb in my living room, with more pain than his mind could bear.

Raquel

Everything happens for a reason. I've always believed that, and yet now I can't find a reason, or not one that makes sense. Glen is dead and we don't know why or how, and we don't know who if anyone is responsible. I'm not sure I even care, whether I give a tinker's damn, though if it's not resolved perhaps I'll have to force myself to mind, because someone could have done it to him. Yet in the end, I'm not convinced it matters, maybe because I'm not convinced he's important enough.

I also don't know if I've lost my sister. She acts as though I haven't yet she'd act in precisely the same way if I had, I imagine. That does matter. A great deal. And I hadn't realized enough about Daddy, which is something else I can't ignore.

'I don't know how to go on without him.' Daddy sat on his favourite armchair in his memorabilia-heavy living room – he used to like to say it was ironic, but I never bought that – with the flesh hanging off his face, crumpled into himself, a deflated Buddha. For the past two days, since getting back from the hospital and the police station, he'd sat there, breaking only to go to the loo. Much longer, and he was going to smell.

'You'll have to. We'll all have to.' Lesley lit a cigarette

from the stub of the one before. She tucked her legs under her on the sofa. I stood by the curtains, inching them open; too much light and Daddy shielded his eyes as though I was blinding him, but if we had to exist in the dark much longer, I'd scream.

'Yes, quite, you'll all go on,' he said. '*Our little life is rounded with a sleep.* Not one of you ever gave a toss.'

'I did.' Delia was sitting at Daddy's feet, sipping the hot Ribena she'd taken to over the past few days.

'Up to a point.' Daddy nodded his concession.

I handed him his whiskey-laced tea from the coffee table. 'Once we know—'

'How do I know it wasn't one of you? Mercy killing or some such bollocks. Or concern that my money was gone, wanting to get your hands on his.'

'*Daddy.*' I moved across the room to take one of Lesley's cigs from her packet without asking. I saw her open her mouth to object to my manners or something equally characteristic, but she put on a smile and handed me her lighter. I lit my ciggie and went back to my post. For two days now, we'd heard these mad accusations, grief apparently being the emotion of melodrama. At first, we'd all reacted in varying horrified ways, but now one of us simply objected with his name.

'How can he just stop breathing? Do people just stop breathing?' Daddy said, appealing to the four photo-lined walls. Daddy with Laurence Olivier, Daddy with Cliff Richard, Daddy with Barbara Windsor, Daddy with Hattie Jacques, Daddy with Cubby Moore; not one of them answered. Even my mother, professionally shot in soft focus, looked down on him impassively. I wondered how easy Dee's mother had found it to live with that bland judgement.

'They don't know.' Lesley sounded weary, with that special exhaustion of playing a part in a too-long run. 'He suffocated and he died, Ken. He died. He had fits, it could easily have happened during a fit. He was navy blue. He might even have done it himself.'

'I don't care if he was sky-blue-pink, he'd *never* do that to me.' For a split second, I thought he might lash out, just as I'd thought so the last time she'd said that. But once again, he didn't. 'Glen-Glen was healthy,' he said. 'Damn it, I thought he'd outlive us all. Or that we'd go together. I never planned for him dying on me.' Tears rolled down his face; it must be sore by now, with all that salt that had dried on it in the last forty-eight hours.

Dee took a tissue from the box, knelt upright to wipe away his tears. He endured it without seeming to notice.

Well, of course little Dee would get it right. Anything I said or did was wrong, wrong, wrongage to the nth. Any man around would be sure to prefer her helpless *acquiescence* to my grasp on reality, frankly. No, that was mean, take it back, it was mean, it was. I'd be next if I wasn't careful. Unthink, unthink, unthink. I tried to smile at her, but she didn't see. You could say Dee was avoiding my eye, but as she always avoided everyone's eye, that didn't tell me a blessed thing.

Lesley checked her watch and left the room, coming back through a few minutes later with a plate of hot sausage rolls that she put too close to the ashtray on the coffee table. Nobody but me took one. I took two.

'I loved him best, you know,' Daddy said. 'I still love him best.'

Dee nodded – of course she did – but me, I smarted. This was a fresh one. Not that it was news exactly, but him saying it confirmed the previously unspoken. Words were very much safer left unsaid. I put out my cig and bit into a sausage roll.

'*Forty thousand brothers,*' he added, '*Could not, with all their…quantity of love, / Make up my,*' he rubbed his palm across his eyes, '*sum.*'

A moo almost of pain.

'No one understood me like he did,' he said.

Bloody ridiculous b – how could Uncle Glen-Glen understand anyone? He'd barely understood he was alive.

'I don't know who I am with him gone,' Daddy said. 'How can the world carry on without him in it?'

'You used to say he couldn't play football, he didn't know where his feet are,' I said, quite nastily really. 'Said he could be a goal post. And that he'd never make a mime artist, much less an opera singer. And—'

'Brotherly banter.' Daddy waved his hand in front of his face, batting Dee away, who stopped wiping his cheeks.

'To *me*, not to him,' I said.

'Brotherly banter *in absentia*.' He should have been angry or defensive maybe, but he just sounded as though he was trying to explain. And failing.

'Ra*quel*,' said Lesley, in her warning voice.

'If someone went in, how did the staff not see?' Daddy said. 'Maybe one of *them* did it. One of them felt the need.'

'Why would anyone need to kill him?' Dee said.

'I don't know, Princess Pea. Charity's the best answer I can hope for. At worst – getting at me? Maybe one of your mothers came back—'

'That's enough, Daddy,' I said. This was another new tack. 'You're just conjuring any old rubbish. We know he had a fit, we know he suffocated, we know it was probably natural causes. Probably, all right, but it's the best we can do at the moment. I understand, I do, you need to know – but this isn't helping any of us. Least of all you.'

'No.' He put his head in his hands and wept. 'He's dead.

I know he's dead. But I can't feel it. How can your hearts not be broken? Made of stone, every last one of them.'

He wept on silently, Dee at his feet, Lesley watching and smoking across from him, me standing by the window, my hand on the curtain.

When I was a little girl, my mother left me. She left our father and she left me and the actress she'd been as well, though I think I'd assumed I'd see her name at the pictures or the theatre. I never did. At Infants – which I'd only just started, months younger than most of the other girls, not even five – the others were mean to me (apart from Janice French), called me The Orphan, and at school dinners for weeks said, *Can't your daddy cook* whenever I greedily finished my chocolate pudding with chocolate custard. They quickly moved on to the next tiny victim, but I never forgot what it was like to be left: it wasn't just about the sorrow and the shame and the confusion, it was about the shape of every part of your life, even the bits that would seem to have nothing to do with what Dee-Dee calls that scratching at your heart.

Now the world had shifted irrevocably once more yet I was blowed if I could see how the death of someone who made so little impact in life had in and of itself done it. It had, though. Glen O'Leary was dead and nothing would ever be the same shape again.

> *Full fathom five thy father lies;*
> *Of his bones are coral made;*
> *Those are pearls that were his eyes:*
> *Nothing of him that doth fade*
> *But doth suffer a sea-change*
> *Into something rich and strange.*

'He was my father and my brother both, my other self and this one before you all now. I loved him and he loved me, and our bond was far beyond that love. To say I'll miss him is to say nothing at all. I can't even say goodbye.'

'KNICKERS.'

A few stifled giggles from the back. Nurses, dutiful on their afternoon off perhaps, or more likely those on shift who could be drafted in.

Oh dear God, someone shut that Tom up.

Daddy bowed his head, professional to the last, and then moved away from the reading stand. The celebrant thanked him with a sympathetic squeeze of the arm and a sycophantic smile, and moved forward to lead us in Uncle Glen-Glen's favourite song. Nelly the bloody Elephant, evidently.

The nurses wouldn't sing, so it was left to the uneasy embarrassed tones of the celebrant, and the four of us plus Tom and Maurice (who on earth invited him?) gamely to chunter our way through.

'*They brought an intelligent elephant*
And Nelly was her name...'

Dee, utterly uncharacteristically, belted out the words as though she was in a pantomime. She sounded pretty fair, actually.

'*One dark* FUH-FUH-FUH-FUCKING ELEPHANT NELEPHANT...'

Why did she have to ask *him*, for heaven's sake?

Maurice leaned over my shoulder from behind during a couple of bars' organ break, and whispered, 'I've sacked him, love. Don't worry.'

'What?'

'Eddie Muir. Let him go from the club. You won't have to see him again.'

Maurice knew about me and Eddie? Who the hell else had Dee told?

'You didn't have to do that, *Nelly the elephant packed her trunk...*'

'Yes I did. You don't want to see him after what he did to your baby sister. Your father told me all about it. Came in to see me. *Trump, trump, trump...*'

Thank heavens for small mercies.

'*Trundled back to the jungle...*' Daddy and Lesley managed to sound as though they were singing a hymn, and were moved by the spirit of suburban worship to boot, Daddy's overdone bass and Lesley's tremolo soprano the worst of possible combinations. I resisted the urge to harmonize.

It was a hideous affair altogether. Ugh. For heaven's sake, an open casket in a crematorium is pure bad taste; instead of anonymous wood, you have to imagine the flames actually burning a face. A beautiful face, still eerily lovely, though a soft shade of blue under the mortician's slap. Open casket. Open verdict. Closed service: we didn't want the press, though the vultures were gathered outside, cameras viciously snapping.

Daddy spent a long time gazing down at that face, then he bent and kissed it full on the lips. 'I'll not weep,' he told the face, and he didn't, not once through the whole service, though *Delia* cried quietly and more or less constantly when she wasn't singing, and Lesley's eyes were red.

'Fn-fn-fn-HIPPIE HIPPOCRITES. FUCK 'EM.' Tom put his hand on Dee's shoulder; she patted his but didn't turn around.

The organ started up again, some generic funereal thing, and the curtains parted, the coffin moving slowly through them into the fiery furnace. Of course I knew that wasn't literally the case, but it was hard to shake the feeling. Daddy stretched out a hand, his exclamation strangled in his throat, and then Glen-Glen was gone. Daddy bowed his head, as though he was finally beaten.

We came out into the sunshine. I slipped my shades out of my bag, put them on, though I wasn't sure it was the done thing at funerals. I'd only ever been to memorial services before, when someone or other mildly famous had died, crowded with the dregs of the profession, and trust me, sunglasses were de rigueur at those. I'd missed Nan's altogether because of Girelli's – *We never close!* – and on account of me loathing the old witch. This funeral was a poor thing, but our own.

Suddenly, I felt my elbow gripped, hard.

'Vardi the chat,' Lesley practically hissed. Look at what? But then I saw: standing by the limo, dressed in black and holding an enormous hat, was MB.

'What the hell's he doing here?'

'How should I know?' She ignored him, and went to look at the flower arrangements. 'Nice wreath from the Home,' she called, patting her stiff hair. Dee and Tom joined her, Maurice hovering fussily on the sidelines with the nurses, but Daddy lumbered over to MB and I thought I'd better go with him. We didn't leave Daddy on his own for a minute these days.

'My sincerest condolences,' MB said, shaking Daddy's hand.

'Well, they won't be very sincere then,' I muttered, loud enough for them both to hear.

'Thank you,' said Daddy, blandly. 'Will you come back to the house for a drink and a bite?'

'No, I won't intrude. Just wanted to pay my respects.'

'It's appreciated.'

'How's the lovely Raquel holding up?'

'We're all doing fine,' I said. 'Now if you'll excuse us—'

'One moment.' He reached up and laid a hand on Daddy's arm. 'Clearly now isn't the time, but you'll need something to take your mind off it. Don't answer right away, but just think about whether you might want to invest further, become a full producer of the show.'

Daddy threw back his great lion head and laughed to the clear blue sky.

'Invest further?' he said. 'You do cheer me up. I wouldn't touch the so-called show with yours, MB. You've got my money – though I imagine lawyers, if I could be bothered, could talk about my diminished responsibility. You're not having his as well. There's no point anymore.' He clapped MB on the shoulder. 'Good try, though. Even for you, spectacularly tasteless and tactless—'

'And inept,' I put in.

'Thank you, darling. And inept.' Still chuckling, Daddy turned and went to join the others at the flowers.

'Think you just blew it,' I said. Whatever it was. So Daddy really had given MB money – that figured. Since the moment he'd announced his retirement, he'd been erratic about finances, as I knew only too well. I wasn't clear quite why he'd decided to do the show, or how much money had actually been poured into it, though Delia said he'd told her all of it (I couldn't see that), but I could tell that MB was very far from happy. He shook his head at me, pointed a finger up to my chest.

'You'll all regret this, missy,' he said. And actually stamped his foot, for all the world an aging child. Yet we hadn't guessed his name.

'Frankly, MB, I've no idea what's going on and right at this minute, I couldn't care less. I've got to go and get drunk now. Nice to see you.'

'Whore!' he yelled to my back, making the family swing round as one.

'WHORE PROZZY WHOREBUM PISS BUM WILLIES,' said Tom.

'Quite so,' Daddy said, and draped an arm fondly around his shoulder.

Back at the house, Tom sat next to Dee on the sofa, a plate of finger sandwiches and things on sticks between them. He had an enormous neat scotch poured by Lesley, Dee had a hot Ribena. Someone, Daddy probably, had put a record on, some jazzy instrumental thing with no voice. Uncharacteristic – the whole family had in common that they preferred music with words. He sat tapping the rhythm on the arm of his chair, absently.

'No lyrics, Daddy,' I said, watching Lesley bustle about with plates and glasses and cups and saucers, even though none of the nurses had come back, and it was just us and Tom and Maurice. 'Unusual for you.'

'I need something other than words to say.'

'That'll be a first. Look at them, Daddy.' I knelt by his chair and nodded across to Dee and Tom. 'Do you think they'll end up together?'

'Oh, I shouldn't think so. Wouldn't matter either way – one of them will die.'

'Well, eventually, yes, but—'

'So why would they put themselves through it?' He reached down heavily for his tumbler. 'They gave me whithkey, whithkey,' he whispered. Then, 'That's not a match, Raquel. You mark your old daddy's words.'

Poor Maurice couldn't have looked more awkward in this tight little family scene, though Tom seemed perfectly at home. 'BOLLOCKS.' My boss stood with his back to the wall, getting redder and redder, smiling benignly in a fearful sort of way, and then scampered off midway through the LP to open the club, leaving half a plate of food and most of a drink untouched.

'Funny fella, that,' said Lesley, when we'd seen him out. 'What did MB want, Raq?'

'To pay his respects, he reckoned. Then he asked for money.'

'Well, that's hardly going to make the bleeding headlines, is it?' Smoothing her cream blouse into her pencil skirt. 'Never been struck on sensitivity, that one – thinks it's for losers. He's got some front though, give him that. Make Jane Russell look flat-chested, him.'

'Is Dee right, did Daddy put money into the show?'

'Yeah, far as I know. Least he'll have Glen-Glen's share now.'

'I think he's gone. MB. Properly gone, I mean.' To my surprise and I think hers, I kissed her on the cheek. We kiss a lot in our family, we call it being affectionate, being close, but it's always centred on greetings, thanks, other concrete reasons. Never just for the sake of it.

'Wouldn't count on it, lovely,' she said, properly smiling and patting my face. 'Still, we can't worry about all that old nonsense today. Got to get on with the job.'

It wasn't clear what job she meant, other than being the Neighbourhood Watch set up to monitor Daddy. I slipped into the kitchen to pour myself a little Bacardi and Coke, one that wouldn't take the back of my throat off, then went back to my vigil next to my father's chair.

The LP had finished. Daddy's player wasn't automatic, so we had the che-ker, che-ker, che-ker as the needle went round on the empty middle grooves.

'I never heard his voice,' he said, flatly. 'Not once. Not

since we were babies. Two or so. I never heard his fucking voice.'

Che-ker, che-ker, che-ker. I could hear Lesley washing up in the kitchen, Dee and Tom whispering now and then on the sofa, though mostly sitting silently except for the odd yelp or squeak from Tom. Through the open window, pigeons warbled as though pretending they were in the countryside. A pigeon's about the only bird I can recognize, apart from a robin redbreast.

'Shall I change the record?' I said as brightly as I could, to the room. 'What shall I put on? Tom? Little? What do you think?'

'Raquel – don't call me Little.' Dee glanced up to meet my eyes, then stared at my mouth. 'Not ever again. My name's Delia.' She spoke in her quiet monotone, but with a new authority. So that's what betrayal does for you. I'd wondered.

'What on earth—' I said, more for form's sake than because I didn't understand.

'You FUCKING LYING BITCH heard her,' Tom said.

Lesley stood at the doorway now, her marigolds dripping Fairy bubbles, clearly desperate to hear better.

'But I've always—'

'I'm twenty-seven years old,' she said. 'I can choose my own name.'

'Oh for God's sake. All right then, *Delia*, what record shall I put on?' But my heart was pumping nineteen to the dozen and I was having a job controlling my breathing. *You're all right, you're all right, everything's all right.*

'Don't matter what they call you, long as they don't call you pigeon pie and eat you up,' said Lesley. 'Talking of pigeons, hark at them out there, noisy beggars. It mating season, anyone know?'

'It does matter, Auntie Lesley.' Dee nodded, still looking at my mouth.

'She's right,' said her stooge. 'FUH-FUH-FUH-fn fn fn...'

'Jesus Christ,' yelled Daddy, standing up so suddenly he knocked his plate and glass to the floor. 'Can none of you see it? Not one of you? *We can't do it.* We can't be like other people, not any of us. The trying's over. Finished. We can't do it any more, there's nothing to pretend for any more. The end.' He swept his arm round in a grand gesture. 'This family's a Freak Show! Should charge admission at the bloody door. Roll up, roll up, ladies and gentlemen, see the freaks in their natural habitat. Only cost you your bloody soul.'

He covered his face in his hands and howled into them, spit flying through the splayed fingers. Dee, Lesley, Tom, me, all frozen as we looked on in horror. The Fabulous O'Learys and guest, together again for one final performance.

Delia

It's a beautiful day out there, really sunny for September. But it's not just that white sun that makes you screw up your eyes and burns the back of your neck through your hair, it's the lovely soft yellow sun, that makes everyone smile and shine. I don't like summer much – this is nicer. I think autumn's my favourite season. You always liked it because of the new shows, touring for Christmas. I remember that from when I was only four or five, how happy you seemed after the summer season was over and you were looking forward to the rest of the year. Eddie's not on my list anymore, so maybe autumn could be, for both of us. I'll have to think about it.

Raquel says it's grotesque that they've moved you into here. *Grotesque*, she actually said that word. I know she means well, but she doesn't understand – of course you'd want his room, now you're out of the hospital. You were lucky to get it, I think – maybe Raquel's right to believe in fate. Where else would you want to be? You can feel close to him here. I understand. I feel it too, though not like you do, I think. No, not like you do.

You're sniffing a lot – are you getting a cold? Do you want my tissue? Oh, it's a pink one – never mind. Maybe you're trying to smell him, though. It does sort of smell of him, but only because it smells of disinfectant. I wonder what it's like, to spend your whole life smelling of something to take the smells away.

I never hear myself speak for this long. Never, not even in my own head, where colours and sounds and bright or dark blank spaces take up far more room than my words ever could. Out loud like this, my voice is thin, isn't it? Thin like my wrists, my fingers. I like it. I'd hate to make fat, greasy sounds that clog up your ears. Hope it doesn't get on your nerves, though, my voice. I was always sure I got on your nerves, just a bit, and I can't think it would be different now.

I've brought you some chocolate. Bourneville. You don't want it? I'll put it on the chest of drawers, look. Daddy, look, the chocolate's on the chest of drawers. Oh, and I nearly forgot – I found your old hip flask, the one some actor gave you. Can't remember his name. I could never remember their names, they all blended into one harsh, glittery, angry sound. Look, I filled it with whiskey. Don't let the nurses find it. You want it? There you are. I'm a good girl sometimes, aren't I? No, I know I'm not a girl, not really, but you're still my daddy. Sorry, I mustn't get silly. I promised Raquel I wouldn't get silly, if I came here.

Did you hear? Princess Diana's just had her second baby, and she's going to call it Harry. That's an old-fashioned name, but I suppose they can't be modern. I would have liked a baby. Does that surprise you? You look a bit surprised, I think. I would have, though. Won't ever have one now – all that's finished with. I won't fall in love again, if I ever did. Probably didn't. I'm just going to try to find something I like doing and do that. Tom says I could go on a jewellery-making course, even do a degree in it. I might. Silver and gems, that would be lovely. I could be happy, I imagine. I can imagine being happy, in a small way. Even

Raquel says it's a good idea. Sometimes I think they gang up on me, Tom and Raquel and Auntie Lesley, but I let them. It makes them happy and it doesn't really bother me. Actually, I'm not sure it makes Tom happy but he can't seem to stop himself joining in, so, you know.

Auntie Lesley's got a girlfriend now. Pam. She's nice, she was a buyer for one of the big shops, but she got laid off. The business isn't doing very well, I think, it might have to close, but Auntie Lesley's so thrilled with herself, I don't think she minds. She's gone a bit giddy and dyed her hair orange. It's meant to be red, she says it's red, but I'm good at colours and it's burnt orange. Uncle Lou must mind, though. I don't know what will happen about money, but something always turns up, doesn't it? Auntie Lesley says she's a grafter and there's always work for grafters, but Tom says that's rubbish. Actually, he says that's total bollocks, which is one of the few times you'll hear him swear and mean it. You always liked that word, didn't you? *Bollocks.* I like it too, it feels clippy-crisp as you say it. But I don't say it much. Auntie Lesley would slap me round the knees.

You tired, Daddy? You look tired, your eyes keep nearly closing. Shall I go, leave you be with your whiskey? Don't forget your chocolate, it's on the chest, look. Daddy, look. Over here. Your favourite.

I'll give you a kiss and go, now. On your head, see. Night, Daddy, sleep tight. Don't let the bed bugs bite. Only it's not night, not yet, but I don't suppose that matters. Nothing much matters in the end, does it? Love you. See you next week, I expect. Though you never know, do you? Don't suppose it matters much either way, but we have to behave as though it might. I've worked it out, Daddy: that's what all the real people do – behave as though it might matter. That's why they always say bad things aren't the end of the world, because they have to act as though hope is important. Mustn't grumble. Could be worse. Something will be round the corner. And inside they're terrified that they're wrong, that it could be worse, that there's nothing round the corner. That this is all there is.

Bye then. Bye. Don't forget your chocolate.

Acknowledgements

Thanks to my draft readers for their generosity and rigour; to my family for never demanding the mainstream; to David and Michele Lambert for hosting many near-perfect writing retreats at Le Verger, and to the community we have found there; to the sisterhood, especially Lizzie and Kelly, for getting it; to Lucy Durneen for being my writing and weirdness twin; to my agent Louise Greenberg for intuiting Holland House would be a good match; to my editor Robert Peett for demonstrating what writers once believed editors to be; to artist Jo Dalton for a cover more beautiful and witty than any I could have imagined.

About the Author

Caron Freeborn was a novelist (*Three Blind Mice, Prohibitions*) until she gradually became a poet instead. Her first full poetry collection was *Georges Perec is my hero* (2015). Against class expectations, she has taught at university level for years, and is writing a poetry textbook. She is also working with photographer Steve Armitage on a project about their home town, Basildon, putting voice poems into his unpeopled pictures. With *Presenting… The Fabulous O'Learys,* Caron Freeborn makes a return to prose fiction.